It's All
in the Details

Praise for Dena Blake

A Spark in the Air

"I was so invested in all these people...this is a feel-good Christmas romance: HEA guaranteed...It's warm and cozy, with just the right generous dash of spice and wee-bit amount of angst to keep things interesting."—*Book And Coffee Addict*

"This was so good! Filled with festive cheer but also truly heartwarming moments...Highly recommend, especially to get you in a festive and giving mood. Loved every second of it and couldn't put it down.!"—*LESBIreviewed*

The Probability of Love

"So much fun!...What a great emotional ride, with magical moments and purely amazing connection between two fantastic women. If you've read other books of Dena's there are a few lovely surprises throughout this great story too, which were an absolute treat and made me smile!"—*LESBIreviewed*

Love by Proxy

"Brilliantly funny and sweet!...This was such an amazing story! Gripping, exciting, full of twists and turns, unexpected events, and most importantly a little touch of comedy. It really was the perfect rom-com. Packed with drama and lots of conflict, nothing was more exhilarating than being on this roller coaster of emotions with Tess and Sophie."—*LESBIreviewed*

Next Exit Home

"I enjoy Dena Blake's writing, and I enjoyed this book a lot...I especially liked this book because the two single mums who have become mums for very different reasons/experiences are strong women. Proving they are super capable to solo parent and raise rockstar kids. There is something very sexy about a single mum grabbing parenthood by the horns and making it work. I really enjoyed that aspect!...Great small-town romance that packs a punch in the enemies to lovers trope! I'll definitely be rereading this one again soon."—*Les Rêveur*

Kiss Me Every Day

"This book was SUCH a fun read!!…This was such a fun, interesting book to read and I thoroughly enjoyed it; the characters were super easy to like, the romance was super cute and I loved seeing each little thing that Wynn changed every day!"—*Sasha & Amber Read*

"Such a fun and an exciting book filled with so much love! This book is just packed with fun and memorable moments I was thinking about for days after reading it. This is one hundred per cent my new favourite Dena Blake book. The pace of the book was excellent, and I felt I was along for the fantastic ride."—*Les Rêveur*

"The sweetest moment in the book is when the titular phrase is uttered…This well written book is an interesting read because of the whole premise of getting repeated opportunities to right wrongs."—*Best Lesfic Reviews*

"Wynn's journey of self-discovery is wonderful to witness. She develops compassion, love and finds happiness. Her character development is phenomenal…If you're looking for a stunning romance book with a female/female romance, then this is definitely the one for you. I highly recommend."—*Literatureaesthetic*

Perfect Timing

"The chemistry between Lynn and Maggie is fantastic…the writing is totally engrossing."—*Best Lesfic Reviews*

"This book is the kind of book you sit down to on a Sunday morning with a cup of tea and the sun shining in your bedroom only to realise at 5 pm you've not left your bed because it was too good to stop reading."
—*Les Rêveur*

"The relationship between Lynn and Maggie developed at an organic pace. I loved all the flirting going on between Maggie and Lynn. I love a good flirty conversation!…I haven't read this author before but I look forward to trying more of her titles."—*Marcia Hull, Librarian (Ponca City Library, Oklahoma)*

Racing Hearts

"I particularly liked Drew with her sexy rough exterior and soft heart… Sex scenes are definitely getting hotter and I think this might be the hottest by Dena Blake to date."—*Les Rêveur*

Just One Moment

"One of the things I liked is that the story is set after the glorious days of falling in love, after the time when everything is exciting. It shows how sometimes, trying to make life better really makes it more complicated…It's also, and mainly, a reminder of how important communication is between partners, and that as solid as trust seems between two lovers, misunderstandings happen very easily."—*Jude in the Stars*

"Blake does angst particularly well and she's wrung every possible ounce out of this one…I found myself getting sucked right into the story—I do love a good bit of angst and enjoy the copious amounts of drama on occasion."—*C-Spot Reviews*

Friends Without Benefits

"This is the book when the Friends to Lovers trope doesn't work out. When you tell your best friend you are in love with her and she doesn't return your feelings. This book is real life and I think I loved it more for that."—*Les Rêveur*

A Country Girl's Heart

"Literally couldn't put this book down, and can't give enough praise for how good this was!!! One of my favourite reads, and I highly recommend to anyone who loves a fantastically clever, intriguing, and exciting romance."—*LESBIreviewed*

Unchained Memories

"There is a lot of angst and the book covers some difficult topics but it does that well. The writing is gripping and the plot flows."—*Melina Bickard, Librarian, Waterloo Library (UK)*

"This story had me cycling between lovely romantic scenes to white-knuckle gripping, on the edge of the seat (or in my case, the bed) scenarios. This story had me rooting for a sequel and I can certainly place my stamp of approval on this novel as a must read book."—*Lesbian Review*

"The pace and character development was perfect for such an involved story line, I couldn't help but turn each page. This book has so many wonderful plot twists that you will be in suspense with every chapter that follows."—*Les Rêveur*

Where the Light Glows

"From first-time author Dena Blake, *Where the Light Glows* is a sure winner."—*A Bookworm's Loft*

"[T]he vivid descriptions of the Pacific Northwest will make readers hungry for food and travel. The chemistry between Mel and Izzy is palpable."—*RT Book Reviews*

"I'm still shocked this was Dena Blake's first novel…It was fantastic… It was written extremely well and more than once I wondered if this was a true account of someone close to the author because it was really raw and realistic. It seemed to flow very naturally and I am truly surprised that this is the author's first novel as it reads like a seasoned writer." —*Les Rêveur*

By the Author

Visit us at www.boldstrokesbooks.com

It's All
in the Details

by

Dena Blake

2023

IT'S ALL IN THE DETAILS

ISBN 13: 978-1-63679-430-3

THIS TRADE PAPERBACK ORIGINAL IS PUBLISHED BY
BOLD STROKES BOOKS, INC.
P.O. BOX 249
VALLEY FALLS, NY 12185

FIRST EDITION: JULY 2023

CREDITS
EDITOR: SHELLEY THRASHER
PRODUCTION DESIGN: STACIA SEAMAN
COVER DESIGN BY TAMMY SEIDICK

Acknowledgments

Weddings have always enchanted me. Watching two people celebrate their love for each other does something to me that I can't explain, and that makes all the bad in the world melt away. The ceremony, the music, the food, and the dancing are traditions I adore. Seeing two people fall in love in the middle of it all is magical.

Shelley Thrasher, my wonderful editor, you were so patient with me when I ran late with drafts and had to make huge additions to edits. Life has been challenging this year, and I can't thank you enough for being so understanding. Rad and Sandy—I'm going to say it again, there's no one I trust my work with more than Bold Strokes Books. To the rest of the team at BSB, you're amazing and I appreciate all you do to make my dreams come true. You really do make me feel like a professional writer!

Kate, Wes, and Haley, I wouldn't be able to keep moving forward on this journey without your support. I love you all more than I could ever put into words.

All my readers out there, thank you from the bottom of my heart for reading my books. I know you have so many choices out there, and it means the world to me that you choose mine.

To Jacky, my newest daughter, thank you so much for your advisement on all things wedding makeup. I would've been lost without your help. Since the first time I met you so very long ago, I loved your sweet soul and vibrant spirit. I'm so glad you found Wes again and captured his heart. You're a beautiful addition to our family.

CHAPTER ONE

L ane Donnelly stood with Iris Jones, her friend and makeup partner, at the front desk waiting to find out the room number of the brides' prep room. The bride had engaged them close to a year ago to do her makeup, along with the rest of the bridal party. This wedding was going to be the event of the season, held at the Rosewood Mansion, one of the most elite hotels in Dallas. Located near the Dallas arts district, the nineteen-twenties estate embodied timeless luxury in the middle of a modern world. The hotel also homed the rich and famous whenever they were in the area. Lane was sure that was due to the decor. Each room felt like one that you would find in someone's home—with books on the shelf, soft linens, and other interesting items throughout the room. It was perfect, so much so that Lane had chosen it for her own wedding.

Iris turned, leaned up against the counter, and scanned the beautifully decorated, welcoming lobby, then fixed her gaze on the roaring fire in the fireplace. "How long do you think this one's going to last?"

"Forever."

"You say that every time." Iris bumped Lane's shoulder.

"Because that is what I choose to believe." Lane waited patiently for the clerk, who seemed to be distracted by another clerk, who didn't appear to be proficient at her job. Probably training.

Iris blew out a breath. "I can't believe after that mother-of-all-effers, Belinda, left you at the altar, you still believe in true love." Iris never failed to bring up Lane's ex-fiancée when a client had a wedding at this particular hotel—the place where Lane had planned to be married. It had taken Iris less than ten minutes this time to mention the subject.

"Belinda didn't actually leave me at the altar, and that was a long time ago, Iris." It was actually a little over six months ago, although it seemed like only yesterday.

"Three days before is close enough." Iris was always reminding Lane that love was far from perfect—and heartbreak was inevitable.

"It wasn't meant to be. I'm probably better off without her." Lane had been devastated, hadn't been able to function for weeks after her ex had disappeared, and still slipped into depression when she thought about it too much. She'd forced herself to seek out therapy to deal with the whole situation. Even so, Lane still believed in true love and that she would find her soul mate someday.

"Do you still have doubts about that?" Iris propped an elbow on the counter as she turned to face her.

"Not really." Lane did wonder what went wrong. She hadn't had any contact with Belinda since it had happened.

It hadn't been the perfect relationship, but what couple could claim that status? Maybe celebrities Ellen and Portia, but she was sure it wasn't always smooth sailing for them either. The only difference was that they had stuck it out and were still together. Belinda, on the other hand, had bolted three days before their wedding for some reason unknown to Lane. She still hadn't worked up the courage to ask Belinda why and wasn't sure she really wanted to know.

"Then stop saying probably." Iris slapped her hand to the counter. "That means you're not sure. I for one know that you're much better off without that jackass."

The clerk startled and fumbled behind the counter. "Sorry for the delay." She quickly slid a key inside a paper jacket, jotted down the room number on the outside, and handed it to Iris.

"Thank you." Lane's stomach roiled as she picked up her makeup case and they exited the lobby toward the cantilevered staircase. "When Belinda left, I lost myself. It took me months to figure out who I was without her. Now that I have, I don't want to ever be that vulnerable again."

"Why not? That's what love is all about." Iris was always contradicting herself. One moment she was telling Lane that being in love was wonderful and the next that it sucked. Lane tended to believe she would have a happily ever after someday, though not right now.

As they ascended the steps, Lane admired the meticulous restored interiors of the mansion. The owners had made sure to retain the intimate ambiance of the private residence it once was while providing an elegant venue for events. After arriving at the door to the bridal prep suite, she glanced at her black velvet V-neck tea-length chiffon dress that fit her waist well and fanned out at the hem. Even though guest attire ranged from very casual to ultra-fancy, Lane always felt underdressed at this particular hotel.

Iris swiped the electronic key across the front of the scanner, and they entered the living-space side of the suite, which was a large, flexible working area designed specifically for weddings, and currently empty. They were early, so the bride was most likely still in the bedroom getting dressed.

Lane scanned the room looking for the best lighting for makeup and settled on the antique square table in the corner accompanied by a padded Victorian-style chair. "I'll set up for the bride over here." She pointed to the bar-height rectangular table on the opposite wall. "Will that work for the bridesmaids?"

Iris nodded. "Yep." She pulled one of the dark curtains open. When it came to makeup, it didn't matter if the venue was indoor or outdoor as long as they had good lighting.

She motioned to the table nearest the window, then pulled the remaining section of curtain all the way open. Sunshine spilled into the room, filling it with light. They had just finished laying out all their palettes, brushes, makeup, and other tools when the bride came into the room, followed by a few of her bridesmaids. She was already beautiful, and Lane would accentuate her features to stand out perfectly on her special day. "Did you do your regular skin care routine this morning?"

"I did." The bride nodded. "Just like you showed me." They'd held a dry run previously, so Lane knew exactly which makeup and color palette they were going with. She applied primer first, then a light layer of foundation, beginning in the center of the face and blending outward, to even her skin tone and reduce the appearance of blemishes, discoloration, and excess redness, although the bride had beautiful skin and didn't need much foundation. Next, she added concealer under the bride's eyes and to a couple of other small imperfections. All the products were a perfect match for her skin tone.

"I've also been drinking lots of water, like you said." The bride smiled widely, resembling a child trying to please her teacher.

"I can tell." Lane grinned back at her. "Your skin's glowing." Lane wouldn't deny her the reward.

There was a knock on the door and one of the bridesmaids answered it. A room-service waiter rolled a cart into the room and began opening a bottle of champagne. Several additional bridesmaids who had opted to do their own makeup came through the open door after him.

"Ooh, the bubbly's here." Lane glanced at the bride. "Are you ready for a glass?"

"Absolutely." The bride smiled. "Help yourself to a glass as well." She stood quickly, and Lane backed up to give her space. "So much water that I have to pee practically every thirty minutes." The bride turned and rushed to the bathroom.

"That's the only drawback." Lane chuckled as she watched her.

It was sweet of the bride to offer her a glass, but she didn't usually partake in the celebration early. It could sometimes make her hand unsteady. Lane crossed the room and reached for a flute of champagne from the cart.

"That's not for you." Helen swiped it from beneath her fingers.

Helen Trent was like a guard dog watching an already protected area. Lane had been hoping she'd be able to avoid the woman this time. Helen had been the planner on the last three weddings Lane had worked. It seemed they were on the same list somewhere. Would it be so bad if Helen were the least bit civil to her? She was always slapping Lane's hand for something or other. Lane considered her spring wedding track the schedule from hell, and Helen was the demon who set everything on fire.

"I'm aware." Lane narrowed her eyes as she picked up the tongs, plucked a strawberry from the tray, dropped it into the glass, and watched the champagne bubbles gather around it.

Helen held tight as Lane grasped it. "I said it's not for you." She pulled it from Lane's grasp, and the champagne spilled out onto her white button-down shirt. "Now look what you've done." She set the glass on the tray.

"Is everything all right over there?" The bride had stopped on her way back from the bathroom to talk to her maid of honor and was now watching them—they both were.

"Everything's fine." Helen smiled that perfect smile of hers. "Just cleaning up a little spill." She blotted the moisture from herself, and button-closed her blue suit to cover the stain.

"I have your glass right here." Lane held up another glass of champagne and dropped a strawberry into it. "Not for me," she ground out through gritted teeth at Helen before she headed back to the area of the room where the bride was now headed as well. Helen glared at her as she handed the glass to the bride. "I'll be right back. I need to get a few palettes from the other bag."

Maintaining eye contact with Helen, Lane walked the short distance to Iris. She wasn't going to let the Wicked Witch of the West intimidate her. "I hear most of the caterers are scared of her." A tidbit she'd overheard during her own wedding planning.

"Of course they are." Iris shivered. "I'm scared of her."

"Well, I'm not." Lane was terrified of Helen, but she wouldn't let anyone know—especially not Helen.

"I still can't believe you chose her as your wedding planner." Iris shrugged. "You'd think she'd be nicer to you after that."

"Belinda chose her." Lane found the colors she was searching for and tossed a palette and brush into a small bag for touchups later. "Just like everything else when it came to the wedding." Helen had been cordial at best during that process, always sticking to what Belinda requested since she was footing most of the bill.

"Thank God you're not still dealing with her." Iris grimaced.

"Looks like I am." And would be as long as she stayed in the wedding-makeup business. Lane watched Helen cross the room and attempt to wrangle the newly arrived, rowdy bridesmaids who'd been joined by the bride. She cursed herself for ogling her long legs with shapely muscles designed specifically for wearing expensive three-inch heels. The woman was ridiculously sexy and elegant, but as soon as she opened her mouth, all that allure was immediately ruined. The first time Lane had met Helen, which was way before she'd become engaged to Belinda, she'd thought it was love at first sight. Once she'd gotten to know her, she'd liked her less and less. Unfortunately, still being the glass-half-full girl she was, Lane always thought Helen might change over time, but every time she saw Helen, her dreams were crushed.

Was it weird to think a beautiful woman should have a beautiful soul as well?

The bride walked back across the room and sat in the chair. "Sorry about that. I needed to hug my girls."

"No sorrys today. This is your day." Lane found the colors she'd planned to use. "Just a bit of eyeliner, shadow, and mascara, and we'll be finished."

The bride closed her eyes instinctively, and Lane applied the eye makeup. She wished all her wedding parties were this easy to please. Her only issue today was Helen, and Lane planned to avoid her for the rest of the evening. "All done." She backed up and handed the bride a mirror.

"I'm beautiful." The bride seemed surprised, as though Lane had performed a magical transformation.

"Of course you are. You were beautiful before." She took the mirror back. "I used a long-lasting foundation that should get you through the evening, and I've added a couple of things to this bag in case you need a touch-up later tonight."

"Thank you so much." The bride stood and gave her a hug before she headed into the other suite to put on her wedding dress.

"You gonna help me put the makeup away?" Iris nudged Lane's shoulder with her hand. "What's going on with you today?"

She watched Helen across the room. "I don't like the way she thinks." Or the way Helen treated her.

"Who? Helen? Thinks in general or about something in particular?" Iris was jabbing at her, as usual.

Lane nodded. "The way she assumes she knows everything."

"Surely she doesn't know everything." Iris glanced at Helen, who was straightening whatever personal items the bridesmaids had brought into the room. "Well, she knows how to push your buttons, but she doesn't know how to make those baby blues pop with her makeup." She looked Helen up and down. "She's attractive for sure, but if you helped her with those eyes, she'd be irresistible."

"I'm not sure that one could ever be irresistible." She was certainly alluring, with her perfect ass and gorgeous legs, hence the reason Lane couldn't seem to keep from looking at her. She had to get her roaming eyes in check.

"Why don't you find out?" Iris handed her an eye shadow palette with warm-toned color shades. "See if she's open to trying something new." She raised an eyebrow. "That might just be your in."

"What makes you think I want an in with her?" That ship had sailed long ago, along with any thoughts of docking it.

"The fact that for the last few events we've worked with her, you can't keep your eyes off her." Iris gave her a sideways smile.

Lane pulled her eyebrows together. "That's not true." She'd been more obvious than she'd thought. She packed a few more items into her bag for when they headed downstairs to the event area of the hotel. Once the bride's makeup was done, Lane usually stayed around until after the beginning of the reception, just in case touchups were needed.

Iris laughed. "Oh, but I think it is."

"Whatever." She didn't intend to touch that one, even if she couldn't keep her mind off the suit coat that hung at the top curve of Helen's perfect ass, and how her skirt stopped just above her knees, allowing her long legs to peek out from beneath it. She fanned herself with a palette box. She needed to get out of there before she did something she'd regret.

❖

The ceremony had gone smoothly, as usual, and now the reception was in full swing. The bride was beautiful on her special day, thanks to a bit of help from Lane. Helen couldn't deny she had the magic touch when it came to bridal makeup. She glanced across the room and caught sight of her. It had been only a week since Helen had seen Lane, but she didn't affect her any differently. To keep her distance, she'd tried to remain at odds with her at each event they worked together since Lane's non-wedding. After the first glimpse she'd had of her today, she'd quickly moved in the opposite direction, but now she couldn't take her eyes off her. Lane was dressed in a low-cut black dress that accentuated her waist nicely. She had wonderful curvy hips hidden beneath the velvet that Helen knew would feel good under her hands, but she needed to keep this relationship professional. Right?

The body language changed between Lane and the man talking to her. Helen moved closer to see what was going on. She wasn't in the habit of eavesdropping, but the man was a little drunk and couldn't seem to keep quiet.

He reared his head back and looked at Lane. "Hey, you want to grab a drink after this?"

Lane gave him a tentative smile. "That's very sweet of you to ask, but I don't think that's wise."

"Why?" The man moved toward Lane.

"You seem a little intoxicated." Lane turned her head to the side and backed up.

Helen leaned closer and listened intently. At least Lane seemed to know how to avoid a bad situation.

"Sure, I've had a glass of champagne or two, but that doesn't change the fact that you're a great conversationalist." He moved closer. "And you have killer green eyes." He took a strand of her hair between his fingers and let it run through them. "Sorry. I've been imagining what it felt like since I first saw you."

What a ridiculous line. Helen glanced over her shoulder and watched him lean in and Lane back up farther. Total fail on his part. She couldn't blame the guy for trying. Lane was the most attractive woman in the room.

"You seem like someone I'd like to get to know." He shook off the rejection and took another sip of champagne as he moved closer to Lane.

Helen caught Lane's attention, trying to let her know that she was nearby if she needed help. They weren't friends, but Helen wouldn't leave her alone in a bad situation.

Lane seemed to understand and returned her attention to the man. "In another life, possibly." She smiled. "However, in this one, my dating circle consists of women."

He didn't speak for a moment, obviously letting the information sink in. Helen did the same. She'd been aware of that fact about Lane but had avoided thinking of her in a dating sense.

"Oh." The man pulled his eyebrows together. "No men at all?"

Helen moved toward them. This situation seemed to be turning in another direction.

Lane held up her hand, waving Helen off. "Not since I was sixteen."

"Sixteen." He gave her a cocky grin. "There's a difference between boys and men, you know."

That was it. Helen shot between them. "Lane. The bride needs a makeup refresh. Do you think you can check on her for me?"

As the man stepped away a bit, Lane narrowed her eyes. "I had this under control."

"I'm sure you did." Helen raised her eyebrows and nodded. "The bride, though. She needs you after all that crying from the toast. Will you check on her, please?"

"Uh. Sure." Lane slipped around her and headed to the bridal table.

The man watched Lane walk away before he focused on Helen. "I was only being friendly."

"I'm sure you were. I think you've had enough champagne." She plucked the glass from the man's hand. "Now you can either go back to your table and have a glass of water, or you can leave. Your choice."

She didn't need anyone getting out of hand this early in the reception. If he persisted, Helen would personally show him to the door.

CHAPTER TWO

L ane drove home on autopilot and found herself in front of Belinda's house for the third time that month. She sat for a minute and stared at the beauty of the front yard. It had been a desolate, brown patch of ragged grass when she'd moved in a couple of years ago during the winter. Lane had planted shrubs, roses, and other perennial flowers that had come to life the following spring. She'd nurtured them daily until hers had become the most beautiful yard on the block. She had to admit that it had turned out much better than she'd expected. Now she got to enjoy it only in passing or when she let her subconscious do the navigating on her drive home, which was happening way too much lately.

Sometimes she wondered if she nurtured the yard more than she'd nurtured her relationship with Belinda and, on occasion, had thoughts about leaving it. It was difficult to let go of what Lane had thought her future was going to be, but she needed dependability in a partner. It took Belinda's one last devastating act for Lane to realize she was everything but dependable. At first, Lane found Belinda's spontaneity refreshing and fun, but as their relationship grew, Lane saw it as irritating. On more than one occasion, Belinda ignored what Lane had decided to do for weekends or even dinner with friends and opted to go off on her own on a different adventure. Belinda rarely stuck to plans.

Lane spotted a shadow inside the house through the curtains and yanked the car into gear. All she needed was to get caught by Belinda in front of her place. A stalker that wouldn't take her ex's calls was unique, wasn't it? Since Lane's breakup with Belinda, she'd been living with Iris a few blocks away. Thank God she had a spare room, but Lane would've slept on the floor at that point to get out of Belinda's place. It had been almost six months since Belinda had broken her heart, and she really needed to get her own place now instead of imposing on Iris. But Iris didn't seem to mind, and she just wasn't ready to be alone yet.

Lane stepped through the doorway of her current home, pulled the band from her hair, and began peeling off items of clothing as she walked into her bedroom. She couldn't wait to get out of this dress. She hung it in the closet and put on a pair of leggings and a crop top. This would do until Darcy, her best friend, texted and let her know where they were going tonight.

She headed into the kitchen of the small, two-bedroom house, pulled open the refrigerator door, and plucked a beer from the shelf, along with a jar of salsa. She was famished. She grabbed the chips from the counter where she'd left them last night and headed to the couch in the living room, where she put her feet up and clicked on the TV before she took her laptop from the side table to check her email. It was her week to respond to any inquiries regarding event makeup.

After logging in, she scrolled through the multiple emails. *Delete, delete, delete.* The spam was out of control. She was just about to log out when a new email popped up from someone named Jessica Adams. The subject line read *Availability for February 4th.*

> *My wedding is scheduled for February 4th of next year, and I was wondering what your availability is for that date. The wedding venue we have chosen is the Dallas Country Club, but we plan to get ready at the Hotel Crescent Court nearby on Crescent Court. At least me, my five bridesmaids, and potentially a few other family members will need their makeup done.*
>
> *I sincerely hope you have this date available, as I have heard great things about your services.*
>
> *Thanks, Jessica*

She thumbed through her bookings in her head and didn't recall being busy then. She leaned sideways, swiped her planner from the end table, found the date, and confirmed they had an opening. If the wedding was at the country club, that meant Helen was probably the event planner. She couldn't afford to pass up bookings, so she'd just have to suck it up and ignore her condescending attitude. She dropped her planner onto the couch before she hit reply and began typing.

Hello Jessica!
Congratulations on your engagement! I'm happy to say that we are available for your big day and would love to work with you.
Attached is our price list and contract for you to look over. We are still honoring this year's prices if you book with us by the end of July. Please don't hesitate to let us know if you have any questions.
Thank you!
Lane & Iris

Just about every bride they had contracts with also had a contract with Helen. It was clear Helen was good at her job or that wouldn't be the case. She googled *Helen Trent*, and a variety of information filled the screen.

Helen had lived in Chicago for a brief time before she moved back to Dallas. She was forty-four years old, but Lane would never have guessed that. She'd thought she was much younger, close to her own age. She scrolled farther down the page, found her business website, and clicked on it. The website was well done, each section grabbing her attention. It popped with color, but not too much color, and provided links to all the typical social media pages. She clicked on each of them, drilling down to each detail, then spun off to Helen's brother's social media as well. He had a beautiful wife and several children that seemed to be very active. There were multiple pictures of Helen with them at outdoor adventures. The resemblance between the two siblings was uncanny. She wasn't immune to the sight of Helen's tanned, defined arms, she zoomed in closer on her face—the woman was beautiful—but Iris wasn't wrong about making her eyes pop with a little makeup. She blew out a breath as she clicked out of the page. She'd gone down a rabbit hole that she wasn't able to dig herself out of. The guy really needed to make his pages private, if only for the sake of his children's privacy. Why did she find Helen Trent's life so interesting? She slapped the laptop closed and tossed it onto the couch next to her before she found her phone and sent a text to her friend Darcy.

Want to go to Ruby's tonight? Ruby's, the most popular bar in town, catered to everyone, and she needed some distraction.

Can't tonight. Something came up with James.

Ugh. *But we had plans?* Lane typed.

The bubbles appeared, and a new text came through from Darcy.

I'm sorry. He said it's important.

Lane sighed. Couple plans were getting in the way again. *I'll need details in the morning.*

Of course. Darcy rarely kept secrets from Lane and vice versa.

Lane typed in a new message to Iris this time. *When will you be home?*

Wrapping up at my mom's now. Iris had gone there after the event to help her with something.

I feel like dancing.

I'm exhausted. How about a movie night instead? Lane had figured that was coming. They'd had a long day, and Iris rarely went to bars anymore since she'd become engaged to Harvey, unless Lane begged her to be her wingman.

But what will my feet do? They're begging me to dance.

I'll pick up some wine on the way home. That'll make them happy.

They'll want pizza with that wine. If Lane wasn't going to distract herself with people, she'd need food.

Okay. I'll get that too. Find a good movie.

Lane dropped her phone to her lap, grabbed the remote, and began scrolling through the movie selections.

CHAPTER THREE

Helen microwaved her meal, poured herself a glass of red wine, put them both on the tray, and carried them into the living room, where she sat watching her favorite show about brides finding exactly the right dress. Her feet were killing her. She really needed to stop wearing heels. She towered above everyone without them, but she liked the authority they gave her. People listened more carefully when she made her presence known.

The titles scrolled rapidly on the TV screen as she held the button down on the remote, trying to find the episode on her DVR that she'd begun to watch last week. She'd recorded the whole season and hadn't had a chance to view many of the segments. After she found the one with the cute consultant she'd been searching for, she settled in. She'd eaten only a few bites of her dinner when her phone buzzed with a text from her brother Will.

Going to grill at Mom and Dad's tonight. Come over.

She glanced at the tiny Lean Cuisine meal on the tray in front of her. *What time?*

I'm getting the kids packed now.

Need me to bring anything?

Nope. Picking up the steaks on the way.

Helen sipped from her glass of red. *I'll bring the wine.*

Perfect came across the screen immediately.

Helen pushed the tray back and stood. She hadn't planned to go out this evening, but a night at the pool with her brother and his brood was always fun. However, it was a tossup as to whether she enjoyed the rest of the family.

❖

Helen dove into the pool and swam several laps before she took the body board from the edge of the pool and tucked it under her arms. Will was running later than he'd indicated, which was okay. That would give her some time to relax in the pool alone. She closed her eyes as she floated to let her mind clear, as she usually did after an event. Only it wasn't easy today. She couldn't shake the vision of Lane from her head. The woman was both incredibly attractive and ridiculously infuriating at the same time. Instead of the usual mindless relaxation she enjoyed, she found herself remembering Lane's face, the outline of her jaw, her gorgeous green eyes, and those luscious lips that looked to be made specifically for kissing and other intimate things. And her neck, long and slender, was perfect for nuzzling—a lead-in to trailing kisses down along her collarbone and beyond.

A splash of water covered her face—a well-needed interruption. She opened her eyes and smiled as a stream of additional splashes followed as several of her nieces and nephews cannonballed into the pool. Will ran across the deck after them, launching a perfect dive into the deep end. This was a pleasant surprise. She hadn't realized she was going to get to see her sister Gwen's kids as well. Will hadn't mentioned them when they'd spoken earlier. She wasn't keen on seeing her sister, since the last time they'd talked, when Gwen had told her exactly what she'd thought about Helen's current career choice. Gwen didn't pull any punches. She was like their mother in that way.

The ability to join in the joy of her siblings' families was the only thing that got Helen over the fact that she didn't have children of her own. She could create a family herself, since she had the money to support a couple of kids but had always imagined having a partner when she moved into that phase of her life. At forty-four, she had become increasingly aware that she might never have the whole family package.

Her brother took a lap before he swam across the pool to where Helen was floating. "Sorry about the splashing." Will had the perfect smile that always cheered her up immediately.

"No, you aren't." She glanced at the kids. "Can't stop 'em, have to join 'em." Helen pushed a blade of water into Will's face before she let go of the board and sank below the surface. She swam like a fish to the ladder, climbed out, and walked to the diving board. "Splash contest." She stepped quickly to the end, bounced off the board, and tucked her legs into her arms.

Her brother followed. "Cannonball away." Billy, Ava, TR, and Lizzie followed, but none of the kids' splashes could compare to Will's. Nor could Helen's. He was the master splasher and had been perfecting his skill since he was a child spending endless hours in the pool.

Next came the races. Everyone lined up at the end of the pool.

"On my go," he said as he propped a foot against the side of the pool behind him. He always found a way to give himself an edge— even against his own children.

Helen did the same and readied herself to race. "No false starts or you're out." She glanced over at Will, and he winked.

"One, two, three." Will hesitated. "Go." He launched himself into the race.

Helen shoved off as well but didn't swim all the way. Instead, she floated to the edge and watched as they raced to the end of the pool, did a flip turn, and swam back. Will would win. He always did. Ever since he was a kid, his need to compete had been strong, as was Gwen's. Yet somehow, she'd been born without that gene.

Will's hand slapped the edge of the pool as he emerged from the water. "Still champion." He cheered as each one of the kids finished the race after him.

"Someday these kids are going to leave you in their wake," she pointed to TR. "Especially him." TR, short for Trent Robert, was Gwen's oldest. He was already over five feet tall and only eleven years old. The combined height genes of their two families seemed to have merged into just one child. Billy at ten years old, Ava at eight, and Lizzie at nine all seemed to be average height for their ages now, but that would soon change as they grew older. Helen climbed out of the pool, walked to the covered cabana area, and took a couple of beers from the mini fridge, along with a small container of lime wedges. She held one up to Will.

He got out of the pool and relaxed into a chair. "Did you have an event today?"

She nodded. "Have them pretty much every Saturday. Sometimes Friday and Sunday too." Though on Sundays she mostly met with clients.

"That's awesome." He squeezed a slice of lime into his beer and shoved it down the neck of the bottle. "Soon you'll be running that country club."

"Eh. Not something I aspire to do." She sipped her beer. "Too much managerial work. I just want to make people happy."

"Have you told Mom that?" He set his beer on the table. "You know she thinks you're going to take the club on, right? She's been priming the board members for months."

"I know." Helen wiped a bead of sweat from her glass. "She's going to be disappointed again." She blew out a breath. "Why can't she just realize I'm happy doing what I do?"

"She's never satisfied. You just have to walk away when she starts."

"It's not that simple. She'd see a lot of my back. It'd be easier if I didn't have a younger brother who superseded anything I did." She grinned. She wasn't jealous in the slightest. In fact, she was happy for Will's success.

"Yes, it would be." He grinned "But you can't stop this legal machine." He used the nickname Helen had given him when he'd begun law school.

"I'm disappointed you didn't put that nickname in neon on the building sign below your name." She traced her finger in the air. "William Trent, Legal Machine."

"I seriously thought about it, but Dad wouldn't allow it." Will shook his head. "He said it would make the other partners jealous."

"He ruins all the fun."

"Right? That was my exact thought." Will laughed. "Seriously, though, you're avoiding the question. Artfully, but still dodging the subject. What's your plan if you're not interested in running the club?"

"I'm going into business for myself." Helen sucked in a deep breath. "I know this sounds weird, but I really do like making people happy." When she'd come upon this job opportunity, event planning for a company called Dreams to Reality, she hadn't been prepared to like it as much as she did. Making people happy on their special days created joy and sent endorphins throughout Helen each and every time she saw the outcome. But now, she was tired of the mother-may-I scenarios Lydia, her boss, put her through when Helen was the one bringing in the money and Lydia was raking in all the profits.

"You need money?" Will raised his eyebrows. "I can talk to Ash. I'm sure she and I have enough to help you get your business off the ground."

"No, but thanks. I have a plan." Helen shook her head. She needed only one more year to make her plan work—to break away from Lydia and Dreams to Reality. She watched her nieces and nephews as they played pool games. "You really lucked out with those kids, you know."

"Yeah. They have their moments, but all in all they're pretty special." He took a pull on his beer. "So, if you're not going to take over the country club, when do you plan to find that special woman and settle down...have some kids of your own?"

"Not in the near future. I'll be busy getting my business going." She shook her head.

"Do it before you make that career move." He shrugged. "Find someone who can support you in it."

"I don't know if that will ever happen. I can't seem to find the right woman." Helen always seemed to attract women looking for support from her rather than the opposite.

"Ever think that maybe *you're* the reason you can't find the perfect woman? You have some pretty high standards." He glanced at her momentarily before he continued to watch the kids. "The perfect woman isn't out there on display for everyone to see. You have to look past some things to get to the heart of a person."

"Is that what you did with Ash?" She leaned back and cocked her head. "Are you saying you didn't marry the perfect woman?"

"No. Ashley is absolutely that." He grinned. "I'm lucky you were involved with what's-her-name when we met, and I got to her first."

"Damn right you are." Helen had introduced Will to Ashley many years ago. They'd met during Helen's accounting phase, but the only two things that came out of that career venture were Helen's ability to create a budget and Ash joining the family. Ash was a gorgeous brunette with a killer body. They were friendly at first, and Helen thought she might have a shot at her until she'd made the mistake of bringing Ash to a family event, where she met Will. After that, Ash only had eyes for him. She'd jokingly told Helen more than once that bringing her home had been her biggest mistake. So, now she rarely brought women to the house when her family was there.

"What about the ones from summer, fall, and winter?" He looked into the sky. "I tried to alphabetize them all, but I got confused."

"I see your point. Don't try. It hurts my head just to think about it. And there were two women last summer. It almost killed me." She wasn't fond of running through all her relationships and the reasons for the breakups.

"Right. That hot brunette was a handful, huh?"

"She was a huge liar. I couldn't trust anything she said." Helen took a drink of her beer. "You have no idea how much of my stuff went missing when she stayed over. Plus, she started contacting the other woman I was seeing." She'd never juggle dating two women again.

"What about the pretty blonde, the one who lived in Fort Worth?" He smiled. "She seemed like a keeper."

"Yeah. I really liked her, but Mom hated her." Helen had thought she might be the one because she was super supportive, but according to her mother, she didn't have enough ambition. Which, in hindsight, was probably exactly what Helen needed in a partner. Two highly driven women in a relationship didn't make for a good support system. Especially when no one was ever home to greet the other one after a hard day of work.

"You need to tell Mom to keep her opinions to herself. After all. She ended up with Dad." He chuckled. "But seriously. In the end, you need to decide who and what makes you happy. You need to stop hopping from woman to woman."

Helen raised an eyebrow. "Hopping?"

Will let out a laugh. "Okay. That sounded bad, but you know what I mean."

"You're one to talk." Helen laughed. "How many women did you go through before you found Ash?"

"Too many." He flattened his lips and nodded. "But now I'm really, really happy."

"I can see that." Helen glanced at the children. "So, did you just stop noticing other woman altogether, or did that just kind of fade?"

"I put Ash front and center in my life because she was important to me." He took in a deep breath and let it out slowly. "I didn't really look at other women after I found her. No one else compared, and I didn't ever want to hurt her in any way."

"Wow. That's very noble thinking." Helen wished she could be as altruistic about the women she dated.

"I knew she was the one—my forever girl—and I didn't want to blow it. So, I deleted all the women out of my contacts and kept it that way."

"You really did go all in." Will seemed to have the perfect life.

"I did, and you should too the next time you're attracted to someone. You're gonna miss out on a whole lot if you don't." He patted her on the knee before he stood. "Lower those initial expectations and get to know someone. You might find *your* forever girl where you never expected." He paced back to the pool and dove in.

Helen envied what Will had with Ash—wanted the same thing to some extent but wasn't sure she'd be able to maintain that kind of relationship with someone. Would she be able to discuss all her decisions with them? Alter her plans if that person wanted her to? She'd always been solely in control of her choices.

Her mother had given up her career to be the perfect wife to her father, the corporate lawyer. Her mother had everything she wanted, but could she exist on her own if she needed to? If she lost her dad or… if he left?

Her sister, Gwen, had done the same, and it was obvious how unfulfilled she was—how unhappy she'd become without having the passion of a career in her life. Gwen hadn't been able to channel that love into a passion for raising her children, as so many other women had done successfully. It seemed to be all or nothing in her family. Did it have to be that way? Maybe she needed to loosen up her expectations a bit and expand her scope. There were plenty of single women out there. It shouldn't be this hard to find someone to love.

Will popped his head out of the water long enough to shout, "Maybe you can strike a truce with Gwen. I'm sure she can introduce you to plenty of women."

"Maybe, but she'll have to make the first move. I'm tired of being talked down to." Her sister was notorious for being passive-aggressive. Even when she gave Helen a compliment, she didn't trust that it was genuine, and criticism usually followed on the back end.

"That's just Gwen. She does that to me too, and look how successful I am." Will grinned.

She held back a smile as she laughed. "A bit full of yourself, aren't you?"

Will launched out of the water to snag the mini football the boys were throwing back and forth. "Heads up," he said as he tossed it to Lizzie, who let it land in the water in front of her, splashing her in the face.

"Uncle Will, *stop*." The last word came out of Lizzie's mouth hard. Lizzie was the prim one of the girls, never wanting to mess up her makeup. That trait came straight from Gwen. Will's daughter, Ava, on the other hand, could hold her own with the boys, always wanting to participate in all the games.

Helen padded to the pool and went down the steps into the water. She inched her way closer to the game, and the next time the ball came TR's way, Helen launched out of the water in front of him and snagged it. Will waved his arms, and she tossed it to him to begin a raging game of keep-away. Ava joined in to complete a triangle, while Lizzie slipped out of the pool and found a lounge chair and her cell phone. Another beautiful afternoon with the Trent offspring.

Chapter Four

L ane stretched out across the mattress, soothing the aching muscles from her shoulders to her calves. It was her first Sunday off in what seemed like forever, and she planned to lounge around in bed as long as she could. She rolled over and pressed her face into her pillow. After Belinda, she was finally getting used to being alone—not completely alone, but without Belinda sleeping next to her in bed. Iris still slept in the other bedroom, it being Iris's house and all. The automatic coffeemaker kicked into gear, filling the house with the aroma of the blond roast she adored.

She picked up her phone, and when it didn't light up with the motion, she realized it was dead. She slid out of bed, taking the phone with her to charge in the kitchen. It sounded when she plugged it in, and the slight hint of a red bar appeared on the screen. It was still alive, just resting, same as her. She didn't notice the text from her best friend, Darcy, until it popped up on the screen after she'd poured her first cup of coffee and taken the first glorious sip of the black nectar that kept her going.

Meet me at The Golden Egg at ten.

Ugh. She was planning to do nothing all morning, with another session of nothing in the afternoon that lasted well into the night. She glanced at the clock. It was still before nine, so she could make it if she wanted to—but did she really want to? After Darcy had ditched her last night, she was still a little irritated. Playing second fiddle all the time was getting old.

She heard laughter, then low voices from Iris's room. She closed her eyes and blew out a breath as she recognized the low, rolling sounds.

Iris's boyfriend, Harvey, must've come over after they'd gone to bed. *Brunch with Darcy it is.* She rushed to the bedroom to get dressed and out of earshot before the main event began. Doing nothing was going to have to wait until this afternoon.

❖

Lane loved the theme of this breakfast spot. With golden eggs and chicken art hand-painted on the walls, it always made her feel like she was in a fairy-tale storybook. Plus, the food was delicious. They had a massive variety of omelets and special versions of hollandaise and benedicts, not to mention the soups and salads if you weren't in the mood for breakfast. She glanced around the restaurant, which was filling up quickly, but Darcy was nowhere in sight, so she snagged a booth and ordered a cup of coffee. After the wine-and-movie night with Iris, she needed copious amounts of coffee.

Darcy swept into the restaurant, grinning widely. "I have some exciting news." She held out her hand and wiggled her fingers, and a beautiful diamond sparkled in the light.

"Oh my God." Lane slid out of the booth, grabbed hold of Darcy's arms, and they jumped up and down like schoolgirls. "I'm so glad James finally got his shit together and asked you." She would excuse the ditching last night for that.

Darcy sat in the booth across from her and admired her ring. "Right? I thought he was never going to ask."

"Did you set a date?" Thoughts of the fun they'd have during the wedding planning spun in Lane's mind.

"September twenty-third." Darcy waved at their usual waitress.

"But that's only a few months away." Lane took in a deep breath, thinking about all the things she would have to accomplish. "We can do it." She took a gulp of coffee and swallowed. "It won't be easy, but I'll get started on a few things tomorrow."

The waitress appeared, placed a cup of coffee in front of Darcy and topped off Lane's, then dropped the pot at the station and returned. "Are you two ready to order?"

"This calls for a celebration." Lane glanced at the waitress. "Mimosas, please." That would take the edge off the mild headache building in her head.

"Half bottle or whole of champagne?"

"Just half," Darcy said. "I have too much to do today for day drinking."

"Coming right up." The waitress spun and headed to the bar.

"Do you have a venue in mind?" Lane knew there were only so many places Darcy would consider. She could be very particular, and it could be difficult finding one this late in the game.

"We're going to have it at my dad's country club." Darcy picked up her coffee and held it between her hands.

"Oh. That's a beautiful place." Lane, having been there many times before, envisioned the ballroom all decked out in wedding decorations of silver and blue, Darcy's favorite colors. "Is it even available? I would think it would have already been booked for months."

Darcy nodded. "My dad's a member of the board, and he pulled a few strings to make it happen." She sipped her coffee and set it back on the table. "Just one more thing." Darcy's fingertips whitened as she held her cup tightly. Must be something big. "I've asked Audrey to be my matron of honor."

"What? Why?" Lane's neck heated as a jolt of anxiety rushed through her. "We'd always talked about you being mine and me being yours." Disappointment hit her hard.

"I know." Darcy rolled her lips in. "But I couldn't get out of it. Since my sister had me as her maid of honor, she expected to be mine. I tried to explain, but she was so excited, and my mother agreed that I should ask her."

"Well, fuck me, then." Lane couldn't hold in her disappointment.

"Lane." Darcy reached across the table and touched her hand. "Don't be like that. You know you're my best friend, and I would do anything for you."

"Except choose me over your sister." Darcy's sister was always about herself. "You know it's going to be a shit show with her at the wheel." Lane flopped back into the booth and crossed her arms.

"That's why I'm still going to need your help."

"So, you want me to be the maid of honor without actually having the title."

"Yes. Unofficially," Darcy said softly as she scrunched her eyebrows and batted her lashes, giving Lane the puppy-dog look she couldn't resist. "I know it's a lot to ask."

It was definitely a lot to ask, but Darcy knew exactly how to pull Lane's heart strings. She always had. "Okay. I'll do it."

"Thank you, thank you, thank you." Darcy popped up, slid into the side of the booth next to Lane, and pulled her into a hug.

"But if she gets in the way—"

"Just give me a heads-up, and I'll take care of it. You'll have carte blanche on everything. With my approval, of course." Darcy slid across the leather, returned to her seat across from Lane, and picked up a menu. "Let's order. I'm starving."

Lane picked up her menu and peeked over the top at Darcy, who was staring down at hers with a huge smile. Lane couldn't muster the same joy. She was still super disappointed, but she would officially be the unofficial maid of honor because Darcy asked.

CHAPTER FIVE

Helen drove through the gates and up the driveway into the circle drive, then put the car in park and killed the engine. Helen's mother, Caroline, had sent a text that simply said she needed to see her. When Helen had responded, her mother hadn't written back. Helen didn't particularly like being summoned, but that was her mom's usual pattern—throw out an SOS and nothing more to make sure Helen showed up. Not the way she wanted to spend her afternoon. She had plenty of things to do for her next event.

The front door was unlocked, as usual. Helen entered and crossed the massive living room and into the kitchen, where her mother sat at the breakfast-nook table drinking coffee.

"You know you're not supposed to have coffee this late in the day." Helen dropped her keys onto the counter before she sat adjacent from her mother and swiped the mug from her hands. "You'll never be able to sleep." She took a sip and enjoyed the warmth spreading throughout her throat.

"Who needs sleep anyway?" Her mom swiped the cup back. "Get yourself a mug. It's fresh."

Helen stood, crossed the kitchen, and took a mug from the cabinet. "That's the spirit. Think of menopause as the gift that keeps on giving."

"I'm not able to drink much in the morning, since your father's doctor said we should cut back." She shivered. "And tea just isn't the same."

"How's Dad doing with the new diet?"

"Let's just say he's used to eating more trans fats than he thought. They're in so many products." Caroline dropped her head back. "I had to buy new glasses to check the fine print on food labels for the words 'trans' and 'hydrogenated.'" The table shook as she dropped a hand to it. "And don't get me started on his salt intake. Needless to say, he's a bit grumpier than usual."

"Dad, grumpy? Never." Helen knew the lifestyle change would be a struggle, but the doctor maintained that they could reduce his risk of developing further health problems by changing his diet. She filled the mug halfway, took a sip, and hissed as the hot liquid burned her tongue. "What's the emergency?"

Caroline relaxed in her chair and crossed her legs. "I need you to handle an event at the country club."

"Okay." Helen sat again. "Just email me the details."

"I will." Caroline nodded. "I wanted to go over some of the particulars with you first."

Helen sipped her coffee. Sounded like this might be a bigger event than usual.

"It's a wedding for a board member's daughter." Caroline hesitated. "And it's in three months."

"What?" Helen choked on her coffee. "That's a ridiculous ask, Mother. It takes months to even find the appropriate people to handle all the details of a wedding." She stood and headed to the formal living room. She needed something stronger than coffee for this conversation.

"That's why I'm asking you." Caroline followed her from the kitchen. "You've been wanting to branch out on your own. This will give you the opportunity."

"I'm not sure this is the opportunity I was looking for." The seal popped as Helen removed the stopper from the Waterford crystal decanter and poured herself a splash of bourbon. "A month ago, you didn't think event planning was a worthy enough career for a Trent, and now you expect me to run around like a crazy woman begging people to do things at the last minute?" She sipped, letting the whiskey burn slowly down her throat. Caroline was always asking for impossible things with unmanageable deadlines that couldn't possibly be met easily. Helen could probably enlist Teigen, her assistant at Dreams to Reality, to help. She could trust her to be discreet—to keep it from her boss, Lydia—but it was still a huge ask.

"I'm not fond of your newfound career choice, but you *are* good at it, and I've supported your decision." Her mother took Helen's hands.

"Just think of it as a way to show your father how successful you've become."

Her mother knew that remark would hit a nerve. Being successful was important to Helen, and having her father—her family—acknowledge that fact was important to her. "Fine, but you might need to make some contacts for me."

"I can absolutely do that." Caroline sat on the couch. "By the way, your father has someone for you to meet." Her mother gave her a smirk. "Thinks he's the perfect man for you." She laughed out loud. "He's invited him to dinner tonight."

"Good grief." Helen shook her head. "Do I have to tell him again?" Growing up, she'd been a daddy's girl—the biggest tomboy on the block—but for some reason her father couldn't grasp the fact that she didn't date men—ever.

"Probably. Your father firmly believes that love is about the person, not the gender. He's always on the lookout for your soul match."

Helen rushed into the kitchen and swiped her keys from the counter. "I hope he's grilling something good, because I'm not staying to ride this one out." She took off toward the door before her mother could protest. No way was she going to sit through a dinner of awkward conversation just to disappoint another man. She pulled open the door and ran straight into her sister, Gwen.

"Leaving so soon?" Gwen moved through the door and closed it behind her. "I think Dad has a surprise for you."

"The exact reason I'm leaving." She should've known that her sister was involved somehow.

"Oh, darn. That's the only reason I came over." Gwen pulled her lip to one side. "I was hoping for a good show."

"Well, then you can take center stage." Helen rolled her eyes. "Maybe he'll be a better match for you than Robert is."

"Robert is my perfect match. You know that."

"All I know is that since you've moved into the stay-at-home-mom role, you've been riding my ass more than ever." Her sister had to be in control of something, and since she wasn't working, she tried to run everyone's life instead.

"I can't help it if you can't find a career and stick with it. You make yourself an easy target."

"Ah. That sisterly love is shining through again." Helen jerked open the door. "Have fun plotting with Dad tonight." She glanced back over her shoulder. "Next time you go hunting for someone for me, make sure she's the right gender."

"Are you coming for the Fourth of July barbecue?" her mother shouted.

"That all depends on the guest list." She pulled the door closed behind her. She wasn't in the mood for any more of her dad's matchmaking or Gwen's criticism.

CHAPTER SIX

L ane glanced around the country club as they entered. "I can't believe you were able to book this place on such short notice."

"I know. I've been dreaming of having my wedding here since I was a kid. Thankfully my dad swings a lot of business their way. Has a lot of work events here. I guess they figure that's worth satisfying him."

"I heard they're booked out until next spring." Lane checked her phone. "I thought Audrey was meeting us?" It was after ten and there was no sign of her.

"She sent me a text. She's going to be late." Darcy shrugged. "Something came up at work."

Well, that's just bullshit. "I guess we can start without her." Lane was still miffed that she was going to be the unofficial maid of honor, putting in all the work and getting none of the credit. She glanced at Darcy. Did she really need more glory than her best friend's gratitude?

Darcy's phone chimed, and she checked her text messages. "That's Helen. She's already here somewhere."

"Helen Trent is your wedding planner?" Could there be another planner named Helen? The probability of that was slim to none.

"Yeah, another contact of my father. Her parents are members of the board."

"*Of course* they are." No wonder Helen was the planner on so many weddings. Lane couldn't believe her rotten luck. Now she was going to have to deal with two difficult people during this wedding process. At least Helen knew what she was doing.

"Every time I saw a bride's blog about this place, I took notes." Darcy pulled out her checklist. "It looks big enough to hold everyone."

"How many people are you inviting?"

"At least two hundred. Probably more. We haven't received the lists from James's parents."

"Wow. That's a lot." Lane hadn't realized the event was going to be that large. "I thought you wanted a more intimate ceremony."

"I did, but James has just as many friends as I do." Darcy shrugged. "Plus, he has a lot of colleagues and clients from work that he wants to invite."

"Clients?" Lane hadn't expected Darcy to invite total strangers. "Really?"

Darcy nodded. "It's kind of expected when you work in finance." She strolled to the wall of French doors that led to the outdoor space. "We can do indoor and outdoor if the guest count rises." She checked off a line on her list. "I've seen pictures of that, and it's really lovely."

"You should do that anyway. People who like the heat can go outside to warm up, and those who don't can stay inside where it's cool." Lane smiled as she opened the doors and stepped outside. The patio was beautiful, lined with columned walls and boxwood shrubs to section it from the walkways surrounding it. "Think how beautiful this will be all lit up with strings of white lights and white-linen-covered tables."

"You're right." Darcy jotted down a note. "Good call." She walked the perimeter. "They can place cocktail tables here as well."

Audrey would never have made that suggestion for sure. Lane tamped down her irritation. "You still want a timeless and classic feel to your wedding day, right?"

"Absolutely, and James agrees, thankfully." Darcy chuckled. "I was glad I didn't have to fight that battle, or I might've had to reconsider the whole engagement." She giggled and then grabbed Lane's arm. "Audrey and I have vastly different tastes. So, I'm going to need your help reining her in if she gets any wild ideas." Her smile was gone—she was serious.

"You got it." That task was going to be even more exhausting than being the maid of honor. "Where is the wedding planner going to meet us?"

Darcy glanced at her phone. "Helen should be here somewhere, and it looks like Audrey has arrived as well." She laced her arm with Lane's "Let's go inside and find them. I can't wait to see the rest of the secrets this place holds."

❖

Helen hit the end button on her phone and rushed toward the ballroom. It had taken her much longer than anticipated to wrap up the unexpected call from another client. Getting someone off the phone politely could be a challenge at times. She hoped Darcy wasn't upset with her for being—she glanced at her watch—almost twenty minutes late. Helen had sent her a text during the call, explaining the situation. Hopefully, Darcy was the forgiving type.

Helen immediately stopped and shivered when she walked into the room. Lane Donnelly was standing with Darcy, pointing at different areas of the ballroom. She'd expected to meet with Darcy and her husband, not her makeup artist. That was unusual, but perhaps Darcy had brought Lane along to look at the bridal area of the venue. She watched them for a few minutes, assessing the dynamics between them. It looked like Lane might be more to Darcy than her makeup artist.

She crossed the room and held out her hand. "Good morning, Darcy. I'm Helen Trent. We spoke on the phone. I'm so sorry to keep you waiting."

"No worries." Darcy took her hand and shook it. "It's nice to finally meet you in person." She turned to Lane. "My fiancé couldn't make it this morning, he's tied up in meetings, so I brought along my best friend, Lane." She pointed to another woman across the room perched in a chair talking on her cell phone. "And that's my sister, Audrey. She's my matron of honor."

Helen glanced across the room and caught a glimpse of Audrey, who seemed to be rather engrossed in her phone conversation. She glanced back to Lane just in time to see Lane roll her eyes. "Would you like to wait for her to finish her call before we take the tour?"

Darcy shook her head. "We can start without her. She can catch up."

"I'll let her know." Lane strutted across the room and tapped her knuckles on the table in front of Audrey, who looked up and lifted a finger. Lane said something to her and hooked a thumb over her shoulder before she spun and headed back toward them.

It seemed that Audrey wasn't a favorite of Lane. In fact, judging from Lane's body language, she didn't seem to like her at all.

Darcy turned to Helen as they waited for Lane to return. "Sounds like you had a high-maintenance bride on your hands this morning."

"Her mother, actually." Helen smiled as Lane joined them again. "Okay. You ready to get started?"

Darcy nodded. "Yep."

"I assume you've been here before, considering your father's position on the board." Helen led them through a few doors, around a corner, and into the large industrial kitchen. The room contained a large eight-burner gas cooking area, several bakery ovens, and a spacious food-preparation area.

"I spent a good part of my childhood in the summer here." Darcy followed Helen, with Lane right behind her.

"Oh? Tennis or swimming?" Helen asked.

"Swimming. I wasn't one for hitting a ball back and forth in the heat."

"I understand. It can get a bit steamy. Large amounts of fluid intake is a must." Helen remembered those searing, torturous days well.

"What's their catering policy?" Darcy glanced around the kitchen.

"Good question." Helen smiled. "I always recommend checking out the catering before booking the venue. Every venue has different requirements. Sometimes if they have an exclusive caterer, they're more expensive than you might be looking to spend." She turned and led them out. "That isn't the case here because they have an open arrangement. We'll be able to look at other food options, if you'd like. We just need to make sure they have a serving staff. I have a list of caterers I work with on a regular basis that you can look through, based on availability, of course."

"What about the cake? Is it possible to purchase that outside of the caterer?" Darcy asked.

"Absolutely. All my contacts allow that without charging a cutting and plating fee. I also have recommendations for some wonderful bakeries." Including the one Helen had contracted for Lane's previous engagement. What had happened to that cake?

"Great. I need those." Darcy jotted something on her list. "I'm not sure what size. We don't have a firm guest count yet."

"While it's true that twenty percent of your invitees typically will decline or, more rudely, not show up, I never suggest banking on a list to accommodate your maximum guest count. I advise that you cut back on the guest list now or create a no-stranger rule to prevent your wedding from becoming the party of the month."

"That actually happens?" Darcy raised her eyebrows.

"I've seen it a few times." Lane nodded. "You'd be surprised at the people who show up as guests of guests that aren't technically invited."

Helen shrugged. "Why should you have to pay for someone to be there that you've never even met?"

"Good point." Darcy made a note. "Not that money's an issue, but we'll thin the list out. There will, however, be some of my fiancé's clients invited that I've never met." Darcy shrugged. "There's no getting around that."

"The tables and chairs are included with the club booking. I have a crew set them up and then flip the room into a cozier atmosphere once dinner is finished." Helen glanced over her shoulder at Darcy. "Don't worry. They're nice chairs, and floor-length linens and napkins are provided as well."

"I'm impressed. I had no idea how many of the details Helen handled," Lane whispered to Darcy.

"Wasn't she your wedding planner?" Darcy's voice rose as she drew her eyebrows together.

"I was." Helen gave Lane a solemn smile. "I'm sorry that happened to you." But was she really? Belinda had been such a nightmare to work with, she could only imagine how she behaved in a relationship…and then there was that other situation. "We'll have a lighted tent set up outside to accommodate the guests and provide additional shelter just in case it rains." Helen opened the doors leading to the courtyard.

"Can we do the ceremony out here?" Darcy walked through the doors into the outside area.

"That's possible, weather permitting. You can decide once we get closer to your wedding date. We don't want you repeating vows swimming in water or saying I-dos in sweltering heat." Helen brushed past her to the center of the area and held her hands out to her sides. "Either way, the tent will have soft, twinkling lights and cascading florals that whisk you and your guests to the fairy-tale wedding you've always dreamed of. The top will also be see-through to allow your guests to be able to look at the stars once the sun goes down." She pointed to the covered walkways that surrounded the courtyard. "Multiple strings of lights will be draped along the outer pathways to keep the area lit well enough to prevent anyone from falling or getting injured."

Darcy took a minute to process all the information, tapping her chin with her pen as she looked over her list. "Does the facility have getting-ready rooms and additional bathrooms? And what about drink set-up? We plan to have an open bar."

Helen led them back into the ballroom. "There's a bridal suite as well as a groom's room, which is equipped with video games to keep him and the groomsmen occupied."

"The girls don't get games?" Lane drew her eyebrows together. "How disappointing."

Darcy rolled her eyes. "You'll be way too busy helping me to play games."

"I'm here to help." Audrey's voice echoed in the room as she crossed the floor toward them.

"Took you long enough." Lane's aggravation shone through again.

"I didn't think I'd ever find you." She gave Lane a fake smile. "You should've left some breadcrumbs."

"No need." Lane returned a smile with the same enthusiasm. "We're just about done here."

"Oh." Audrey's shoulders dropped. "You'll have to fill me in on everything, since you didn't wait."

"There's plenty more to do." Helen closed the doors to the courtyard. "How about the four of us meet here early next week? We can work out more of the details, do some food and cake tasting." Helen glanced at Darcy. "You should bring James for that as well."

"He's pretty much left all the details to me." Darcy fidgeted. "It seems a bit overwhelming so far."

"Don't worry." Helen touched Darcy's arm. "I'll make sure everything goes smoothly. I don't work for the venue. I work exclusively for you."

"That's good news." Darcy blew out a breath. "I can't begin to know how you handle all these details yourself. Does someone help you with all the arrangements?"

Helen nodded. "I have a part-time assistant to handle some things, but I do most of it." She looked at her Day-Timer to make sure she hadn't neglected to mention any details, and she had. "I almost forgot. There's also plenty of on-site parking with no extra charge. Cars can be left overnight if guests feel they need to find an alternate way to travel home or to a hotel. They just need to plan to pick up their cars before noon the next day." She led them back to the lobby area of the club. "Can I answer any more questions?"

"Nope. I think you've pretty much covered everything." Darcy glanced at Audrey and Lane. "Any questions from either of you?"

"I'm good." Lane smiled. "Not my first rodeo." Helen knew that all too well.

Audrey shook her head. "But she reserves the right to ask more questions in the future." She seemed to be still stinging from being left behind.

"Of course. Darcy is welcome to call me anytime, as is either one of you two." Helen handed each of them her card and then focused on Darcy.

Audrey took the card quickly as an obnoxious ring came from her phone. She stuffed the card into her purse before she pressed her phone to her ear and began talking.

"Sorry about her. I appreciate all your help. I know the reception will be spectacular." Darcy turned and headed out the door, with Audrey close behind.

Lane stopped and turned to Helen. "Thank you for taking such good care of her."

"Absolutely. It's my pleasure to make Darcy's wedding day as special as possible."

"Right." Lane smiled. "I believe at least two of us have that goal in common." She turned and went out the door.

Lane seemed more interested in Darcy's wedding than Audrey did, and she wasn't even the maid of honor. Pleasing the bride could be a difficult task, but trying to please both her sister and her best friend could be a disaster. How was she going to get around the bride's sister, who seemed a bit entitled and more interested in her own life than Darcy's wedding?

CHAPTER SEVEN

Lane got comfortable in her chair but didn't look at the menu. This was the best Italian place in town, and she already knew what she was going to order. "I'm so glad you suggested dinner, Iris. I had the most ridiculous day dealing with Audrey."

"I can't believe Darcy chose her instead of you. You'll be my maid of honor no matter what." Iris reached across the table and patted her hand. "Even though we haven't been friends since childhood, I feel like we've known each other forever."

"I feel that way too." Over the years Lane's friendship with Darcy hadn't changed. They were still close, but Iris had become closer. The issue wasn't necessarily that Darcy had chosen her sister. Sure. That hurt. But Audrey was high maintenance and difficult on top of that.

The waiter appeared. "Would you ladies like something to drink?"

Lane glanced up. "We'll have a bottle of the Napa Valley merlot." Their usual choice. They never finished the whole bottle, but it was cheaper than buying it by the glass. She always had the waiter re-cork it and send the remaining wine home with Iris to enjoy later. Now that they were roomies, they could enjoy the rest together.

Lane took a second look as a woman dressed in black skinny jeans and a form-fitting light-pink blouse approached the hostess stand. Tall—slim—gorgeous—the woman turned—Helen. Lane straightened in her seat. What the hell was that? She'd thought of Helen in various ways—mean, cranky, condescending—but she'd pushed hot and sexy from her thoughts long ago. She realized her mouth was hanging open, then quickly looked away. Life just wasn't fair. The most attractive woman she'd seen in forever had an ego a mile high and possibly a significant other. A detail that she'd never really considered until now. Why hadn't she? What was wrong with her? Was Helen involved? Lane had never had any reason to check. Had never seen Helen with *anyone*. She continued to stare, too curious to let her curiosity go now.

"Isn't that Helen over there?" Iris asked.

Lane glanced at Iris and quickly back to the hostess stand. "Yes. Hide." She held up her menu in front of her face. "We need to get out of here."

Iris continued to watch as Helen crossed the restaurant to her table. "I say we stay to see who she's meeting. I bet she's not single. That body isn't wasted—shouldn't be, for sure."

"Could just be meeting a client or a friend."

"In a place like this? No way." The ambiance was perfect for romance.

"You and I are here." Iris cocked her head. "Is there something you need to tell me? Do you have a secret crush on me?"

"Yes." Lane lowered her voice and pressed her hand across her heart. "I've wanted you since we first met."

Iris rolled her eyes. "Right. I forgot. We're here because you love the ravioli, and your stomach does all the talking for you now."

Lane peeked over the top of the menu at Helen.

"Stop staring," Iris whispered. "Unless you want to ask her to join us?"

She didn't know whether to invite Helen over or not. Could she make dinner conversation with her? "I don't want to embarrass her." That was her only excuse, and it was a lame one.

"So, instead, you'd let her sit there eating dinner all alone?" Iris frowned.

"Clearly, she's waiting for someone." Lane noticed the place setting that remained across the table from Helen. "Maybe they're just late." Helen seemed calm and relaxed, not worried in the slightest about anyone else in the restaurant. The hostess appeared and removed the second place setting.

"Looks like she's not meeting anyone." Iris grinned at her across the table. "You're cleared to invite."

Shit. Lane could never be comfortable eating alone in a restaurant— and being stood up would solidify her feelings of discomfort. A few caustic friends had long ago imprinted on her the stigma that only sad, friendless people got stood up and had to eat alone at a restaurant.

"I've never seen her out of a buttoned-down two-piece suit. She really is beautiful." Iris stared across the restaurant. "Get her out of that shirt and I'm sure there's treasure to be had." Iris was always the first to notice Lane watching Helen. Staring seemed to have become an uncontrollable act tonight—for both of them. "If I weren't straight, I'd be all over her."

The waiter delivered the bottle of wine, opened it, and poured a small amount into Lane's glass.

Lane took a sip and nodded at the waiter. He filled Iris's glass and added more to Lane's.

"Does Harvey know you check out women?"

"Absolutely. We appreciate views together." Iris sipped her wine.

"I'm with you on a good view." Lane smoothed the dress across her breasts. "How's my view?"

"Spectacular."

"Maybe you should switch-hit once in a while."

"Done that. I have a better average with men."

"Really? How did I not know that?"

"It was a long time ago. She pursued me big-time." Iris rolled her eyes. "It was hot but short-lived."

"I could've introduced you to plenty of women." Lane shrugged. "What am I saying? If I had half the charm you have with women, I wouldn't be single right now."

"Maybe you should re-introduce yourself." Iris looked her up and down, then reached over and unbuttoned a couple of buttons on the cotton cardigan Lane was wearing over her dress. "Add a little sexy to that wardrobe of yours—show off that view. It's ninety degrees outside."

Lane quickly rebuttoned her sweater, leaving only one additional button unfastened. "I told you, I'm not looking."

"While you're not, women will be. At you." Iris was silent for a moment. "He proposed."

"What? Why didn't you tell me?" Lane noted Iris's blank expression. "You don't seem happy about it."

"I'm not sure I am."

"Why not?"

"After marriage comes kids, and then what? I like my life the way it is. I'm not sure I'm ready to turn domestic."

"That's not always true. Have you told him that?"

"I think so." She bounced her head from shoulder to shoulder. "Maybe not in so many words."

"You absolutely cannot accept until you do. I like Harvey, and I don't want you doing to him what Belinda did to me." Lane took a sip of wine.

"I would never do that." Iris picked up her own glass.

"Good. Then talk to him. Tonight."

Iris nodded. "I will." She clinked her glass with Lane's before she sipped.

"*Right* after we're done here," Lane insisted. Iris didn't always do what she said.

"I said I would, and I will." Iris's voice rose. "So, you agree?"

"Agree on what?" Lane lowered her glass to the table and relaxed into her chair.

"That Helen's beautiful." Iris cocked her head toward Helen's table, where she was still sitting alone.

"I've never disputed that." In fact, more than once, Lane had dreamed about removing that button-downed suit Helen always wore. She had one in every color, but Lane was especially fond of the way the navy-blue one fit her. It seemed to be a little snugger than the others. "You're avoiding the subject."

"So are you. Just because I'm straight doesn't mean I can't appreciate a beautiful woman when I see one." Iris glanced at Helen. "She's still alone. If she's single, she might be good for you."

"I appreciate you looking out for me, but I'm not interested in dating anyone."

"Who said anything about dating?" Iris grinned as she raised her glass to her lips. "I'm only suggesting you get into the sack with her."

"Iris. Stop." Lane glanced at Helen again. She *was* gorgeous, Lane couldn't deny that, but her condescending attitude was unbearable. That wasn't a good combination in bed.

"Come on. You need a fling or something to get you back in the game." Iris took her napkin from her lap and dropped it on the table. "I'm going to invite her to join us."

The table rattled as Lane lurched to grab Iris's hand. "No. I'll do it." She stood, straightened her dress, and crossed the restaurant.

When Lane approached the table and Helen looked up at her, she realized that she hadn't prepared what she intended to say.

Something came out of Helen's mouth, but Lane didn't comprehend it. Helen's forehead creased. "Are you okay?"

"Yes. Sorry. I'm fine." She had no idea how to interact socially with Helen. After all, Helen had never been particularly nice to her. "Iris and I saw that...I mean we thought you might like to join us for dinner. Unless you're meeting someone, of course."

Helen glanced at the empty seat across from her. "Seems they've been held up." She pushed away from the table. "I'd love to join you."

Now what? Lane hadn't expected Helen to take her up on it. "Okay. Great." Did she really just say great? "We're right over here." She led Helen to the table.

Helen took the seat across from Lane, which meant eye contact throughout their meal. The ravioli she'd planned to order didn't excite her anymore.

The waiter appeared just in time to avoid an awkward silence. He took a place setting and wineglass from another table and set it in front of Helen before he picked up the bottle. "Wine?"

Helen covered her glass with her palm. "I'll just order a separate glass."

"Absolutely not." Iris signaled the waiter to pour. "Unless you don't like merlot."

"Merlot is good with me." Helen removed her hand, and the waiter filled her glass.

"Are we ready to order?" the waiter asked.

Helen glanced at the menu lying on the table, but it appeared she didn't need one either. "I'll have the ravioli."

"You like ravioli?" Iris asked.

Helen nodded. "It's the best dish on the menu here."

"That's so funny." Iris glanced at Lane. "Lane thinks so too."

"Cheers to good food." Helen held up her glass, clearly waiting for Lane to clink her glass against it. Lane did as Helen silently beckoned, and they both took a drink. "Mmm. This is good." She twisted the bottle to look at the label. "I haven't tried this one before. I'll have to add it to my list of favorites."

Was Helen actually being nice? Lane had expected arrogance, criticism, judgment, but she hadn't expected complimentary—at all. Iris kicked Lane under the table and winked at her when she glanced her way. Nothing was going to come of this, but Lane would play along to satisfy Iris.

CHAPTER EIGHT

Helen stared across the table at Lane, more nervous than usual. She'd been surprised to see Lane and Iris when she entered the restaurant. She hadn't looked their way and had tried to avoid interaction, but Lane had made that impossible. She didn't know why she'd accepted her invitation to dine with them. Maybe it was the sincerity in Lane's eyes that did it. Maybe it was the fact that she didn't want Lane to know she was dining alone. Why did that matter? Plenty of people dined by themselves, right? Helen had been doing it for so long it had become routine. Good food was meant to be enjoyed with appropriate ambiance. She'd never cared what anyone thought before. Why now? Why Lane? Because she was a beautiful, vibrant, single woman whom she didn't want to know she lacked a social life.

"The last wedding we worked together was beautiful." Lane sipped her wine and regarded Helen. "I have to admit you're good at your job."

"I'm not sure quite how to respond to that." Helen laughed at the backhanded compliment. "Thank you?"

Lane stiffened, and Iris covered her hand with hers. "I think Lane meant that the bride was pretty demanding, and you didn't let it faze you at all."

"Yes. She was quite a handful." Lane blew out a breath. "I had to redo her makeup twice because she kept crying."

"You wouldn't know it. She looked beautiful." Helen was always impressed with Lane's makeup skills. She could erase a bride's skin imperfections without making them look like they were wearing any makeup at all.

Lane smiled. "The second time around I used my most potent waterproof products."

"That seemed to have done the trick." Helen twirled the stem of her wineglass with her fingers. "How did you two get into the bridal-makeup business?"

"That's a long story." Lane tapped the table with her fingertips.

"I'm listening." Helen sipped her wine before she leaned in and clasped her hands together on the table.

"Okay." Lane blew out a breath. "My first *real* job out of college was at a local public relations firm as a copy editor. I considered myself lucky to land a job that paid well so early in my career. Only problem was that it was boring as hell, and because of that, my work wasn't stellar. After struggling with myself about it, I finally left."

"You just left? Without another job offer?" Helen asked.

Lane nodded. "Not the smartest action to take. After about six months of part-time jobs, including serving in a restaurant, working for a catering company, and even telemarketing to help pay the bills while I lived with Iris, I took a job at a high-end department store selling and doing makeup on customers. I started part-time because that was literally all they had available. I did whatever they needed me to do—run errands, get coffee, even clean makeup stations. One of the full-time makeup artists didn't show up for work one day, and I stepped in to help out. I was lucky enough to be noticed by the manager, and she brought me on full-time after that."

Lane had more moxie than Helen realized. She would've never left a perfectly good-paying job without having secured another beforehand. No matter how much she hated it.

"And…" Iris tilted her head and stared at Lane.

"And my family owns a commercial plumbing business, so I went to work there to supplement my income." Lane lowered her gaze to the tablecloth as she ran her finger across the crease. "Still work there. The pay is great."

Why was Lane keeping that tidbit a secret? Was she embarrassed to admit that she'd needed help with her goals—that she wasn't making enough profit to sustain herself—or was she trying to hide some family dynamic? Helen was no stranger to any of those feelings. Either way, Helen had been through similar circumstances in some of her early careers, and no one's family could be more toxic than her own. "That experience must come in handy for planning your own business model."

Lane raised her gaze from the table. "How did you get into event planning?" Lane seemed sincere.

Helen tilted her head from side to side. "In college I was all over the map. I knew what I didn't want to do, but I had trouble narrowing down exactly what I did want to do. I was interested in so many different areas. It was kind of expected that I go into law like my dad, but defending corporate millionaires didn't appeal to me."

"I can understand that. What else were you interested in?" Lane rolled her lips together, an action Helen couldn't deny was alluring even though she knew Lane hadn't intended it to be.

"At one point I thought about becoming a travel guide." Helen crossed her legs to calm the buzzing in her system.

"That sounds like fun."

"I thought so too at first. Taking vacations all over the world sounds exciting until you look at the logistics of it. You're on a plane, boat, or in a car for a good portion of the time. Besides, when I travel, I like to enjoy the trip, not work it." Helen finished her wine and pushed her glass forward.

Lane picked up the bottle and refilled all their glasses. "That makes sense."

"I took a few classes in public relations and marketing, and then I finished college in the mass media and communications track, which helped when I decided to go this route. I did everything I could to gain experience. Volunteered with a local nonprofit to help plan fund-raising events and found ways to get involved with event planning, even if it was just a small party." Helen relaxed into her chair again. "I needed to be able to organize an event from start to finish. I wanted to be prepared when the right opportunity presented itself." *And to be sure it was really something I wanted to do.* She didn't know if she could survive another career change—didn't think she wanted to.

"So how did you end up here…I mean where you are now, working at Dreams to Reality?" Lane propped her elbows on the table, seeming sincerely interested.

Helen contemplated her answer—needed to edit the details. She wasn't about to tell Lane and Iris that she'd moved back to Dallas from

Chicago over a year ago after an unfortunate scandal with her former employer. She should've known better than to get involved with the boss—especially one who took advantage of her. She'd ended up doing all the work and getting none of the rewards. Not much different than now, except without the personal perks. After one too many broken promises, she'd tucked her tail between her legs and headed back home, where she knew the territory—where she thought she'd have the support of her family. Helen had no idea how she'd let herself become so vulnerable, and she'd promised herself that she'd never let it happen again.

"My mother asked me to plan a party for her, and I liked the feeling of accomplishment it gave me." That wasn't a lie. Her mother had asked, and Helen had never had another job with such a rewarding feeling. Lane didn't need to know she'd been unemployed at the time. "Everyone enjoyed themselves, and I decided that I wanted to continue making people happy." The endorphins that rushed her when a party came together were enough to charge her system for weeks to come. She was even flying high now from today's planning session with Darcy. "I've never been able to get that feeling from any other job."

"I feel that too." Lane gazed into her eyes. "It's something you can't beat."

Conversation stalled momentarily as they stared at each other. Then their food arrived—two plates of ravioli and one fettuccini Alfredo.

"Look at that." Iris grinned. "I can't get over the fact that you both ordered the ravioli."

"How about that," Helen said and smiled lightly at Lane.

"Parmesan?" The waiter held up a block of cheese and a grater.

Everyone nodded, and he began grating cheese over each plate.

Helen picked up her fork but waited and watched Lane. She wanted to see if Lane had just chosen something from the menu or if she truly enjoyed the dish as much as Helen did.

Lane cut one of the raviolis in half and slid the portion into her mouth. She let out a soft moan as she chewed and then immediately covered her mouth. "Sorry, but this is my absolute favorite dish."

An odd shiver coursed through Helen. It was her favorite too. She came to this restaurant specifically for the ravioli, and the house salad, which was pretty good too. Helen suddenly found herself thinking about Lane dining with her at some of her other favorite restaurants. The little Chinese place, where she loved to eat lunch, the breakfast place near the building where she lived—she shoved herself out of the thought. She didn't know Lane well enough to be sure of any of her preferences, but she wanted to see her reaction to the ravioli again.

"What do you have in mind for Darcy?" Helen speared a chunk of ravioli, put it into her mouth, and held back a similar sound of delight as she let the flavors in her mouth bring her taste buds to life. The chef skillfully had dosed a balance of multiple ingredients, including meat, vegetables, cheese, spices, and aromatic herbs. It was the perfect blend. She found it amazing that, historically, one of the theories regarding the dish was that it was created to recycle leftovers.

Lane set her fork on the side of the plate and wiped her mouth with the linen napkin from her lap. "Elegant, yet relaxing, fun. I want it to be a stress-free event for her. I want her to have an unforgettable experience, so everything needs to be original—something new and different from your average wedding." She took a sip of wine.

Lane seemed to be passionate about making Darcy's wedding an event she would never forget. Helen admired her for that thoughtfulness.

Iris spun a bit of fettuccine onto her fork. "Do you think you can give Lane everything she wants?"

Helen didn't move her gaze from Lane. "I think I can satisfy her needs." She tugged her lip into a subtle smile. It had been a long time since Helen had flirted, but it seemed to be coming back to her easily— and unexpectedly. "I promise to do my very best."

Lane cleared her throat and broke eye contact. "I'm sure you will. No one knows the bride better than her wedding planner."

"In this case, that seems to be her sister. At least she thinks she does." Helen cut a ravioli in half and speared it with her fork. "But setting that situation aside, I think, with your help, we can make Darcy's wedding a spectacular event." Helen glanced across the table at Lane and winked. "Don't you think so?"

Lane blinked rapidly. "Yes. I believe we can." Seemed she hadn't been flirted with in a while either.

Helen grinned and held in a laugh. Even though she'd planned to dine alone—had no plans for conversation with anyone tonight, specifically someone who triggered all her buttons in more ways than one—Helen was having a surprisingly delightful evening. She hadn't intended to make Lane uncomfortable, but it seemed she might have done so. Made herself a little uneasy as well by moving into uncharted territory. For some reason she was enjoying the blush in Lane's cheeks and the fact that she'd made it happen.

❖

When Helen got home, she sat for a minute and analyzed the evening. Having a nice dinner alone hadn't been in the cards tonight, and although Helen found social dining a bit draining, she hadn't minded the company. When she'd first started dining alone, it had taken some getting used to, but she'd grown tired of missing out on a restaurant she wanted to try because she had no one to go with. Now she enjoyed her moments of solitude. Dining out alone, indulging in one of her favorite meals in the atmosphere in which it was intended, was much more enjoyable than getting takeout or having a meal delivered and eating at home in front of the TV watching wedding reality shows. She was able to wear what she wanted—no heels or fancy suits—and eat exactly what she wanted. She didn't need to worry about being embarrassed by having food on her face or have to compromise her food choices for anyone.

Oddly, she hadn't worried about any of that while dining with Lane and Iris tonight either. Their company had been enjoyable and pleasant—an unexpected turn. She stood, went to the kitchen, and tugged open the refrigerator to get a bottle of water. Individual packages of cheesecake, cheese sticks, and carrots and dip filled one of the shelves. She really did live a solitary life. She slid open the freezer drawer and plucked a fruit bar from the box nestled between the multiple Healthy Choice Power Bowls. After the evening she'd spent tonight, suddenly solitude didn't seem so inviting, and she was looking forward to seeing Lane again.

CHAPTER NINE

A s Lane and Audrey entered the ballroom area of the country club, Helen focused on Lane, dressed in a red floral swing dress with a royal-blue midriff cardigan covering her shoulders. Helen let her gaze drift down Lane's back to her shapely legs. She seemed more attractive today, maybe because of Lane's disposition change Friday night. But when Lane turned, she didn't have her usual relaxed look. In fact, she seemed uncomfortably awkward. Sort of like her expression when she'd approached Helen at the restaurant. Thankfully, that look had soon dissipated as their eyes met. When Helen had found out she was going to have double time with Lane for this event, she'd been dreading this wedding. Surprisingly, dinner Friday night with Lane and Iris had been pleasant. She only hoped that theme would continue trending throughout the planning process today. She took in a deep breath as she walked toward them.

"Where's Darcy?" Helen glanced around the lobby of the club.

"Darcy doesn't have time to check out the food, so I'm going to do it for her." Audrey's crass response was unexpected.

"Oh. Darcy didn't mention a conflict when I spoke to her yesterday." Helen was sensing much more animosity between Lane and Audrey than she'd realized.

"Something came up at work." Lane didn't elaborate.

"I understand." Helen dipped her chin. "Several good caterers are on contract at the club that should be able to present a nice buffet or sit-down dinner."

"That sounds way too fancy," Audrey said.

Helen glanced at Lane briefly before addressing Audrey. "What do you have in mind?"

"Carnival food." Audrey shrugged as she held her hands up in front of her like the choice was a no-brainer. "Darcy loves the food at the state fair."

Lane's mouth dropped open. "Darcy *does not* want turkey legs and roasted corn at her wedding reception."

"Sure, she does. We can rent a bouncy castle and set up a beer-pong table. Cornhole too." Audrey pointed to the doors leading to the courtyard. "The castle would fit perfectly out there."

"No. Absolutely not." Lane lunged forward toward Audrey. Helen's arm hit her in the chest as she tried to crash through it. "You're not going to ruin your sister's special day."

That approach probably wasn't the "new and different" scenario that Lane had envisioned during their last meeting. Helen lowered her arm. "Why don't we make a list and run it by Darcy?"

"O…kay." Audrey eyed Lane. "Add a photo booth to that list."

"That's actually not a bad idea." Helen searched her bag, took out an old receipt and pen, and then jotted a few notes on the back of it. "We can set it up in the lobby."

Audrey's phone rang, and she turned away and answered it. She nodded a few times before she dropped the phone from her ear and spun around. "I need to go."

"What?" Lane was irritated. "You just laid out all these crazy plans, and now you're going to bolt?"

"It's unavoidable." Audrey moved forward and narrowed her eyes. "You just remember who the maid of honor is here."

"It's *matron* of honor, if you're married." Lane rolled her eyes. "You don't even know that."

"Whatever." Audrey shrugged. "She picked me, *not you,* which makes me in charge. So, get over yourself and do what I say."

"Now, settle down, you two." Helen hadn't planned to referee today. "I'm sure we can arrange some things that Darcy will be happy with."

"I'm glad someone is the voice of reason." Audrey tucked her phone into her back pocket. "I have to go. You can catch an Uber home, can't you, Lane?"

"I don't really have a choice, do I?" Lane shook her head.

Audrey glanced over her shoulder as she raced out. "Let me know what you find based on the suggestions I made."

"I will." Helen watched Lane stare at Audrey as she left the room.

"You're not actually going to take anything she suggested seriously, are you?"

Helen glanced at her list and then held it for Lane to read.

Lane cocked her head. "You only wrote down the photo booth."

"I didn't catch everything she said. Did you?" Helen raised an eyebrow as she waited for an answer, hoping they were on the same page without her having to say it out loud.

"Nope." Lane grinned. "Nothing else at all."

"Okay, then." She dropped the list into her bag. "Let's get on our way. We can take my car."

"Good, because I came with Audrey."

"I gathered that." Helen pulled open the door and let Lane exit before her. Audrey didn't seem like the kind of girl who stayed with her friends when she went out either.

Once they reached Helen's car, she hit the clicker to unlock the doors and looked through the window of the back seat. "Do you mind if I run by my place really quick to pick up my Day-Timer? I can't find it anywhere." Helen glanced around the car. "I must've left it on the counter this morning." Helen pulled open the door for Lane. "Maybe we can check a few more things off the list while Audrey is occupied elsewhere."

Lane nodded. "That's fine."

Helen wouldn't invite Lane up—or would she? It would be rude to leave her in the car. Her apartment was clean for the most part.

"I can see that Audrey irritates the hell out of you."

"She really does rub me raw." Lane gritted her teeth.

"Just a word of advice for future meetings with her. If you counter her on everything, you might risk being excluded from Darcy's wedding, but Audrey will most likely be included no matter what." Helen looked straight ahead as she drove. "So, I suggest you be as civil as possible during this process."

"Darcy wouldn't kick me out. We've been friends for too long." Lane was adamant.

"I wouldn't be so sure about that." Helen glanced at Lane and then back to the road. "I've seen friendships crumble due to disagreements with family."

Helen had no plans to follow any of Audrey's suggestions, and it seemed that Lane was going to be a good ally in her quest to provide Darcy with the wedding of her dreams as long as she was able to keep the conflict under control.

Chapter Ten

A fter they parked, Lane followed Helen from the car to the building and into the elevator. Helen lived in the East Quarter, the building nestled between the Farmers Market, Downtown Dallas, Deep Ellum, and the Central Business district. It was surrounded by historic buildings essential to the main culture and commerce of Dallas. Lane had expected nothing less but had underestimated the opulence of the building. She would never in a million years be able to afford to live in a place as lavish as this. Even the lobby, with its leather sofas, midcentury modern chairs, angular coffee tables, and specialty lighting, was dripping money. "Upscale living" was a massive understatement.

Lane had never really thought about where Helen lived, just assumed the evil queen lived in a dark castle somewhere. She was going to have to stop thinking of Helen that way, especially after she'd been so nice to her Friday night…and this morning. She squeezed her eyes shut and popped them open again to adjust her internal view. Her anxiety kicked in as they took the short elevator ride to Helen's apartment. Suddenly she felt as though she didn't know how to interact with her. Knowing about her living space had somehow catapulted Helen to a different plane. Why was she even here?

"You okay?" Helen seemed to notice her discomfort.

She nodded as the elevator door opened and she stepped into the foyer that housed the door to Helen's apartment.

Helen unlocked the door and held it open for her. "Make yourself at home. I'll just be a minute." She took a left and went down a long hallway.

Lane glanced around the expansive apartment, which was nothing like the lobby. With spiced-oak hardwood flooring, it was decorated in warm colors with a wheat-colored fabric couch and loveseat centering the room, as well as a large mahogany bookcase covering the full length of one wall. What she saw before her didn't reflect the Helen she knew. There was also a pair of sable tweed club chairs and an ottoman nestled in the corner near the bookcase. The perfect spot to escape into the imaginary world of fiction. It seemed warm and enchanting, nothing like Helen at all. Lane crossed the room to the floor-to-ceiling windows to admire the expansive view of the Dallas skyline, then wandered to the bookcase and plucked a random book from one of the shelves. She glanced at the back cover and read the blurb—a romance—one that Lane was sure she'd seen at the movies. She hadn't thought of Helen as someone to curl up with a good book on a rainy evening, especially not a romance. Lane's stomach sank as she realized that she hadn't thought much past Helen's gruff exterior at all. She hadn't given Helen the chance to be human in her eyes, which was clearly a bad decision. She sighed and slipped the book back onto the shelf. What she wouldn't give for a collection like this.

"You like to read?" Helen's voice startled her as she moved across the room to her side.

"I do." Lane glanced at Helen, then back at the bookcase. "I was just admiring your collection. I don't have near this many." Helen had some of the newer books Lane had put on her wish list.

"Feel free to borrow one if you'd like." Helen slid the book Lane had been looking at from the shelf. "They made a movie out of this one, but you should read it anyway. They left out a few scenes I found interesting." She handed it to Lane.

"Thank you." The gesture stunned her, actually made her feel a little tingly all over. "I'll start on it tonight and get it back to you next week." Then maybe Lane could trade it for another she hadn't read. She turned to see that Helen had changed clothes. Skinny jeans, a half-tucked white button-down blouse, and penny loafers had replaced the stiff two-piece suit made in assorted colors and pointy shoes. The tingle returned. She hadn't seen a more attractive butch in ages.

"No hurry." Helen grabbed her Day-Timer from the table and turned to the door. "But we should get going if we're going to make our first appointment."

"Uh, right." Lane held the book to her chest to settle herself and followed. She needed to remember the *bitch* Helen was just underneath that beautiful exterior and could reemerge at any moment.

"Has Darcy discussed her thoughts with you on food for the reception?" Helen pushed the button for the elevator before turning and locking the door.

Lane found herself staring at Helen's ass as she secured her apartment. When had she become the woman who ogled other women? She cleared her throat and turned toward the elevator. "She wants a traditional sit-down dinner." Through the years, Lane and Darcy had had many conversations about each other's wedding plans. "None of that buffet stuff."

"I thought as much. So, we'll try my favorite caterer first." The door opened, and Helen waited for Lane to step into the elevator.

"You have a favorite?" Lane didn't know why that tidbit surprised her.

Helen nodded. "I have them ranked from one to ten, and this one is number one." She turned to the business cards in her Day Timer and pointed to one.

Lane made a mental note of the name on the card. "What do you use for your ranking criteria?" She was curious about what was important to Helen.

"Great-tasting food, flexibility, and ease to work with."

That sounded reasonable. "What if your favorite isn't available or Darcy doesn't like the food?"

Helen dropped her Day-Timer into her bag and smiled. "Then we move on to the next one on the list, but I think both you and Darcy will be happy with this one."

❖

"I'm not a big fan of broccoli." Lane poked one of the mini trees with her fork and held it up for scrutiny.

"Neither am I, but this will make you a convert." Helen picked up a fork. "Go ahead. Try it."

Lane eyed the singed green appetizer again before giving it a try. A burst of ginger and pineapple hit her tongue, and she giggled in delight. She popped another piece into her mouth and closed her eyes as the flavors exploded in her mouth. "On second thought, maybe we should keep the broccoli to ourselves and stick to something more traditional, like asparagus, for the reception."

"It'll pair well with steak, chicken, or salmon." Helen forked a head of broccoli and slipped it into her mouth.

"She also mentioned lobster." Darcy enjoyed elegant food.

"If she wants to serve her guests the best of the best, lobster is an option." Helen flipped to a page in the caterer's book. "They usually place the lobster atop a bed of risotto or serve it with clarified butter. We'll have to make sure to include a second choice of steak or chicken for the guests allergic to shellfish."

"I think she has some vegan friends as well." Lane speared the last piece of broccoli, cut it in two, and pushed half toward Helen.

"No problem there. We can add a vegan zucchini lasagna as well." Helen scooped up the remaining piece of broccoli.

"Gluten-free?" Lane squinted as she asked.

"This caterer can accommodate that as well." Helen smiled. "Now you know why they're my number-one pick. Outside of the delicious food, of course."

Lane was amazed. Helen didn't falter. Her knowledge of everything wedding was impressive. "How do you remember all these details?"

"It's more about the experience than the memory." Helen poked a finger to her temple. "I've handled enough weddings to know what works and what doesn't." She flipped through the binder pages. "We can also set up a grazing table. Darcy and James seem to enjoy the finer things in life, and what better way to celebrate than with charcuterie?" She flipped the page and moved the binder to give Lane a better view. "These giant meat and cheese spreads have mesmerized wedding guests for the past few years and are sure to be a hit with theirs."

"I would have to agree. That's impressive." Lane's mouth was watering just looking at the photo. "Darcy said James is inviting some clients as well."

"We'll need to arrange for food for the staff also. They'll be working most of the day." Helen flipped to a section in the back of the book.

"I wasn't aware of that." Belinda had done most of the planning for their reception. "Will they eat the same food as the guests?"

"Not usually." Helen pointed to a page in the book "Roast chicken is usually a good choice."

"Do they have a table in the reception area? Mingle with the guests?"

"No. We'll have a staging area for them to eat and take breaks." Helen jotted a couple of notes in her Day-Timer. "You seem to have a good grasp on what Darcy wants." Helen's voice rose into a playful demeanor. "Much more so than her sister."

Lane sat back in her chair and studied Helen—contemplated her next words. "Why are you being so nice? I mean, you rarely talk to me at events."

Helen shrugged. "Because I'm running out of reasons we shouldn't get along."

Lane crossed her arms across her chest. "You had a list of reasons *not* to be nice to me?"

"Not you in particular." Helen shook her head. "It's just easier to deal with people professionally if I don't become friendly with them."

"And you're changing that now because...?" Lane honestly wanted to know.

"Because we have a mutual problem in Audrey, and we're going to have to form some kind of alliance to get around her." Helen closed the book and pushed it to the middle of the table. "I take other people's happiness very seriously."

"I see." Lane hadn't thought about having an ally in making sure Darcy's wedding didn't turn out to be a disaster. And it would be if Audrey had control.

"We can put it all together, but none of it means anything if we're not doing it for someone to enjoy." Helen stood. "And I'm not about to let Audrey ruin that for Darcy or the rest of us."

What she said made perfect sense.

Helen walked over to the counter to talk to the caterer and continued making notes. Lane watched her interact, surprised at the heat rising within her. The woman was becoming more attractive with each passing day.

Chapter Eleven

Lane slid into the passenger seat and waited for Helen to fire the engine. She had no idea where they were going next, but she hoped it was somewhere they wouldn't end up being in such close proximity.

"Task days are like road trips that never end." Helen put the car into gear.

"You go on many road trips?" Lane knew absolutely nothing about Helen but had recently discovered she wanted to know everything.

"Road trips are fun. Great scenery, lots of adventure, and no time limits. I love them." Helen glanced over her shoulder at the road and pulled away from the curb. "But, sadly, no. I don't have much free time to go on very many."

"I'm good with road trips, but I love to fly someplace tropical." Lane had been looking forward to her honeymoon more than to the wedding. Probably another sign that it wasn't meant to be.

"Where's Darcy planning to spend her honeymoon?"

"Italy."

"Oh." Helen didn't smile, kept her eyes on the road. "That should be nice."

"Have you been there?" Lane sensed some backstory that Helen wasn't sharing.

"Yes." Helen smiled lightly. "I went there once…with someone I thought could be…never mind. It's not a good story."

"Please tell me." Lane wanted to know what had made Helen so sad all of a sudden. *Who* had broken her heart.

"It was a glorious trip. We backpacked, rode the rails, and sailed." Helen seemed to be inside her head again. "Until the last couple of days. I thought we were moving toward something together, but I couldn't have been more wrong. *She* thought it was one last fling." She blew out a breath. "So, I spent the last couple of days by myself." She glanced over at Lane, pulled her lips into a tight grin. "Taking a trip with someone in hope of creating a fantasy out of a struggling reality wasn't a good idea. When you get back from paradise, or in my case before I got home, the enchantment fades quickly, and reality kicks you hard in the ass."

Lane knew that feeling well. "I'm so sorry that happened to you." She wanted to reach across the console and take Helen's hand to comfort her—let her know she understood. Because she did. Bad memories outweighed the good, making them fade quickly. Would she ever be able to think about Belinda without getting a knot in her stomach? Would the experience in Italy ever change for Helen as well?

Helen pulled into the parking lot and slid the shifter into park. "I believe you're feeling sorry for me, but don't. It's all water under the bridge now." She pointed toward the pathway into the park. "The gazebo on the other side of the footbridge is a nice area where a few couples I've worked with have chosen to take pictures."

As they got out of the car, Helen reached into the back seat and grabbed her bag, along with a blanket. Lane wasn't sure why she needed it, since the sun was ridiculously hot. Perhaps she planned to take some pictures to show Darcy. The scent of freshly mowed grass filled Lane's head as they walked to the middle of the footbridge that crossed the pond.

"This is a lovely spot for engagement photos. Do you know if Darcy has had any pictures taken yet?"

Lane nodded. "A few candid photos, but nothing professional." That was surprising, because Darcy was all about perfection.

"Then let's put this place on the list." Helen took out her phone and typed in a note. "We can have these done pretty quickly, and then she'll have something to include in her thank-you notes." She tucked her phone into her bag. "We can also use them to create a small display at the reception." Helen paused for a moment and glanced at Lane. "What do you think?"

"Darcy will love it here." Lane glanced at the beauty of her surroundings. Flowers sprouted up in several areas around the pond, the water was clear of debris, and several geese and ducks were gliding along the surface. "I hadn't thought of either of those things." She fanned herself with her hand as the sun reflected off the surface.

"That's why you have me." Helen smiled and motioned her to the other side of the pond. "There's a little spot over there under a few trees where we can cool off. I never plan midday photo shoots here. It's a beautiful place, but the heat gets a little much during the day. Brides tend to melt under this sun."

"Even the best makeup can't stand up to Dallas summer heat." Lane had been at many engagement shoots where the bride-to-be had fallen victim to dripping foundation.

Helen spread the blanket on the ground, then kicked off her shoes and settled onto it. "Come. Sit." She patted the blanket before she took a small, insulated container from her bag. "I brought a few snacks. Task days can get long and boring." Helen handed her a small bag of pre-made sandwich crackers, then retrieved a bag of apple slices, a small stick of salami, and a tiny container of kalamata olives. She reached in again and retrieved two bottles of water.

Lane peeked into the bag. "You have a mini fridge in there?" It seemed to hold an endless supply of goodies.

"No. But that's a thought." She glanced in the direction of the parking lot. "Maybe I should invest in one for my car, so I don't starve on days like these."

Lane laughed. Thoughtful and funny. Much more than she'd expected from the frigid bitch she'd been working with for the past few years.

Helen took her phone from her bag and scooted closer. "Let's take a selfie to show Darcy how beautiful the setting is."

"Okay." Lane leaned in and smiled. Was this Helen's usual method of convincing brides to buy in?

Helen checked the photo. "Perfect." She handed her phone to Lane. "Text it to yourself." She hesitated as though she'd crossed an invisible line. "Then I'll have your number for future planning."

The picture of them *was* perfect. Helen's usual lip-flattening had transitioned into a soft, genuine smile, and her eyes, enhanced with a subtle black line, were mesmerizing. If someone hadn't met them before, they'd never know they weren't friends. In fact, a newcomer wouldn't believe they'd been more like enemies until just a short time ago.

"Okay." Lane hit the share icon, typed in her number, and hit send before she handed Helen back her phone. "Do you come here...to this spot otherwise? I mean, outside of photo shoots?"

Helen tugged her lip to one side. "Are you asking me if I bring women here?"

"No. Yes." Lane shook her head. "I mean, maybe." She stared at the pond. How was she going to get out of this one? "You could just come here by yourself to enjoy the serenity of it all."

"I do spend some time here alone, to think. Outside of that, I haven't brought anyone here besides clients...and you."

"Oh? Why not? It's such a beautiful spot." A place Lane would frequent again, for sure.

"I don't date a lot." Helen shrugged as she took another cracker from the plastic bag. "I rarely find someone I click with...enjoy their company."

"Maybe if people didn't have to chisel through that thick exterior, you'd socialize more." Today was the first time Lane had seen Helen relax at all.

Helen stopped, her cracker halfway to her mouth, reversed her motion, and set it on the napkin. "Thick exterior? I think you could give me a run for my money in that department."

"That's not true." She let her mouth drop open. "I'm very friendly."

Helen picked up her cracker again. "Then it's just me who gets the brick wall?" She gave her a short glance before she shifted her gaze to the pond.

Lane took in a deep breath. "You can be very condescending at events. You make me feel like I'm not worthy of being there."

"Not my intent." Helen snapped her gaze back to Lane. "I just get very focused on making sure the bride gets the wedding she's anticipated." She pinched a napkin with her fingers. "I apologize if I ever made you feel that way."

"Thank you for that." Lane chewed on her bottom lip. "I'm sure I get in your way more than I should." Lane had tried her best to be civil to Helen, but some days she'd let her irritation get the best of her—pushing her to purposefully get in Helen's way much more than usual.

"It's possible." Helen pulled her lips into a sideways smile. "I'll work on not letting my focus seem personal in the future."

Lane held a laugh. "I'll work on not taking your focus personally in the future."

They finished their food in silence, Lane not knowing exactly where this newfound easiness was going. She'd never imagined having a cozy, impromptu picnic with Helen—she'd never seen herself doing anything pleasant with Helen at all—but this experience right here, among the trees and nature, was indeed lovely…and oddly comfortable.

CHAPTER TWELVE

I hope you saved room for dessert." Helen pulled into a space in front of the bakery. It was a small, quaint place in a secluded part of town, but it had the best bakery items and cakes in the area. Helen had found them by chance when a larger bakery she previously used often couldn't make a cake in time for one of her weddings. It was a hidden gem that wouldn't stay that way for long.

They both got out of the car, and Helen rushed to the door, opened it, and let Lane enter before her. But maybe she shouldn't have. After all, this wasn't a date. She tamped down her anxiety. She would've done the same for the bride.

"I'll be right back." Helen went around the counter into the back and returned quickly. "What kind of cake do you like?" She remembered that Lane and Belinda had chosen white cake with almond buttercream frosting for their wedding reception.

"I like them all." Lane glanced at the bakery case. "If I'd had my way, I would've had all of these."

"But didn't you choose plain, white cake?" Helen was sure that was what they'd planned.

Lane shook her head. "Belinda wanted that, so that's what we ordered. I just went along because I was tired of arguing over everything." She stared at the cakes in the case. "That's probably the only good thing I got from that whole wedding fiasco. The cake was paid for, so I contacted the bakery and changed the order. I got a different flavor for each week following the wedding date." She glanced at Helen. "Because, you know, there wasn't an actual wedding."

Helen nodded and slowly raked her teeth across her bottom lip.

"I'm so sorry about that." So sorry…for reasons that Lane wasn't even aware of. It seemed that Belinda had never told Lane about their chance encounter. About their conversation. Any of it. She didn't dare ask if Lane knew. Only time would tell if she did.

"Don't be." Lane snapped her gaze back to Helen and smiled softly. "I ate decadent cake for six weeks straight. That and plenty of wine was a wonderful way to get over it." She tugged at her blouse. "I gained twenty pounds."

"I hadn't noticed. You look great." Helen envied Lane's positive attitude. Lane seemed to be able to take any situation and turn it around, something Helen struggled with. "You seem to have recovered well."

"I'm not going to lie. I was miserable for a while." Lane leaned closer to the case, scrutinizing the cakes. "At times I didn't shower for days. I went from being numb to feeling everything."

Helen hadn't expected anything less. If the same thing had happened to her—if she had been dumped three days before her wedding—she wouldn't have been able to see the upside of any of it, cake included. After her last breakup, she hadn't eaten for days. "I hope you won't settle for anything you don't want in the future, especially at your wedding."

"I don't plan to settle ever again, but I don't see another wedding in my future anytime soon." Lane focused on Helen. "I hope you still charged her in full for your services."

"We worked out an arrangement." After Helen's conversation with Belinda shortly before the wedding, she hadn't argued the cost. Helen regretted that Lane had become part of the debris field that Belinda left behind. She'd truly hoped for a different outcome.

A woman came from the back of the bakery with a tray of cake samples. "Here you go." She set them on a small table in the corner of the bakery. "Just let me know which one of those choices will work." She glanced at Lane. "Didn't we already make a cake for you?"

"Yes. I believe you did," Helen said, not wanting Lane to have to go into the whole scenario again. "Darcy's tied up this morning, so Lane is helping me with a few things."

The woman scrunched her face. "We kind of prefer the bride or groom be present at the tasting."

Helen pulled out a chair for Lane before she slid into the one adjacent from her. "Well, neither of them is available, so let's not waste all this wonderful cake." She picked up a knife and cut one of the pieces in half.

The woman shook her head and headed into the back.

Helen scooped up a piece of chocolate cake filled with raspberry and chocolate ganache and put it into her mouth. She moaned as her favorite flavors sent a tingle of satisfaction through her.

Lane grinned. "You like that one, huh?"

"This one is my absolute favorite." She pointed to the remaining bite. "Try it before I eat the rest." She always went for dark chocolate cake. The raspberry filling and chocolate buttercream frosting only made it more decadent.

Lane scooped up the bite and slid it into her mouth. Helen focused on Lane's lips as they dragged across the fork, wiping it clean as she pulled it out of her mouth. It was Lane's turn to enjoy the decadence as she licked a remnant of chocolate buttercream frosting from her upper lip, and Helen's body lit up in places she hadn't expected. She'd always found Lane attractive physically but not otherwise. That seemed to be changing.

"You're right. This one is delicious." Lane went for the vanilla with strawberries next. "I love any kind of cake with fancy fruit filling."

"A girl after my own heart." The two of them would have no trouble agreeing on a cake. Hopefully, Darcy would be all in on their choice. Helen was glad Audrey had bailed on today's errands, because if she hadn't, she wouldn't have been able to get to know Lane. Helen eyed the other half of the vanilla cake. "So, you're not thinking about giving your relationship with Belinda another shot?" She hadn't planned to delve into Lane's personal life, but with the way her body was reacting to Lane right now, she needed to know.

"Absolutely not. It was the right move for both of us. Just took me some time to realize it." Lane took a bite of the coffee and cognac cake. "This one is pretty tasty too."

A jolt hit Helen directly in her midsection. That meant she could hope—for exactly what, she wasn't sure. "May I ask why? You seemed pretty upset about the whole thing when you saw her at your friend's wedding not long ago." She snagged the rest of the piece as she recalled Lane's inability to focus on the bride's makeup when Belinda arrived. At least Belinda had the common sense not to bring a plus one to the event.

"Yeah. I'm sorry about that. I'd hoped to be done before she showed up. I had a weak moment and was just feeling sorry for myself." She smiled softly. "In the end, it was good that she called it off. For whatever reason. I'm much happier now."

"I'm really glad to hear that." She truly was. Even though Helen believed that Lane and Belinda weren't a good match, she truly wanted Lane to be happy. The past few months had probably been hard on her. Several women from her chosen wedding party were getting married in succession, and both Lane and Belinda had been invited to each wedding.

They tasted several more flavors in silence, Helen watching Lane take bites and press her fork to the plates to scrape up the last of the crumbs. It was like a weirdly erotic tasting show that Helen couldn't look away from.

"Have we made a choice?" The woman from the bakery startled Helen out of her blissful daze.

"I think we've narrowed it down to these three." Helen pointed to the chocolate with raspberry filling, the strawberry-filled white cake, and the coffee and cognac. "Can you box up some samples to take to the bride?"

"Oh, and add the salted caramel, black and white, as well." Lane pushed the plate toward Helen. "Taste it."

Helen complied and let the flavors roll over her tongue. "Another good choice." Helen smiled at Lane, trying to keep her newfound feelings in check.

"I'll get that right out." The woman spun and headed back into the kitchen.

Lane leaned closer, whispered, "She looks thrilled," in Helen's ear, and chuckled.

The sweet, low laugh that came from Lane put Helen's body into overdrive once again. She didn't know if her libido would be able to survive many more days like this. The jolt coursing through her was electric. This situation was going to be more difficult than she imagined. Her reaction to Lane was ridiculous. With her heart racing, she tried to concentrate on the task at hand, which was to ignore how good Lane smelled.

CHAPTER THIRTEEN

Lane wasn't sure what had changed between her and Helen over the course of only a few hours. She hadn't expected to enjoy the day— any of it—but she had enjoyed it immensely. Before she could get up the courage to mention that fact, Helen pulled up to the curb at Iris's house and put the car into park.

"You up for more errands tomorrow?" Helen's voice was soft and unsure. Lane had heard her sound confident, cool, and aloof, but she had never heard Helen sound insecure before. Another new discovery.

"Absolutely. I'll bring lunch." She opened the door and climbed out of the car.

"That's sweet of you, but I thought we'd grab something at this little place I know of while we're out. It's near where we're going."

She leaned to look through the window at Helen. "Oh. Okay." That would save her a trip to the market tonight. When she got inside, she'd let her father know she'd be out again tomorrow. The plumbing business could survive another day without her.

"Pick you up at ten?" Helen's voice had a lilt to it. Another unexpected sound.

"Sounds perfect." That would give her time to shower and pick out a nice outfit to wear in the morning. She didn't know where this was going or where she wanted it to go. All she knew was that her feelings for Helen were changing. Helen wasn't the cocky, know-it-all asshole Lane had experienced in the past, and she had no idea why she seemed so different today.

Thinking about how well the day had gone as she slid her key into the lock, Lane couldn't help smiling. She was finding out that there was a whole lot more to Helen than she knew, and it seemed she'd only scratched the surface. When she pushed the door open and went inside, Iris met her halfway into the living room.

"Where have you been?" Iris looked worried. "I've been calling all over."

Lane took her phone from her bag and glanced at the screen. "Sorry. I didn't realize the battery was dead." She crossed the room and connected it to the charging cable on the counter.

"You told me you were going to ditch Audrey early."

"She actually ditched me." Lane glanced at her phone as the messages came through. "I was out scouting with Helen."

"You were *alone* with Helen?" Iris rushed toward her. "How was that?"

"Enlightening." Lane brushed past Iris on her way to the refrigerator, pulled it open, reached in, and took out a bottle of water. "She's a lot different than I expected." She propped herself on one of the bar stools.

"Good different?" Iris tilted her head.

Lane took a drink of water, letting the question settle in her brain. "I think so." The memory of vivid blue eyes floated through her head. It was surprising how pleasant it felt to converse with Helen, to learn more about her. She took another quick sip and screwed the top on the bottle. "She's not the ice queen I thought she was."

"I knew it." Iris danced around the room.

"Honestly, the whole day was perfect." Maybe too perfect. Her system buzzed as Helen's smile appeared in her mind.

"Awesome." Iris drummed her palms on the counter. "We'd already decided she's your type, and now she's perfect."

"I said the *day* was perfect." Although Helen had been pretty perfect throughout it. "One good day does not a lifetime make." She shouldn't have said anything. Iris would spiral on this idea for days.

"What's the harm with enjoying her company? Tall, beautiful, and butch, with killer legs." Iris was being ridiculous. "I see sex on the horizon for you."

Helen was all that, for sure. She slid off the bar stool. "We were just making wedding arrangements for Darcy. Don't read more into it than what it actually is." Although the possibilities hadn't escaped Lane's thoughts.

"That's where it all starts." Iris slapped her lightly on the ass. "You irresistibly sexy thing."

"Stop." Lane went into the bedroom to change, listening to Iris's catcalling as she closed the door behind her. Was today the start of something? What would happen if they slept together, and it wasn't good? Every event from then on would be awkward. That was nothing new…but would it be more awkward than it was before? Why was she already jumping to sex? They'd enjoyed each other's company—that's all. Her therapist's voice popped into her head. *This is an opportunity to move past the rejection left by Belinda…to feel wanted again.* The professional repeated this mantra regularly, and Lane knew she was right. She hadn't had such a strong visceral response to any other woman—even Belinda.

❖

Helen envied Lane's friendship with Iris, wished she had someone to talk to after a delightful day with a…what exactly was Lane? A friend, enemy, love interest? She really needed to call someone to get this situation under control—in her own mind, if nowhere else. Helen had scrolled through her contacts in her phone—Delia, Julie, Max, Samantha, and a dozen more—not one of which she would call to just pass the time, let alone discuss another woman. She didn't consider any of them friends. She'd either made a clean break or never responded when they tried to contact her.

Heartbreak wasn't her style, so she'd always cut a woman loose when things began getting serious. In hindsight, that reaction appeared to be a mistake. Now she had no one for company besides her family. The only one who truly understood her was her brother Will, and he rarely had time to spend with her outside of work and his immediate family. She was sure Ash would let him out for a night if she asked, but getting him to actually go would be difficult. Will valued his time with his family—treated it like it was a gold doubloon he'd discovered on a long-lost shipwreck. That was the kind of future Helen wanted for herself, a woman—a family that she always wanted to be with—to come home to.

She hit Will's contact button on her phone, put it on speaker, and waited for him to pick up.

"Hey, sis. What's up?"

"I've got something running on the spin cycle in my head and need some advice." That was an understatement.

"You want to come over for dinner? Ash is making her famous spaghetti and meatballs." Ash was a magnificent cook.

"Seriously? It's the middle of summer. Why aren't you grilling?" It had been at least ninety degrees outside today, although she hadn't noticed while picnicking in the shade with Lane.

"Because Ash wanted pasta, so we're having pasta. Who am I to complain if she wants to cook?" Will was so easy. He could change plans within minutes without any complaint.

Ash did make the best meatballs around, and even though she was still kind of full from her picnic with Lane, she could squeeze in one or two. "Okay. I'll bring some wine."

"Great. See you soon." Will ended the call.

Helen plucked a couple of bottles of red from the wine rack in the kitchen and set them on the counter before she went into the bathroom. She glanced in the mirror. She'd put on mascara and eyeliner this morning. She didn't always, but she'd wanted to look good for her meeting with Lane. She'd never really cared about that before, but around Lane she'd become hyper-aware of how she looked. Weird. After taking a makeup-remover cloth from the package, she stared at her reflection again and tucked the cloth back under the lid. The makeup really brought out the blue in her eyes. She shrugged, flipped off the light, and left the room. Maybe Will and Ash could help her make sense of her feelings.

CHAPTER FOURTEEN

L ane paced across the living room, then waited by the front window impatiently, peering out onto the street for a moment. Helen had sent her a text an hour ago, letting her know she was on her way.

"She here yet?" Iris asked from the kitchen.

"Nope." Lane dropped her bag onto the couch.

"Is she late?" Iris picked up her phone and glanced at the screen.

"It's barely ten. What time does the dance studio open?" She pushed Lane's half-empty coffee cup toward her. "You want some more coffee?"

"Nope." She'd already brushed her teeth. "It opens at ten." She'd already had two cups. Lane took the cup to the sink, dumped the remnants, and put it into the dishwasher. "I'm sure she's thrilled that Darcy chose a different dance instructor than Helen's usual."

"How do you know that?"

"Darcy told me." It seemed Darcy was going rogue on not only that, but she was allowing Audrey to choose the band as well.

"So, maybe Helen's picking up Darcy first."

Was that the plan? Why wasn't Darcy picking up Lane? Why weren't they just meeting Helen at the studio? "I thought she was."

"Or...maybe you're going to have another solo day with Helen." Iris wiggled her eyebrows. "Wouldn't that be fun?"

"Stop." Lane shook her head. "You're incorrigible." That thought had popped into Lane's head more than once last night, but she'd quickly pushed it away. She didn't like Helen—didn't want to spend alone time with her—didn't have any interest in her outside of planning

Darcy's wedding. Right? Warmth rushed her as thoughts of Helen's caring nature, which she'd discovered only yesterday, floated through her mind. *Shit.* Her phone chimed, and she glanced at the screen. "Gotta go. She's here." She flew out the door before Iris could inject any more unwanted thoughts into her head.

As Lane headed to the curb, the window rolled down on Helen's shiny, blue-pearl Acura TLX. The color and car fit her perfectly, as did her whisper-pink sleeveless silk blouse. Helen was a master of putting together an outfit, which made Lane feel underdressed in her mint-green scoop-neck cap-sleeve sheath dress. It was the middle of summer and way too hot for anything fancier.

Helen smiled as Lane approached. "Sorry I'm late. I went by Darcy's, but she wasn't ready yet. Said she'd pick up Audrey and meet us there."

Just the mention of Audrey made all the good feelings fade and created a huge knot in Lane's stomach. The woman was going to ruin everything for Darcy—and Lane. Lane pulled open the door and slid into the passenger seat.

"Do you know anything about the dance studio or the band Darcy recommended?" Helen punched the address into the GPS app on her phone. "I haven't used either before."

"Just that one of our mutual friends engaged the instructor for her wedding party, and they had a lot of fun." Lane yanked on the seatbelt and fastened it. "I have no idea about the band."

"Were you in the wedding party?"

"No. Just Darcy."

"Sounds like Darcy was more mutual than you."

That comment hit Lane abruptly, and she felt the need to explain. "I met her through Darcy." Lane shrugged. "Can't be best friends with everyone you know." Why had she lied to Helen about such a simple fact? Was she worried about what Helen would think? That tidbit, on top of not being chosen as Darcy's maid of honor, made Lane feel inadequate.

"True." Helen put the car into drive and looked over her shoulder at the road.

"Wait." Lane blew out a sigh. "I wasn't being truthful with you about that."

Helen put the car back into park and gave Lane her full attention. "I'm listening."

"It was actually the other way around. I introduced them, and Darcy became fast friends with the bride."

Helen's forehead wrinkled. "Why did you feel the need to lie about it?"

"I'd kind of been left as the third wheel of the friendship, which was awkward and, honestly, hurtful. So I eventually backed out of the group." The statement was enlightening. She realized that no matter how long they'd been friends, Darcy was easily swayed by the attention from others.

"Perfectly understandable." Helen's eyes were soft. "Best friends don't usually come in threes."

"Right, and that left me as a wedding guest rather than a bridesmaid." She hadn't expected to be anything more, but it still stung to be left out.

"I'm sorry you were excluded like that." Helen touched Lane's knee, and warmth spread throughout her. "I know from experience it's not a good feeling."

"No. It isn't." Lane glanced at Helen's hand, which was still on her knee. Where was this compassion coming from? Helen had never been this nice to her before.

"I was hoping you'd had some experience with the band. I guess we'll just have to see when we get there." Helen put the car into gear and pulled into traffic.

There she was, the old Helen, back to the business at hand. The mixed signals she was emitting were giving Lane whiplash.

Helen seemed skeptical when they pulled up in front of the studio. It was located in an older part of town, where the neighborhood seemed a bit run down. The inside of the windows was blanketed from top to bottom with pink curtains. The outsides were painted with various dance classes and schedules. "Doesn't look very impressive." She got out of the car. "Let's hope the inside is nicer."

"I'll reserve my judgment for the instructor." Lane followed Helen to the door.

"You're a better woman than I am." Helen tugged open the door and allowed Lane to enter before her.

No one was behind the counter as they entered the small reception area separated from the studio. They stood for a few minutes waiting. Helen finally moved around the counter, her cream-colored pleated, wide-leg pants flowing gracefully as she walked, and stuck her head through the door to the studio. "Anyone here?"

"Ladies." A man dressed all in black rushed toward them. "What can I do for you?" He motioned them inside.

Lane's heels clicked as she crossed the hardwood floor. The studio was much larger than she'd anticipated. It was a simple, elegant space with an exposed brick wall at the back and chandeliers hanging from the ceiling. Ballet barres lined one side of the room, while the one directly across from it was covered with floor-to-ceiling mirrors.

"We need to see about dance lessons for a wedding party."

"You came to the right place. My name is Eduardo. I'm the owner."

"Eduardo." Helen dipped her chin. "I'm Helen and this is Lane."

"Has either of you danced before?"

"I've danced quite a bit." Helen glanced at Lane. "It's the most romantic part of the wedding. Wouldn't you agree?"

"I would, but I'm not much of a dancer." She was all thumbs when it came to her feet.

"Well, then let's see how you two dance together," Eduardo said.

"But—" Apparently he thought they were a couple.

"No buts." The man pulled them both to the center of the room and had them face each other.

"Oh, no. I can't." Lane backed up. "I'm not a very good dancer."

The instructor put his hand on Lane's back and moved her toward Helen. "It's not about being perfect. It's about enjoying the dance." He took Helen's hand and placed it on Lane's waist.

Lane froze at the warmth of Helen's touch and stilled herself from the zap coursing through her. She hadn't expected anything like this today at all.

Eduardo placed Lane's hand on Helen's shoulder before he rushed across the room and started the music. "Show Lane your experience," he told Helen.

They fumbled at first and then moved into a natural rhythm with each other. Time and space disappeared as they danced across the floor. With Helen leading her, Lane could float like this forever.

"Wonderful." Eduardo smiled as the music faded. "You see? Dance allows you to use the body as an instrument of expression and communication. It enables people to let their inner feelings shine."

"I didn't realize I could move like that." The heat rose in Lane's cheeks.

"You have a good leader. The dance might be intricate and ceremonial or expressively erotic, but you need to be fluid, smooth, and graceful." The instructor took Lane's hand and placed it on Helen's hip. "Like the silk in Helen's blouse—soft and sensual."

Lane touched the fabric, brushing the curve of Helen's waist in the process. "I see what you mean." She slowly drew her hand away. "It's nice." What was underneath was a thousand times more than nice. Soft, yet strong. She stared a Helen for a moment, then backed up.

Helen moved closer, and Lane backed up farther. Lane had tried to convince herself that it was only the proximity and the theme of the events where she saw Helen that made her attractive, but that excuse was wearing thin. Today and yesterday had made it clear that even when she saw Helen outside of those events, she'd begun to impact her the same way.

Lane cleared her throat. "We should really get going. The band awaits."

"Right. The band." As she turned to Eduardo, Helen smoothed her shirt as though she were calming a tingle from her waist. "I have a bride and groom and possibly a bridal party that need dance lessons."

"Oh. You two aren't...?" He glanced from Helen to Lane and back again.

"No. We're planning the wedding."

Did Helen just say we *as though they were a team?*

"When is the date?" Eduardo walked toward the front area of the studio.

"September twenty-third," Helen said as she followed.

"That doesn't give us much time." He looked at the ceiling. "They'll likely need anywhere between three to nine lessons to feel confident learning the rhythm and the timing of the music. I would suggest a class once a week to start, and then, depending on their comfort level, we can adjust to more if needed." He seemed to know what he was talking about. "They'll have to learn the dance steps, how to lead or follow, and more complex moves like spins and dips if they want to dazzle the guests." He held his hands up and shook them.

"Can you write up a quote and send it to me at my email address?" Helen handed Eduardo her card. "The sooner the better, so we can get them started." She didn't wait for a response as she rushed to the door. It seemed Helen was feeling the heat as well.

CHAPTER FIFTEEN

As soon as they were in the car, Helen hit the button on her phone for Darcy. She hadn't expected to be alone with Lane all day again, and their proximity in the dance studio had become closer than she'd intended. The phone rang several times before it went to voice mail.

"Darcy," they said simultaneously, then glanced at each other before Helen continued. "We're good on the dance lessons. The owner is very nice, and he can set up weekly classes until the date. Now we're headed to see the band. Please meet us there." She ended the call.

"Did Darcy say she wants a band?" Lane looked at her as though she'd just suggested Darcy wear a hot-pink wedding dress.

"Audrey set up this appointment." Another dead-end Helen was forced to pursue. "Apparently, she saw this band at a party and thought they were fabulous."

"That's not surprising. Even though they're sisters, Audrey and Darcy are very different. I always thought she wanted a DJ so they could have a variety of music."

She'd expressed the same interest to Helen. "A DJ would be a better fit for Darcy, but we'll talk to the band agent, see a few demos to satisfy Audrey, and go from there." As far as Helen was concerned, they should ditch every one of Audrey's suggestions. She had no idea why Darcy had chosen Audrey over Lane as her maid of honor. They seemed to have vastly different ideas, but Helen would make sure Darcy had a beautiful wedding in spite of Audrey.

Lane's phone chirped and she looked at the screen. "Darcy said they're running late. They won't be there until around one o'clock."

"Oh." Helen stared out the windshield. "Do you want to grab

some lunch? I know a quaint little Chinese place close by." It seemed the Fates were keeping them alone together for some reason.

"Sure. Chinese is my favorite after Italian."

Helen chuckled. "Mine too." This connection with Lane was becoming unreal. "The agent has a website. Once we get to the restaurant, we can view the band on my phone if they have a demo."

"Sounds like a plan."

Once there, they were seated at table for two in the corner. It was before noon, but the place was small, and they were already filling up. It looked more like a dive on the outside, but the inside, with its red, black, and gold decor, was comfortable and clean.

Once seated they each perused the menu for a moment before the waitress appeared with two glasses of water. "The usual for you?"

Helen nodded. "Yes, thanks." She didn't want Lane to get the impression that she ate out a lot, but there was no getting around it now.

The waitress glanced at Lane. "And for you?"

Lane looked up and smiled. "I'll have the lunch special with egg drop soup, General Tso's chicken, and fried rice."

"Two of the usuals coming right up. Anything else?" the waitress asked.

Lane leaned forward and raised her eyebrows. "Let's get an order of dumplings too."

"Great idea." Helen glanced at the waitress. "Dumplings as well." Helen leaned forward as well, as though they were telling the most sacred of secrets. "They have the best General Tso's chicken I've ever tasted. I've never been able to find it this good anywhere, even when I travel out of town."

Lane widened her eyes. "And the fried rice is to die for."

"You read my mind." It seemed Lane was familiar with the restaurant. The place seemed to be more popular than Helen thought. It was nice to have a kindred spirit when it came to food.

"So, what kind of music do you prefer at weddings?" Helen sipped her water.

"Darcy has mentioned to me more than once that she'd like a DJ." Lane fiddled with the package of chopsticks lying next to the fork. "She thinks bands skew the music—make it sound different than it was intended."

Lane truly was the best person to make Darcy's wedding the fairy tale of her dreams. "I know what Darcy likes. She gave me a detailed list in addition to my questionnaire. I want to know what you like?" Lane had also chosen a DJ for her wedding music, or was that another of her ex, Belinda's, choices?

"Me?" Lane held her hand to her chest. "I'm not sure that matters here."

"It might not, but I'd still like to know."

"Honestly, I like the kind of music that traditional big bands play. Something along the lines of the Rat Pack era. There's nothing like the bounce of a standing bass and a mid-range crooner."

"I'd have to agree with you." Helen caught sight of the waitress coming from the kitchen with their soup and took the napkin from the table and placed it on her lap. "I don't think Audrey has the first clue about what Darcy wants."

"From the things she's suggested, it seems like she has some kind of childhood score to settle." Lane scrunched her nose. "I mean, I'm all for a good corn dog on a stick at the county fair, but not at a formal wedding."

"Right." Helen laughed. "They need to be at least bite-sized on toothpicks."

"Maybe we should throw those on the appetizer menu just to satisfy her." Lane shrugged.

"Or maybe we can add them to the kids' menu and seat her with them?"

"Even better." Lane chuckled as she spooned a bit of soup into her mouth.

They ate the rest of their soup in silence, stealing glances at each other between bites. This was feeling more like a date than work. It was time to crush that perception and get back to it. Helen took out her phone and pulled up the link Audrey had given her for the music. She scrolled through the videos, found the band, and hit the play button. Heavy-metal music blared through the speaker.

"Absolutely not." Lane's carefree expression immediately sobered, and she dropped her spoon. "I am *not* going to let Audrey ruin Darcy's wedding."

Helen quickly hit the pause button and lowered the volume before she glanced around the place to see if they'd disturbed anyone. Then Lane laughed abruptly. The sound caught Helen off guard and made her entire body react.

"I'm sorry." Still laughing, Lane rocked back in her chair. "But don't you just love the sound of the wedding march played by a metal band?"

Helen couldn't help but smile as she shook her head. "Audrey definitely must have a vendetta against her sister. This whole backwoods-carnival theme is getting a little much."

Lane laughed even louder, grabbing her napkin to cover her mouth. "Being brutally honest, are we?"

"Yeah. I probably shouldn't have said that." Helen tilted her head. "But I get the feeling that I can trust you."

"You can. I'm not any happier than you are about Audrey's suggestions, and I'm more than willing to work with you on getting around her."

Helen held out her hand. "Okay, then. Let's do it."

Lane took Helen's hand and held it longer than necessary, which sent a little jolt up through her arm and down deep in her belly. Their eyes met and held for a few moments before Helen took her hand away. Fun and light had just turned to awkward.

Their food arrived just in time. Lane picked up her fork. "This looks delicious." She dug into the fried rice.

"It never disappoints." Helen fiddled with her chopsticks for a minute, not seeming to be able to get them situated right in her fingers. What the hell? She was nervous and couldn't hold the damn sticks. She dropped them to the table and grabbed her fork.

❖

Helen didn't really see any sense in meeting with the band agent but wanted to watch Darcy's reaction to Audrey's choice. Also, it was entirely possible that she might need this particular agent as a contact at another event in the future…other than a wedding, of course.

"Come in." The agent met them at the door and ushered them to an old wooden desk with two chairs in front of it. A large flat-screen TV was hanging on the wall beside it.

As they sat, the agent went to the other side and did the same.

Helen was disappointed to see that Darcy and Audrey hadn't arrived yet.

"So, you two are looking for a wedding band?"

"Oh no," Lane said quickly. "Not us. My friend Darcy."

"Hmm…My instincts are usually better than that." He assessed them, and suddenly Helen felt very vulnerable. "Oh, well, the heart that waits can stand the test of time."

What exactly did he mean by that? Helen hadn't been waiting for anyone, let alone Lane.

"Since your bride is running late, would you like to listen to something in the interim?" The agent clicked a few keys on his computer.

Lane's voice flew through Helen's head. *Don't you just love the sound of the wedding march played by a metal band?* Ugh. She glanced at Lane. The only sound she loved recently was the sound of Lane's laugh as she'd said it.

"Do you have any big band or Rat Pack band demos we can listen to?" Helen asked. They might as well make the best of their time while they waited for Darcy and the wedding killer.

The agent pulled up a video on the big screen and clicked play. Helen relaxed in her chair, closed her eyes, and listened to a very good impression of Dean Martin flowing through the speakers.

"You really do enjoy doing this, don't you?" Lane's voice startled Helen out of her bliss.

Helen opened her eyes and nodded. "It's important. At weddings we all gather around friends and family to celebrate with the people we love. Music is a big part of that experience."

Lane stared at her as she rolled her lips in, then bit the lower one as she opened her mouth to speak. "Which part do you like better? The setting up or the party?"

"I love the planning and setting-up process just as much as the party. No. That's not true. Honestly, I don't miss doing the process as much as I miss the people I do it with." Helen glanced at the poster of a band dressed in grunge-wear. "We take all of this and put it together for people to enjoy."

"No matter what they like?" Lane laughed. "I've never thought of you as such a sentimental person."

Helen raised an eyebrow, unsure how to take that comment.

"I mean, I like it—what I'm seeing in you now." Lane touched Helen's arm gently. "It's just that you're always all business, and I didn't realize there was more to it for you."

"What about you?" Helen really wanted to know.

"I understand what you mean about the people—outside of my own wedding planning—which, in the end, didn't turn out well." Lane glanced at the agent and then back at Helen. "I've never been this involved from the start. I'm beginning to love both parts. Thanks for including me." Lane seemed sincere as she stared into her eyes.

Helen broke eye contact and stood. She needed to slow down whatever was happening between her and Lane. They seemed to be syncing in every way. "It looks like the bride has been detained elsewhere. Thank you for your time. I have your card. I'll be in touch to reschedule." She glanced at Lane. "That's it for today. I'll take you home."

Helen wished she could delete that bad experience from Lane's memory and erase it forever—wished she could take back her part in it. Love was difficult enough without having your heart shattered into a million pieces right before what would have been one of the happiest days of Lane's life.

CHAPTER SIXTEEN

It had been only three days since Lane had been with Helen, but she'd been eager to see more of her—more of this new person that Helen was revealing to her. It had been like slowly peeling an orange and enjoying the spritz of fresh citrus in the air with each piece of rind she removed. Today's wedding was at one of Lane's favorite places, a beautiful ranch located on the outskirts of Dallas. The venue was gorgeous, the pergolas decorated with strung greens and flowers that would be lit with sparkly lights as the reception went into the darkness of night. Under the massive tent, also strung with lights, each place setting was arranged meticulously in front of each chair at the round tables that surrounded the dance floor. Lane was impressed, as usual, at Helen's choice of linen, fine crystal, and china for the event. The woman had impeccable taste.

Iris had been there earlier to assist with the bridal party's makeup, but she'd had plans with Harvey tonight, so she'd left soon after the ceremony, Lane staying to keep the bride's makeup fresh. She glanced across the room and watched Helen as she skillfully made sure dinner had been cleared and the tented area rearranged for the night of dancing to come. She glanced at her phone to check the time. Once the clock hit nine, Lane would be able to leave. Her stomach did a weird, tingly twirl when she looked up to see Belinda coming across the lawn toward her. The person most in the world she didn't want to see—ever.

"Lane. I didn't expect to see you here." Belinda smiled widely. "That's not completely true. I saw you when I came in. I've been avoiding you." Her voice was low and sugary, just the way she remembered it.

Lane settled the unwanted butterflies in her stomach. "Sounds like a good plan. No need to change it now." She looked past her to make sure the bride's makeup was holding up.

"I didn't mean for things to happen between us the way they did. I'd like to talk to you about it some time." Belinda's smile didn't let on that she took any accountability for the way she'd left.

"That's not going to happen. I'm working." Not that Lane wanted to talk to Belinda about anything, especially their non-wedding.

"I can see you need more time to get over it." Belinda tilted her head and scrunched her eyebrows together.

"An eternity won't be enough." Being stuck with a wedding to cancel hadn't been on her to-do list six months ago, and paying for part of it as well wasn't in her budget. "I need to check the bride's makeup." She took in a deep breath. "Please stay away from me." She walked to the bride, took a quick look at her, made a few touch-ups, and then went straight to the bar.

It was probably a good thing Belinda had called off the wedding. Lane's gut had told her not to marry her anyway. There had been so many red flags—different schedules, different interests, different sex drives. Not to mention all of Belinda's boring corporate friends. The only good thing she got from the relationship was makeup clients.

The sex had been bad from the start, and it hadn't gotten any better with time. Everyone in Lane's family liked Belinda, though, as did her friends, except Iris. Was that her goal in life—to make her friends and family happy rather than herself?

She'd made a pros-and-cons list not long before the wedding date and convinced herself that the good outweighed the bad, when clearly it hadn't, or she would've been back with Belinda and married by now. Since the split, it had become clear they had nothing in common and were sexually incompatible as well. Belinda never sat still, hated to read, and rarely took time to enjoy the beauty around her. Energetic was an understatement.

She should be thankful Belinda had ended it, and maybe deep down she was, but she hadn't gotten over the humiliation of the experience. Plus, canceling a wedding three days before wasn't easy without any help from the other bride. At least Helen had been there. She supposed the comfort of the routine had kept her in the relationship for so long. In hindsight she should be thanking Belinda for ending it. Otherwise, she'd still be trapped in a mundane existence that she hated—a punishing life of office work and boredom that Belinda had wanted her to move toward to fit in with her lifestyle. Lane had been weak at the time and taken the opportunity Belinda had found for her but realized soon after that she could never do that job permanently. She was much happier setting her own schedule at her family's business and helping people on their happiest of days.

The initial attraction to Belinda was obvious, but now Lane wondered why she'd let herself get sucked into it all so easily. Belinda was exciting, vibrant, and so alive. Every moment with her had been an adventure until it became too much. There was absolutely no downtime with her, no recovery period to re-energize, to let herself think or do any of the things that, deep down, Lane loved to do. Everything she cherished in her life became second and no longer important to either of them. She'd lost herself in a relationship that she'd unknowingly hated at the time.

Then, once all her friends began to pair off and get married, it seemed like the natural thing for them to do as well, even if they weren't perfectly compatible. As Lane had slipped into her thirties, she didn't want to be single. Two years into the engagement, it was clear she hadn't recognized the full depth of the loneliness and depression she'd fallen into. It had taken only one month after Belinda had canceled the wedding for Lane to realize that she didn't miss her—at all. Sure, she missed the concept of the relationship—having someone to come home to—but in reality, she'd never really had that with Belinda.

Iris had always said that a woman wanted only two things when a relationship ended, either to be out of it totally or to have it not be over. Lane was still somewhere in between, wishing the whole thing had been different in some way—thinking she could've changed it somehow.

Lane stood at the bar drinking the last of her second glass of champagne within the span of ten minutes. She was tired of the whole event—tired of all the happiness surrounding love. Love hadn't been happy for her. It had made her lonely and bitter. She wanted to go home—now. She fiddled with her phone, trying to find the Uber app, but her focus was fuzzy. Frustrated, she glanced up and blinked a few times to clear her vision. Helen came into view across the room, and she bolted across to her, bumping into happy dancers as she crossed the floor.

"Can you call me an Uber?" Lane slurred the words more than she'd expected. She should've eaten more today and probably stayed away from the champagne.

Helen assessed her. "I'm done here. I'll take you home."

Fuck. Helen knew she was drunk. That was totally unprofessional. "That's not necessary. Just call me a ride, and I'll be fine."

"I know you will." Helen moved her toward the door. "But I'd like the company, if you don't mind."

"Okay." It was clear that riding with Helen was the only way she was getting home tonight. She stumbled as she crossed the threshold and twisted her ankle. Pain filled her, and she thought she was going to be sick.

Thank God Helen caught her arm before she went totally down. "You okay?"

Lane shook her head. "My ankle." Bile rose in her throat. "I think I sprained it."

"We'll head to the ER on the way home." Helen wrapped her arm around her, walked her to the car, and helped her inside.

Could this evening get any worse? First, she'd had an awkward encounter with Belinda, and now a clumsy stumble was forcing Helen to deliver her to the ER and then home. *Damn, Lane. Get your shit together.*

❖

Helen pulled up in front of Lane's sister's house and killed the engine. Lane had insisted they go there since it was closer to the hospital, and Helen wasn't in the mood to argue. She reached over and nudged Lane's shoulder. "We're here." She'd immediately fallen asleep after they left the ER. Thankfully her ankle had only been sprained.

"What is so wrong with me that Belinda didn't want me?"

Helen had no idea where that had come from. Lane must have been dreaming. "Nothing's wrong with you." Helen helped Lane out of the car, then tucked her under her shoulder and walked her to the door. Warmth filled her as Lane's arms wrapped around her waist. "Belinda is a total idiot for letting you go." The woman didn't deserve someone as nice as Lane. Helen had never met anyone more optimistic and genuine.

Lane stared at her. "You think so?" She fumbled with her keys.

"Uh-huh." Helen nodded, took the keys from her, and unlocked the door. The house was dark. It didn't look like her sister was home. "I wouldn't have said it if I didn't." She flipped on the light and helped Lane, whose weight had gone slack, into the house. "Those are some pretty strong pain meds they gave you, aren't they?"

"Yeah. I probably should've told the doctor about the glass or two of champagne I had earlier."

"Yes. You probably should have." Helen grinned. "Now, let's get you into bed." She walked her toward the hallway.

Lane grabbed the counter as they passed it and giggled.

"What's so funny?" Helen was glad to find that Lane was a happy drunk.

"I never thought I'd hear that sentence from you."

"I never thought I'd be saying it either." Helen had never dreamed she'd be in the position of escorting Lane home at all.

"The couch is my bed tonight." Lane turned her gaze to Helen and blinked to focus. "This is my sister's house, remember?"

"Right. It was closer to the ER." Helen glanced around and didn't see a sign of anyone else. "Where's your sister?"

"Out living life. Partying until the wee hours." Lane slumped against her. "She's still young and beautiful." Clearly, Lane had entered wallow land.

"Okay then." Helen walked her to the couch and laid her back against the cushion before she lifted her legs onto the other end, propping the injured ankle on a cushion. She sat on the edge of the couch and brushed Lane's hair out of her face.

Lane gazed up at her. "You're actually very attractive."

"Thank you." Helen tilted her head. "I think." She grinned at the unexpected and awkward compliment.

"Long legs, beautiful eyes, and..." Lane closed her eyes. She seemed to have passed out. Then she bolted up and gripped Helen's shoulder and the back of the couch. "I have a problem."

"Oh." Helen blinked. "You want to tell me about it?"

"No." Lane shook her head. "You're the one person I don't want to tell."

"Okay. Then why don't you lie back and get some sleep."

Lane pinched her eyes together and opened them widely. "I really like you, and I shouldn't. You're the most infuriating woman I've ever met." Her eyes rolled back, and her lids closed as she fell into Helen. She was out. Helen had the most beautiful Domaine Chandon fire-breathing dragon making tiny snores in her ear.

"That's good." Helen brushed her fingers across Lane's cheek. "Because I like you too." She'd been trying to avoid this situation, but it seemed to be moving along all on its own, even with all the roadblocks she'd put in place to prevent it. However, she'd stumbled upon a pretty big roadblock this evening. Helen hadn't realized the effect Belinda still had on Lane. That was definitely something to consider moving forward. Everything seemed a little messier now, and Helen didn't want any confrontations with Belinda. But she would leave the door open and wait until Lane was ready to walk through it. She caught the whiff of alcohol on Lane's breath and squeezed her eyes closed before she laid Lane back onto the couch.

It looked like Helen would be spending the night at Lane's sister's as well. She couldn't very well leave her alone in this condition. Considering her sprained ankle, Lane would need help in the morning if her sister didn't come home. She glanced around the room and scoped out the recliner. At least Lane hadn't hit her head, and Helen didn't need to wake her up every hour, make sure she wasn't slurring her words. The slurring had occurred before the fall—because of Belinda.

CHAPTER SEVENTEEN

Lane struggled to open her eyes as she pressed her tongue to the roof of her mouth, searching for some kind of moisture. The scent of something delicious floated through her head. What the hell? Her sister never cooked breakfast. She peeked over the top of the couch and froze when she saw Helen at the stove cooking and her sister at the table shoveling pancakes into her mouth. Lane quickly dropped her head back to the couch and squeezed her eyes shut when the wave of an ache rolled through it. Champagne always gave her a headache. She waited a minute before she reached up, grabbed the back of the couch, and pulled herself up to a sitting position.

"Hey. You're awake." Amy pointed at Helen. "This woman makes the best pancakes." She stuffed the end of a rolled one into her mouth and chewed. "If I didn't have a brunch date, I'd eat the whole stack." She talked through her chew as she walked toward her. "This woman is a goddess. You should hold on to her." She kissed Lane on the cheek. "Gotta go. Love you, sis." And she was out the door.

Lane glanced up at Helen. Amy was right. She was a goddess. Short salt-and-pepper hair, tanned face, strong arms, and gorgeous blue eyes. If Lane had met her in a bar, she'd be all over her.

Helen brought a plate of pancakes to the living room and set it on the coffee table. "Eat, and then I'll take you home."

"You don't have to do that. I can get an Uber."

"Nope. I'll take you. You have a meeting with a new bride this morning."

"How do you know that?" Had Lane told her last night?

Helen pointed to Lane's planner, which was wide open on the table. "Your planner fell out of your bag. Today was bookmarked, and I took a look."

"I'll need to cancel. Not sure I can get around on this foot." She wiggled it, felt a touch of soreness, but nothing like the pain she'd had last night.

"Absolutely not. Never turn business away." Helen's condescending tone returned.

"I'm not turning it away," Lane said softly, retreating. "I'm just canceling for today."

"You'd be letting the bride know you're unreliable and giving her time to see someone else." Helen raised an eyebrow. "You don't want that, do you?"

"No. I hadn't thought about it that way." Lane touched her ankle, which had now turned a pretty purple. "I'll need help. I'll call Iris to come get me."

"No need to interrupt her morning plans. I'll help you."

"I'm sorry about last night." Lane had to look away while she spoke. "Drinking at a client's wedding is unprofessional." Even if it was only a couple of glasses, the emotions that drove it were bothering her.

"We all make mistakes," Helen said flatly. "No one noticed. I got you out of there quickly." She glanced at Lane's ankle. "This was our only obstacle."

That was a relief. Lane jammed a few bites of pancakes into her mouth and chewed. Then she fell back against the couch and let the delicious flavor fill her. "These are fantastic." She pointed at them with her fork.

"I don't cook a lot, but when I do, it's breakfast." Helen laughed, and Lane became acutely aware of her own body's response.

Visions of breakfast in bed with naked Helen flew through Lane's head, and she heated from head to toe. She really needed to get laid. It had been way too long. She watched Helen. Was she a possibility—was that a possibility? Helen, naked in her bed? She pinched her eyes shut and shook the thought away. Helen would probably want to give her step-by-step instructions. Lane wasn't good at being led in bed. But oddly, that idea wasn't unappealing to her at this moment.

She quickly finished the rest of the pancakes on the plate. "I should change." She and her sister were about the same size and swapped clothes often. She stood, put her weight on her ankle, and winced when pain shot up her leg.

"Let me help you." Helen tucked herself under Lane's arm, which didn't even feel awkward. They seemed to fit together nicely. Another unexpected fact. When Helen slipped her arm around Lane's waist, a jolt shot right to her midsection. *Wow.* Helen's effect on her had changed from irritation to illumination. No way would she be able to admit that to her out loud. Not yet anyway.

When they reached the hallway, Lane grasped the molding on each side of the entrance. "I got it from here."

Helen followed her and waited by the door as she opened the closet and thumbed through the clothes. She stopped at a pretty flower-patterned dress of Amy's that she'd worn before.

"Put that one on. It looks good on you."

Did Helen actually just compliment her? When had Helen noticed her dress? She took the hanger from the closet. "Okay." She glanced at Helen, not about to strip down to her undies and change in front of her. "Just give me a minute."

"I think you should go with your sister's fanciest flip-flops today." Helen backed out of the room, pulling the door closed.

After changing, Lane hobbled to the bathroom and brushed her teeth with one of the spare toothbrushes her sister kept in the drawer. Amy made a habit of taking more than one each time she went to the dentist. Lane rinsed her mouth and then stared at herself in the mirror. "Well, aren't you a sight this morning." She rubbed a cotton swab beneath her eyes to remove the faded eyeliner and then ran a brush through her hair to flatten the unruly waves created by her night on the couch. She added more weight to her ankle as she walked to the door. It was still sensitive, but the pain was bearable. "Ready or not, here I come." She sucked in a deep breath and held onto the molding as she opened the door. "I'm ready when you are." She entered the hallway, immediately met by a concerned Helen rushing toward her.

"Okay." Helen held out her hand. "Then let's go."

Lane took Helen's hand and let her warmth rush through her. It didn't surprise her that it felt good. She should just stop fighting it. Belinda wasn't a nurturer, and Lane had come to realize that was something she wanted in a relationship.

"I need to run by my place to change." Helen glanced at Lane. "We have time, right?"

"Yes. We have plenty of time." Lane gripped Helen as she helped her hobble across the room and out the door. Today was destined to be another day in paradise.

❖

Lane sat on the couch with her foot resting comfortably on the cushion and stared across at the massive bookcase she'd admired the first time she'd been in Helen's apartment. If it weren't for the pain in her ankle, she'd be up perusing the titles again. The pain wasn't horrible, but staying off her feet as much as possible would most likely help her heal quickly. She probably should've ignored Helen's advice and stayed home, but what she'd said made sense, and she couldn't afford to lose the business.

She'd hoped Helen would be okay with Iris picking her up and taking her to the morning appointment. Lane was reluctant to spend any more time with Helen than she had to. She didn't want to like her, but that was becoming harder to prevent. It was funny. She'd assumed that Helen disliked her in equal measure, but evidently Lane had miscalculated Helen's ability to move past her feelings, if indeed that was how she felt. It also became clear that Lane didn't dislike her at all. Love and hate were connecting them more than she'd realized. She needed to keep her feelings in the friend zone for now.

Helen appeared from the hallway holding a box of medical supplies. "We should probably wrap your ankle." She sat at the end of the couch and lifted Lane's foot into her lap.

"It'll be fine." Lane stifled a gasp as Helen's fingertips roamed lightly over the skin of her ankle as she assessed it. A low rumble began in her belly. Was this foot-play or foreplay? She dropped her head back onto the cushion. Who knew it could be such a turn-on?

Helen glanced up, brows wrinkled. "Does that hurt?"

Lane straightened. "No. It tickles a bit." She planted a hand on her belly to settle herself.

"Good." Helen proceeded to wrap an ACE bandage around Lane's ankle. Not too tight, not too loose. "It's not the most attractive job, but it should give you some support for the day."

"Thank you for this…and for taking me to my appointment." Lane was overwhelmed by Helen's attentiveness today. Last week, they'd been all over town, and Helen had been more than good company.

There wasn't much conversation, besides a comment here and there about the rising heat, on the ride to the venue. When they arrived, Lane was able to get out of the car and inside with minimal help from Helen, who was hovering closely.

The bride was already there and rushed toward Lane as she entered. "Thanks for meeting me here. I wanted to check out the bridal room. I heard it's beautiful since the renovation."

"I'm curious to see it as well." Lane hobbled toward the bride.

The bride glanced at Lane's foot. "Oh, no. What happened to your ankle?"

"It's just a sprain." Lane waved toward her foot. "Should be good to go before your big day." It felt much better since Helen had wrapped it.

Helen followed them into the bridal suite. "Wow. They really did a good job."

Painted in a creamy ivory shade, it was fully equipped with a fireplace, flat-screen TV, sitting area, kitchenette with a bar, and gown display. One side of the room had several salon chairs in front of a solid mirror and counter to provide easy hair and makeup stations. All the vanity space a girl could need. The adjacent wall was lined with floor-to-ceiling windows, which provided a beautiful view of a flower garden and pond.

"The lighting is perfect." Even without the lights mounted above the mirrors, Lane was sure the natural sunlight would make the room glow at any time of day. "A bride could easily get spoiled in this room."

Helen waited for Lane to get situated in one of the chairs. "Do you mind if I wander around and take a look at the place? I haven't been here since they remodeled."

"Go ahead. I'll be fine." Lane waved her on.

"Great. I'll be back before you're finished." Helen went to the door.

"Check out the groom's suite while you're looking around. They spoil the men too. The brochure says they have two flat-screen TVs, theater seating, a kitchenette with a bar, and a pool table."

"What more could a man need?" Helen grinned and left the room.

Lane turned her attention to the bride. "I bet you're getting excited." She'd already done a trial makeup run with her before her bridal shower. They'd decided to tweak the eyeliner and go with false lashes to bring her eyes out a bit more. She was going to be a beautiful bride.

"I am, but I'm more stressed than I expected." She flipped her hair back. "I didn't realize there was so much to do in advance."

"Oh. Well, you know Helen, who was just here?" Lane motioned toward the door. "She's an event planner. I could see if she's available to help?"

"Would you?"

"Sure." Lane nodded. "I'm not sure what she charges."

"At this point, I'm not worried about cost. I just don't want to be exhausted for my wedding."

"We can talk to her when she comes back."

The bride's phone buzzed, and she read a text. "I'm sorry. I have to go. I'm meeting some friends for brunch, and they're waiting." She moved toward the door.

Lane started to get up. "Let me find Helen."

"Take your time." The bride held up her hand. "Don't worry about locking up. The owner will do it. She's around here somewhere finishing some repairs." She looked over her shoulder. "Can you send me Helen's contact information?"

"Sure. I'll text it to you." Lane watched her rush out the door before she hobbled to the makeup area and studied it for a moment. All her makeup and multiple brushes would fit nicely here. They really had done a good job of renovating this room. She headed out of the room to see the rest of the place and to find Helen.

Lane didn't come across her until she happened to look in the coat closet. Helen was standing in the middle staring up at the shelves. "Of all places, I didn't expect to find you in here."

Helen spun around. "Can you believe how big this room is? You could hang a thousand guests' coats in it easily."

"I hadn't thought about that before." Lane was becoming more and more impressed by Helen. She really did think of every detail. But what impressed Lane even more was that this didn't seem to be just a job to her. Helen seemed to truly care about making couples happy.

"I've handled so many winter weddings where guests have had to leave their coats in their cars or, worse yet, hang them on the backs of their chairs."

"That's a crazy tripping nightmare." The vision of women catching heels on overcoats filled Lane's head.

"Right?" Helen's forehead creased. "That's all a couple needs—for someone to get injured on their special day."

Lane entered the room, and as she moved closer to Helen, she stumbled and fell against her, hands landing Helen's on shoulders. She stared into those beautiful baby blues. She could get lost in them for sure. The warmth of Helen's strong hands holding her by the waist was more than she could take. She murmured, "Oh, hell." Then she swooped forward, took Helen's face in her hands gently, and kissed her lightly, glanced into her eyes, and then kissed her again. Helen's lips were soft and pliable. They gave with each of Lane's movements. She relaxed into Helen, and all hints of resistance were gone. When Helen's tongue met hers as it slipped into her mouth, she tangled her fingers in Helen's hair and lost her thoughts for the next few moments as her mind spun. She gripped Helen's shoulders for balance as heat spiraled in her belly and settled between her thighs. *Holy shit.* She hadn't expected their kiss to be so good.

"Sorry. I was just curious what that would be like."

Helen blinked several times. "And?"

"And I have to admit, against all my instincts, that it was pretty nice." Lane pressed her fingers to her mouth.

"Against all your instincts?" Helen moved closer.

Lane felt a rush at the sexy look Helen gave her and almost couldn't catch her breath. "Well, maybe not all of them." Lane's heart beat rapidly. There was so much more to Helen than she'd realized.

"That's the best news I've heard all day." Helen took her into her arms and kissed her again—longer—deeper.

The buzz that zapped through Lane made her weak—made her want to melt into Helen and let her do so much more.

When the kiss broke, Helen shook her head and grinned. "I can't believe I'm making out in the coat-check room. Do you know how many people I've chastised for doing this?" Helen's soft chuckle matched her easy smile.

Lane couldn't believe how much a laugh could transform a woman. Over the past few days, Helen had turned from an ice queen into an enjoyable, beautiful person. Maybe mindless sex was what she needed. But would sex with Helen really be mindless?

"It's totally wrong, but it feels good, doesn't it?" Lane moved closer—stared into Helen's gorgeous blue eyes. She grabbed Helen's hips and pulled her toward her in a desperate motion. She wanted another taste of the gorgeous woman standing before her.

Helen took Lane's cue and kissed her again. Tongues mingled and soft whimpers escaped from her throat as the kiss became deeper. When Lane slipped her leg between Helen's thighs, she ended the kiss abruptly.

"We should stop," Helen choked out between rapid breaths. "Your bride might…"

"She left. Seems brunch is on everyone's schedule today." Lane backed up and straightened her dress. "Good call, though." She blew out a slow breath. Her mind was buzzing, and the dark, sexy look in Helen's eyes was undeniable. "The owner is still around here somewhere." She had to stop herself from ignoring all her instincts and diving into another earth-shattering kiss. A quickie in the coat closet wouldn't do for all the things she wanted to do to Helen. Lane needed to think…This woman could be the end of her if she let this go any further right now.

❖

Helen tossed her keys onto the marble coffee table in her parents' living room before she flopped onto the couch behind it. She didn't know what she'd been thinking earlier. She and Lane could've been caught and lost any future contracts for that venue in a split second. She shook her head at herself as she relaxed against the cushion and spread her arms across the top of the couch. Lane was the first woman in so very long to make her skin tingle…stomach tighten…heart race.

Last night had made it obvious that Lane was probably still in love with her ex-fiancée—if not love, then some other kind of emotional connection. Just the same, Helen dropped her head back, closed her eyes, and savored the moment. When Lane had kissed her, the blood from Helen's brain had immediately drained to more important areas.

Lane's gaze had dropped to Helen's lips as she came closer, and she couldn't move—didn't want to. Then Lane's tongue had slipped across her lips and dipped into her mouth, and the throb between her legs had rocketed to an all-time high. She'd let herself fall into it, feel every moment of it, from the softness of Lane's lips to her magical tongue as it slipped into her mouth. Sweet Lord, she'd forgotten how good it felt to be kissed so thoroughly and with such care and glorious passion. Their kisses had grown bolder with each touch, and having Lane's thigh between her legs almost sent her over the edge. She'd been kissed by many women in her life, but never, ever like that. She was lucky to get out of there without locking the door and stroking Lane in all the places she'd been dreaming of lately.

"What are you grinning about?" Her mother's voice yanked her from her bliss.

Helen snapped her eyes open. "I didn't realize I was." She straightened and crossed her ankles. "I was just envisioning the next wedding I'm planning."

"You seem to be becoming very busy with those." Her mother stood at the bar. "Drink?"

"No, thank you. I still have work to do." Alcohol would just let her sink into the ever-increasing fantasies she was having about Lane. "I'd like a little background on the wedding you so urgently pushed me into taking." It wasn't the first time, and she was sure it wouldn't be the last.

"For whom?" Caroline filled a highball glass with ice and doused it with vodka.

"Darcy Hampton."

"Oh, right. Her mother's a friend from long ago." Caroline sat in the chair adjacent from the couch and glanced out the window. "It's a lovely day, isn't it?"

"Yes, it is." It had been much lovelier a couple of hours ago when Helen had been tangled up with Lane at the country club…in the coat closet. She bit back a grin. "Darcy seems to be a typical bride. What can you tell me about her sister, the matron of honor?"

"She's chosen Audrey as her matron of honor? That's interesting." Caroline sipped her drink as she stared out the window.

The back of Helen's neck burned. She knew there was more behind the request. "Mother, you need to tell me all the details about Audrey."

She seemed to be contemplating her next words. "Has she been helpful?"

"Honestly, she's been a big pain in my ass." And was on her way to being blacklisted from all the planning.

Her mother raised an eyebrow. "I'm not surprised." She set her drink on the side table. "She's always been the challenging one in that family."

"I'm not sure Darcy chose Audrey to be her matron of honor of her own accord. I think she was pressured into it by both Audrey and her mother." That fact was becoming clearer by the day. "Her friend Lane would've been a better choice."

"That's not surprising either." Caroline relaxed into her chair. "What Audrey wants, Audrey gets."

That information seemed to gel with what Helen had already seen. "Why in the world would you ask me to handle this mess?"

"As I said, her mother and I go way back." Caroline sipped her drink.

"How far back?" Something fishy was going on here.

"To my sorority days."

"You owe her for something, don't you?"

"Let's just say neither one of us was an angel, and we both have a lot of knowledge about each other." Caroline's lips quirked into a slight smile.

"Are you going to tell me what it is?" Maybe she should have a drink after all.

"Absolutely not." She laughed as she set her drink on the table. "I *will* tell you that Audrey is easily distracted. Find her something to do to keep her busy. It'll keep you from running down a few rabbit holes because of her zany ideas."

Helen could certainly do that. She knew of plenty of mundane tasks that went along with wedding planning. "Just remember." She stood and straightened her blouse. "Now, *you* owe *me*."

"You collect on that debt every day when I run interference with your dad and his matchmaking."

Helen let out a laugh. "True, but still. This ask of delivering a suitable wedding in a ridiculous timeline is a big one. And as I said, Audrey is a significant pain in my ass." She grabbed her keys and looked over her shoulder as she left the room. "*Huge.*"

"I know you can do it. I have faith in you." Caroline's voice floated into the foyer from the living room.

"I wish I had that much faith in myself," Helen whispered as she went out the door. Faith enough to keep her distance from Lane so she could get this wedding under control.

❖

Lane had settled in on the couch with her foot propped on a pillow on the coffee table. She'd grabbed provisions from the kitchen—cheese, crackers, chips, and a soda. She fished around the cushions. All she needed was the remote, and she'd be set for the afternoon. Iris was out when she arrived home, which was good. She'd want to know where Lane had spent last night, and that was going to be a tricky one to explain. She was still trying to figure out what had possessed her to kiss Helen in the coat closet. She'd always acknowledged that Helen was attractive, but she'd always been able to control her desires. Helen was nothing like she'd been in the past—she seemed to be changing right before her eyes and becoming more attractive each day.

She hadn't even had a chance to finish her snacks when she heard the door open. "You home?" Iris's voice vibrated through the house.

"On the couch."

"You've got some explaining to do." After a minute Iris appeared in the living room. "What did you do to your foot?" Iris rushed to the couch and sat next to her.

"Something jumped out in front of me last night." Thankfully Helen had been there to catch her. She sighed. "Belinda showed up, and I had a few glasses of champagne."

Iris's eyes widened. "Oh, no. What'd she say?"

"She wanted to talk." Lane ripped a piece of cheese in half and put it into her mouth.

"And?" Iris leaned forward, took the other half of the cheese, and ate it.

"And I told her no. She made some comment about me not being over her." Lane took in a deep breath. "I told her to fuck off and went to the bar."

"Good for you." Iris settled in next to her. "I see salt-and-pepper pastures coming your way."

Helen popped into her head—then the kiss. She shifted. "I kissed Helen today."

"Woohoo. Running with that ball, are you?" Iris laughed. "How was it?"

Lane chewed on her bottom lip. "It was so much better than I ever imagined." Wonder, excitement, joy, and amazement flooded her, just as they had earlier.

"Here we go." Iris let out a huge laugh and began humming the wedding march.

Lane swatted her arm. "Stop it. It was just a kiss." She sighed, excited and scared by the whole experience. "A fucking crazy fantastic kiss, but just a kiss nonetheless."

"Yeah, baby." Iris wasn't going to let this go.

"Where do I go from here?" What if Helen didn't enjoy it? What if she didn't want to pursue anything else? What if Helen did? Lane set the plate of cheese on the cushion as her stomach rumbled.

"Forward, my dear, forward. Never backward." Iris pointed both her index fingers in front of her.

"I don't think so." Not yet anyway. "I need to let this one cool off a bit." If that was even possible.

"Good luck with that." Iris stood. "Those fantasies of yours have been brewing so long, they're going to be hard to suppress." Iris headed into her bedroom. "Let me know how that works out for you."

"It'll be fine. I'll just avoid her." Lane pulled her feet from the coffee table and winced as her ankle hit the floor. She gripped the edge of the couch. That was going to be impossible.

CHAPTER EIGHTEEN

A week had gone by, and Lane found herself working another wedding with Helen, which wasn't unusual, just a bit more uncomfortable today. After her uncontrollable urge to kiss Helen last week, Lane had thought it best to keep her distance. Since she hadn't heard from Helen, she assumed she'd thought the same. So far today, they'd both been successful.

Lane and Iris had just finished with the last of the bridesmaids. Everyone was set, but she wanted to touch up the bride's makeup one last time. She pushed open the door from the adjoining room slightly but didn't enter when she heard the frantic voice of the bride. Helen was with her.

"I have no idea why I'm doing this. I'm not even sure it's the right thing to do." The bride paced the room.

Helen put her hands on the bride's shoulders. "You love him, don't you?"

"I love him so much, but I just wanted to have a small celebration. All of this is overwhelming." The bride raised her hands in the air.

"After a three-minute walk down the aisle and a ten-minute ceremony, it'll be over, and you can party until the cows come home."

"I never wanted this huge show. His mother is just—" The bride's helpless sigh morphed into a low growl.

"You're not marrying his mother. By tomorrow night she'll be back in Chicago, and you'll be married to your soul mate." Helen lifted the bride's chin with her finger. "That's what you want, isn't it?"

The bride gave her a slow smile and nodded. "It is."

Helen stepped back and gave the bride a once-over. "Your fiancé is a lucky man."

Lane pulled the door closed slightly as Iris put her hands to her chest. "Wow. Helen really is different than we thought. I can see now why you kissed her."

Lane blew out a breath. "I don't know if I'm ready yet to be loved. You know it's been such a long road with the Belinda mess."

"You're ready. You have been for a while, even before you broke up with her." Iris stared into her eyes. "She was bad for you, made you question who you are as a person."

"I can't deny that." Lane took in a deep breath. "I think she's damaged me in ways."

"Stop that." Iris grabbed her by the shoulders. "There's nothing wrong with you. She's the one who's screwed up. You just need to realize it's okay to talk about how you feel and what you want." She let her hands trail down Lane's arms to her hands.

"Yeah. I never could do that with her." She'd been too afraid Belinda would leave. Which she did anyway.

Iris glanced through the crack in the doorway at Helen. "Well, you sure don't have any issues about being brutally honest with Helen."

"That's because we're not fucking."

"Not yet anyway." Iris gave her a sly smile.

Lane let out a short laugh. "You're so sure of this, aren't you?"

"Have I ever been wrong?" Iris fancied herself somewhat of a matchmaker.

"There was that one time with Pam and Colin." They were friends of theirs that, for various reasons, neither of them had thought of as a couple.

"That wasn't my fault. He dressed way too metrosexual to be straight."

"He did at that." Lane smiled as she watched Helen continue talking to the bride, who was smiling now.

"You can't tell me that he hadn't slept with at least one man before."

"No. I can't tell you that." Lane shook her head. "Never researched him enough to know." She startled as the door opened into her and Helen appeared.

Everything slowed as Helen fumbled around her, trying to catch her balance. Tiny lines sprouted next to Helen's eyes as she smiled. An adorable detail she hadn't noticed before. Lane took Helen's face in her hands and kissed her long and soft. When she was finished, she stared into Helen's eyes, catching a bit of confusion in them. She'd never been so forward with anyone before—never been the aggressor with any woman she'd been attracted to.

Lane backed away, heard Iris laughing in the distance. "Absolutely sure."

It was like a crazy dream sequence, and she'd suddenly realized that Helen was the one. She'd finally found the woman she could see herself spending the rest of her life with, and she was the one woman who exasperated her the most in life. What the hell was she going to do? It wasn't like she could avoid her. They would be thrown together at least weekly for the next two months.

"I have to check on the bride." Lane brushed past Helen and entered the room. Her breath hitched, as it always did, at the sight of the gorgeous wedding dress. Warmth spread though her, and she held her hands to her chest and stared at the bride. "Oh my gosh. You're so beautiful." The bride was gorgeous, but the warmth Lane was feeling had nothing to do with her. It was all due to the exchange she'd seen, the kiss, and Helen. She was turning out to be much more compassionate than Lane had ever thought possible.

❖

Helen stood back and scanned the room, all the things that had gone wrong floating through her head. Morning weddings were more stressful for her since she didn't have as much prep time before the event. She'd been distracted by Lane and lost sight of a few things she'd meant to do, which put the timing off slightly.

"Everything turned out beautifully, didn't it?"

Helen shook her head. "In the end, it did, but there were plenty of things that I wish I could've done better."

"Look at them?" Lane pointed to the wedding party. "The bride and groom are having a spectacular day because of you. That in itself is a great compliment to your skills."

"I just helped them along." Their happiness was genuine, and Helen could see it every time she caught sight of them. That made her happy.

"Believe me, you did more than that. Do you know how many weddings I've worked that haven't turned out half this nicely?"

Helen raised an eyebrow. "Oh, really?"

"Plenty. They happen in backyards, parks, and even camp-grounds." Lane shivered. "The bugs can be relentless at those."

Helen laughed. "I bet that can be a real problem." She'd been involved in a few wedding disasters. Some things are out of anyone's control.

Lane's eyebrows pulled together. "You ever see a bride toss her bouquet and take off running like a crazy woman because of a bumblebee?"

Helen grinned. "I can't say that I have."

"Well, I have, and it's not pretty. Turns out it's exactly like yelling fire in a crowded theater, except outside. Panic takes over, and your whole wedding setup is ruined."

"To think that a cute little insect can put that kind of fear into so many people." Helen rolled her lips in, holding back a laugh. "And you were there doing the bride's makeup?"

"That, and other things. Sometimes I help with setup and cleanup."

Helen had no idea that Lane did more. "Maybe I should engage your services some time?" But then again, that could make her events even more disastrous.

"I doubt that you'll need them. You always have everything under control." Lane smiled softly. "What you did for the bride today was very sweet."

"She just needed to calm her nerves." Helen didn't really have everything under control. She just knew how to put up a good front. But she'd never enjoyed any compliment more than the one she'd just received from Lane. She didn't know why, but she was beginning to value Lane's opinion, and that meant a lot to her.

"Would you like to have dinner with me tonight—after this event wraps up?" Helen raised her eyebrows. "I'd really like to explore this thing happening between us a little more."

"Yes. I would." Lane took in a deep breath. "I think we should... at least discuss it."

"Okay. Great. We can go to Basilico." The same place they'd had dinner with Iris. If things went awry, at least she'd be someplace familiar. She spotted an empty tray at the buffet table. "I can pick you up, say at six?" She waited for Lane to nod before rushing toward the kitchen to check on the food situation.

CHAPTER NINETEEN

L ane was ready and waiting when Helen arrived at Iris's place to pick her up promptly at six o'clock. Lane answered the door quickly after she heard the knock.

"Hi." She couldn't help giving Helen the head-to-toe once-over. Helen was dressed in khaki capri pants and a baby-blue button-down shirt, which matched Lane's navy polka-dot V-neck midi dress. She'd originally chosen a black slip dress but then decided that was too sexy for whatever kind of date this was with Helen.

"Hi." Helen blinked and cleared her throat. "You ready?"

"Yes. Just let me grab my bag." Lane turned quickly and found it on the couch.

They walked together down the pathway to Helen's car, which was parked on the street. Helen opened the door for Lane to slide in before she circled the front of the car and got into the driver's seat.

"I'm starving." Helen fired the engine.

"You didn't have a chance to eat at the wedding?" That didn't surprise Lane. Helen was very busy.

Helen shook her head. "Not today."

"I always eat before events. I never know if I'll have an opportunity to grab something during the day." She hadn't eaten much before last week's wedding when she'd run into Belinda, and look where that had gotten her—drunk and escorted home by Helen via the ER. Lane flattened her dress across her legs, trying to calm her nerves.

"That's good advice." Helen gave her a sideways glance. "I'll try to do that next time."

Helen's phone in the console buzzed, and it rang through the speakers. She quickly hit the toggle button on her steering wheel, sending the call to voice mail. "My brother. I'll call him back later."

"You have a brother?" Lane hadn't remembered that.

Helen nodded. "One brother, one sister. You?"

"Two brothers and three sisters." Whom she adored most of the time.

"Five siblings." Helen's eyes remained on the road. "That's quite a family to get along with. I have trouble with only the two."

"We fought a fair amount as kids, but as we've grown older, we've become closer." Moving out of the house had helped that along.

"Your dad's plumbing business must do pretty well." Helen stopped at a red light and glanced her way.

"He's branched out into commercial HVAC as well. It's a good living." She could never remember a time where she'd felt that she had to do without.

"That's great." The light turned green, and Helen looked back toward the road and hit the gas again.

The rest of the drive was short, and the conversation remained light. It seemed that neither one of them was ready yet to discuss what their kisses meant until other people were around them. They were apparently both playing it safe.

The restaurant was busy, as usual on a Saturday night, at least from what Lane could tell. When she dined there, she was usually earlier or later than the dinner crowd.

"Good evening." The man looked at the list on the counter. "I don't see an order for you."

"We're eating in tonight," Helen said, and glanced at Lane. "I'm sorry. I forgot to make a reservation."

"No problem at all." He plucked a couple of menus from the stack and led them to a table for two at the edge of the dining room. "Will this be okay?"

"It's perfect. Thanks." Helen smiled.

Lane noted the small red glow from the candle holder. The location was more romantic than she'd intended for the evening—the conversation they needed to have—but she couldn't very well ask to be moved, or Helen would wonder why.

Helen waited for Lane to sit and then settled into the chair across from her.

Lane picked up the menu and set it down again. "I don't really have to look at the menu. I always order the same thing."

Helen tilted her head. "Really? Me too."

Lane shook her head. "I have to limit myself on how often I come here, or I'll blow all my dining-out funds at the beginning of each month." She'd eat here every night if she had the money and opportunity.

Helen placed her menu on top of Lane's. Seemed neither of them needed to make a choice. "In addition to the ravioli, why don't we branch out and order the pasta chips?"

It was sweet that Helen had remembered her favorite dish. "Sounds good to me. I'm starving, but my eyes are always bigger than my stomach. So maybe we shouldn't."

"Then let's forgo them tonight to save room for dessert."

"Sounds like a plan." Lane glanced around for the waitress, who seemed to notice and came their way quickly, bringing a basket of bread and a dish of butter.

"Wine for you ladies tonight?"

"Water for me, please." Lane wanted to keep her mind focused for this conversation.

"The same for me." Helen glanced up at the waitress. "We're ready to order."

"Great." The waitress smiled. "What can I get you?"

"We'll both have the ravioli, and I'd like a green salad with house dressing." Helen ordered for them both.

"Soup or salad for you?" the waitress asked Lane.

"I think I'll have the minestrone tonight." She tore off a piece of bread and buttered it, biding her time while the waitress wrote down the order and walked away. "So…what's going on here…I mean, between us?"

"We're having a nice dinner together." Helen reached for a piece of bread. "Can't we do that?"

"You know what I'm talking about. We've kissed twice, and I'm not sure what's happening." Lane felt the ridge of the tablecloth crease and ran her finger slowly down it.

"You tell me." Helen tilted her head slightly. "You've initiated it both times."

Lane rolled her lips in and nodded. "I guess I did. But I don't know how you feel about it." She smoothed the tablecloth and then began fidgeting with her silverware, changing the position of the small and large forks.

"I didn't hate it, if that's what you're looking for." Helen relaxed into her chair. "I have to admit the kisses were unexpected but were actually quite nice."

"Really?" A spark of relief laced with joy fluttered through her.

Helen leaned forward, reached across the table, and took Lane's hand, moving it away from the silverware she'd suddenly become obsessed with. "I haven't been able to stop thinking about them—about you."

Lane pulled her lips into a cockeyed smile. "That makes two of us."

"So where do we go from here?" Helen raised her eyebrows.

The waitress appeared with their soup and salad. Such bad timing. Lane retracted her hand and glanced across the table at Helen. "We can share if you'd like." She wasn't exactly sure why she'd offered. She never did with Belinda.

"I'd like that." Helen took her napkin from the table and laid it across her lap before she picked up her fork and dug into the salad. "This is delicious, as usual."

"They have the best homemade dressing." A vinaigrette stored in wine bottles, which they sold as well. "I have a half-full bottle in the refrigerator at home." Lane spooned a taste of minestrone into her mouth.

"As do I." Helen grinned.

Lane glanced up as she spooned another bite into her mouth. The commonalities between them were getting ridiculous.

"When is your next event?"

"Tomorrow at the Deep Ellum Art Gallery."

"Huh. I don't have that one." Helen scrunched her forehead. "I guess you'll be working with another planner."

Lane shook her head as she swallowed. "They don't have one. It's a small wedding that they coordinated themselves."

"Does everything look good with the planning?"

Lane nodded. "They did an excellent job. I'm impressed by how organized they are. They had a checklist and all."

"Great." Helen smiled. "But don't let that news get around, or I'll be out of a job."

Lane laughed. She really did enjoy Helen's company, even though they were skirting the main discussion. They continued with their soup and salad in silence, eating the appropriate amount of each before switching dishes. It was like they'd been dining together for years.

Soon after that, their main course arrived. Lane cut one of the meat dumplings in half and slid it into her mouth. She let out a sigh, enjoying the first bite of her ravioli as though she'd never had it before.

Helen smiled. "My thoughts exactly."

"Sorry." Lane covered her mouth. "But how do they make this so good *every time?*"

"The same chef has been here for a long while. I guess he has his pinches and dashes down to a science." Helen ate a bite of ravioli.

"Do you think he's mastered strokes as well?" Lane couldn't believe that came out of her mouth. She was beginning to get comfortable with Helen.

Helen let out an unrestrained laugh and almost choked on her food, grabbing her napkin quickly before taking a drink of water. "I guess we'll have to order dessert and find out."

A tingle slowly began in Lane's belly at the spontaneous, unfiltered sound, and she wanted to make Helen laugh a thousand times more. "Did you hear about the woman who choked on her ravioli? She pasta way...get it? *Passed away?*"

Helen shook her head and chuckled again. "You're hysterical."

Lane had never felt she was good at flirting, but Helen was playing along even if she wasn't, which made her feel confident and good about herself. She ate a few more bites, then set down her fork. "That night when Iris and I ran into you here." She hesitated. "Were you eating alone, or were you meeting someone?" She shouldn't ask, it was really none of her business, but she wanted to know.

Helen wiped her mouth with her napkin. "I was eating alone."

A wave of sadness hit Lane at the thought of Helen having to do that, and she set down her fork. "I could never be that brave."

"Why not?" Helen reached for her water.

"I don't know. Maybe I'd be worried about what other people would think." She'd definitely be self-conscious.

"No need to worry about that." Helen glanced around the restaurant. "Other customers are way too focused on their own food, and the people they're with, to pay attention to you."

"It still feels awkward." Lane could see Helen was right.

"They might notice you because you're beautiful, and they might wonder who's lucky enough to be in your company." Helen motioned toward herself. "But at the risk of offending you, I'm going to repeat myself. Most people don't even notice someone dining alone."

"Look at you." Lane laughed. "Complimenting and offending all in the same breath. Not many people can pull that off in such a polite and positive way."

"What can I say? It's a gift." Helen's grin was ridiculous. "You want to get dessert here? Or I know a quaint coffee bar that serves a wonderful chocolate mousse."

"I'm in for that. It'll give my stomach time to free up a tiny space." And at least another hour with Helen, which was an unusually pleasant thought.

They finished their meal while exchanging small bits of conversation about the weather and other menial subjects before Helen signaled the waitress for the check. When she dropped it off, Lane reached for her wallet.

"I asked you." Helen waved her off. "My treat." Helen inserted some cash and closed the leather holder. "I'm going to run to the ladies' room. Do you want to wait here, or should I meet you at the front?" Helen was being so attentive.

"I'll meet you by the hostess station." That would be the best move. Waiting alone at the table for Helen to come back would be awkward.

It had been a wonderful night so far. Even though this had become more of a date than Lane had intended, she was looking forward to the finish. Helen was turning out to be so much more than she'd expected. And so very, very different.

Lane felt a hand on her shoulder and swung around, expecting to find Helen, but to her surprise she saw Belinda standing before her, grinning. These coincidental run-ins were becoming suspicious. She had a lot of nerve coming to Lane's favorite restaurant after the way she'd left her.

"Lane. How are you?" Belinda's voice was soft and sweet, just the way she'd spoken when she'd seen her last week. "I've been meaning to get back in touch with you."

"Oh." Lane had no idea why Belinda would even think that was okay.

"Yeah." Belinda rolled her lips in. "I'm really sorry about everything."

Lane raised her eyebrows. "You mean the way you left me three days before our wedding?" She couldn't keep the anger from seeping into her words.

"I got nervous and made a horrible mistake. Over the past six months, I've thought a lot about who and what I want in my life."

"Good for you." So had Lane, and it wasn't Belinda.

"Can you ever forgive me, find a place for me in your heart again? I know this is a ridiculous ask, but I can't see my life without you," Belinda pleaded. "Even if you decide it's only friendship."

Wait. Was Belinda asking Lane for another chance—with her? Lane's heart pounded as the back of her neck tingled. "You left three days before our wedding. And took our honeymoon with another woman."

"I was confused." Belinda's voice cracked.

"You were confused? Imagine how I felt." She moved into Belinda's space. "I'm not anymore. I'm seeing someone who makes me very happy."

"Who?" Belinda's eyebrows rocketed up. Her demeanor changed quickly when Helen approached. "Helen," she said stiffly.

"Belinda." Helen responded just as stiffly before she touched Lane's shoulder and smiled. "I'll get the car."

"I'll be right out." Lane let her gaze roam Helen's backside as she walked away. When she glanced back to Belinda, she realized she'd just given herself away.

"That's who you're dating? Well, isn't that just peachy?" Belinda let out a hearty laugh. "It all makes sense now."

"What makes sense?"

"I can't believe you're dating the wedding planner who sent me running from getting married—to you." Belinda's mouth dropped open.

"What?"

"Oh. She hasn't told you?" Belinda lifted an eyebrow. "Helen is the one who had me second-guessing our marriage."

"I doubt that." Could it be true? Just today Lane had seen Helen calm a bride's nerves. Why would she do the opposite to Belinda?

"No. Really." Belinda pointed to the door Helen had gone through. "She's the one who prompted my doubts. I ran into her the week before, and she questioned me about us—had me wondering if I could truly make you happy." Belinda took Lane's hands and squeezed. "I made a mistake—a huge mistake. Just give me another chance. I'll make it up to you. I promise."

Lane pulled her hands from Belinda's grasp. "I have to go." She rushed to the door, then stopped. She couldn't ride home with Helen. She was too angry, and she needed to think. If she got into that car right now, they would have an explosive argument, and she wouldn't give Belinda that satisfaction. She took a quick right and circled the perimeter of the restaurant until she found the entrance to the kitchen. Dishes crashed as she rushed past a waiter to the back door and outside. Then she ran to the closest hotel and grabbed a cab home.

CHAPTER TWENTY

Helen had been waiting in the car for close to fifteen minutes, with still no sign of Lane. Clearly it had been a mistake to leave her alone with her ex. She killed the engine, got out of the car, and went back inside the restaurant. No sight of Lane. She scanned the restaurant—not there. Where could she be? She rushed to the restroom and ran headfirst into Belinda. "Where's Lane?"

"Last I saw her, she was running through the restaurant and into the kitchen."

"Shit." Helen's stomach lurched to her throat.

"Karma's a bitch." Belinda glared at her.

"What the hell did you tell her?" The back of Helen's neck heated. Anything Belinda told Lane would have been out of context. Belinda was a master at spinning tales.

"Enough to know that you're a snake."

"As memory serves me, you're the snake. I just moved Lane out of your striking distance." Helen rushed to the door. She refused to debate the semantics of what had happened between Belinda and Lane. Belinda had made the choice. Helen had only presented her with the details of what she'd discovered and how she would communicate it to Lane.

She drove directly to Lane's house, rushed up the walk, and banged on the door. The door pulled open, and she was met by an angry Iris.

"She doesn't want to talk to you." Iris frowned. "Which is sad because I was rooting for you."

She hadn't expected that from Iris. She hadn't expected any of this. "Please, just let me in so I can explain."

"Give me a reason—something I can believe about why you did what you did." Iris blocked the doorway, gripping the molding with her fingers.

"You know Belinda. There's no way she was faithful to Lane." Helen remembered the disappointment when she'd discovered her infidelity. She hadn't wanted to see Lane get hurt.

Iris bit her bottom lip. "You know that for sure?"

"I caught her." Helen enunciated each word slowly.

The door opened wider, and Iris stepped aside, then pointed down the hallway. "Last door on the left. No pun intended."

Helen could very well be walking into her own kind of horror story—a life without Lane. She knocked on the door. "Lane. It's me, Helen."

"I know who it is." Lane's voice came through loud and clear. "I don't want to talk to you."

"Please let me explain." Helen needed a chance to make this right.

The door flew open. "You let my fiancée bolt." Lane narrowed her eyes. "No. You didn't just let her. You told her to leave me."

"I was just—"

"Just what?" Lane was angrier than Helen had ever seen her. "Do you make it a habit of advising brides on marriage—to leave their fiancées?"

"She didn't love you." Helen shrunk a little. "I didn't want you to get hurt." She'd thought it was the right thing to do at the time. Maybe she was wrong.

"I got hurt all right—hurt and embarrassed. Do you know what it feels like to have to tell all your guests not to come to one of the biggest events in your life? A moment you've been planning for months?"

"No. I don't, but would you have rather married her and then been divorced a few months later?" Helen's voice wavered, bile pushing to her throat. That fact was harsh but would've been true.

"Wow." Lane's mouth dropped open, and she blew out a breath. "You seem to have a whole lot of knowledge into what my future would've been like." She grasped the knob and started to close the door.

Helen wedged herself in the gap. "I caught her with someone else." The words came out quietly. She hadn't wanted to tell Lane, but she probably should have. At the time, she wasn't sure Lane would believe her—wasn't sure she would now.

Lane's gaze snapped to Helen's. "You what?" Apparently, Belinda hadn't disclosed that tidbit when she'd told Lane about Helen's participation in her leaving.

"I saw her at a restaurant with someone else in a very romantic situation." Helen bit her bottom lip. She didn't want to go into detail, but it was obvious they were involved.

Lane narrowed her eyes. "And you just thought it was your duty to take that information and blackmail her with it?"

"No." Helen shook her head. This wasn't going well at all. "I told her what I saw, and she admitted that she was unsure about the whole commitment of marriage."

"Why in the world would you do that without talking to me?" Lane leaned against the door. She looked like a balloon with a slow leak, deflating bit by bit with each second.

"Because you were so beautiful, naive, and in love." Helen glanced away. "I couldn't bear to hurt you." She moved closer and brushed a stray strand of hair from Lane's cheek. "You were going to be the perfect wife, and I just couldn't stand the thought of her breaking your heart someday."

"But you thought it was okay to crush it right before my wedding?" Lane backed up. "How could you even think I would forgive that?"

"I didn't know if you would. I wasn't concerned with that at the time, but now your forgiveness means everything to me." That was something Helen could only hope for. "I broke my number-one rule...I fell in love with the bride." She probably should've kept that to herself, but losing Lane would crush *her*.

"What? Until recently, whenever we've worked the same events, you've hardly been nice to me."

"I know. My defense mechanism." Helen took in a deep breath. "I tried to keep my distance and was doing fine until Darcy's wedding planning. Then I couldn't get away from you."

Lane closed her eyes briefly. "You need to go."

Helen backed out of the doorway. "Can I call you tomorrow or the next day?" She would give Lane as much time as she needed.

"I don't know. I need to think." Lane rolled her lips in and closed the door.

Helen turned to find Iris leaning against the wall at the end of the hall. "I'm sure you hate me too."

"No. I actually have a bit of admiration for you that I didn't before." Iris pushed off the wall. "That took a lot of guts to admit, even though you were forced into it."

"I should've told her about Belinda, but she was so vulnerable. I didn't want to make the situation any worse than it already was." She blew out a breath. "I didn't know any other way to protect her."

"We have that in common. I don't want to see Lane get hurt either—even by you." Iris led Helen to the door. "I'll talk to her because neither of us likes Belinda, and we both love Lane."

Helen's hands were shaking when she reached her car. She sat still for a moment, gripping the steering wheel. She'd known this would come back to bite her in the ass, but that hadn't been her greatest worry at the time. Now she might have lost Lane's trust, and that hurt more than she could've ever imagined.

❖

Another knock on the door. "I don't want to talk to you." Seemed that Helen wasn't giving up.

"She's gone. It's just me." Iris's voice came through the door.

Lane scooted off the bed, got up, and unlocked the door for Iris to enter. "I guess you caught all that?" She'd heard the words but hadn't let them sink in.

Iris pushed through the door. "That was a helluva declaration of love." Her mouth dropped open.

"This whole situation is unbelievable." Lane put her hand to her forehead and paced the bedroom. "Why couldn't she have just been truthful with me at the time?"

Iris shrugged. "Would you have listened to her—believed her if she'd told you?"

"Probably not. I was so wrapped up in getting married that I'd lost all sight of our actual relationship." Lane rolled her eyes. "Which had turned to shit for both of us, apparently. I was just too oblivious to recognize it."

"You would've been married to a fucking cheater." Iris clenched her teeth. "I never really liked her."

"Belinda asked me to take her back." Lane bit her lip. She hadn't expected that, nor had she expected her own flat-out rejection of the idea. As little as a month ago, she'd have been willing to try again with Belinda. She wasn't at all sure what she wanted now. *Damn you, Helen!*

"What the fuck?" Iris's brows rose quickly. "You're seriously not going to make that mistake again, are you?"

"No." Lane shook her head and closed her eyes. "I feel nothing but anger toward her." That wasn't a lie. The hurt was gone now. Was that because of what was happening with Helen?

"So, what are you going to do about Helen?" Iris had the magic question.

"Right now, I honestly don't know." In some twisted way, Helen had her best interests at heart, didn't she?

"For what it's worth, I think you should accept her apology. It seems like she was just looking out for you."

"While causing me a lot of heartache along the way." Plus, Helen seemed to be benefitting from the breakup now. Not that Lane regarded herself as a benefit of anything.

"You can't really blame Helen for the breakup. You were headed in that direction eventually anyway." Iris sat on the bed next to her. "Belinda's the one who broke your heart. If she was really committed to you, she wouldn't have bolted."

"I know." Everything Iris said was true. How could she blame Helen for not seeing what was right before her eyes—for her own stupidity.

"And you're the one who kissed her…" Iris grinned. "*Twice.*"

"Right." Lane *had* been the one to initiate both wonderful kisses. Why had she done that? Was she just lonely—needed to get laid— wanted to finally have her way with the ice queen? No. None of that applied. It was more than that. Helen was different than she'd been before—than when Lane had been engaged—than even two weeks ago.

"I haven't seen you this happy in a long time. Not since you left the honeymoon phase with Belinda." Iris stood and walked to the door. "Think long and hard before you let Helen go."

Would she have let Helen get that close if she'd known about her participation in the collapse of her relationship with Belinda? *"I broke my number-one rule…I fell in love with the bride."* Helen's words echoed in her head.

Lane had a lot of thinking to do. Helen had probably stopped her from making the worst decision of her life, but the way she'd gone about it had been so wrong. Nevertheless, each night when she crawled into her bed all alone, it was Helen that came into her thoughts now. What would it be like to make love to Helen—to let Helen make love to her? She wasn't ready to let those thoughts go.

Chapter Twenty-One

Helen pulled up in front of Will's house. She didn't want to be alone today. That would put her in a place to second-guess every decision she'd made regarding Lane again. She'd done enough of that during her night of fitful sleep. At the time, she really hadn't thought calling Belinda out had been the wrong thing to do. Having the bride bolt had been the furthest thing from her mind. Helen had honestly thought Belinda would take a step back and realize what she had with Lane—what she was going to fuck up if she continued seeing other women. Boy, had she been wrong about it all.

She strolled up the pathway to the door, rang the bell, and waited for someone to answer.

The door pulled open, and Will stood before her. "Where were you last night? I thought you were coming over for movie night. I called you at least a dozen times." He wasn't angry. Will rarely got mad at her.

"I saw that. Sorry." She'd forgotten to let him know she wasn't coming. "Didn't you get my text?"

"I did, but it was late and vague." He flattened his lips.

"Yeah. I had dinner with someone and didn't want to be rude, so I typed it in when I went to get the car." Before Helen entered, she glanced out the window at the storm clouds, which fit her mood perfectly. "What is up with this weather?"

"Went to get the car?" Will's eyebrows rose. "You had a date?"

"Yeah, but it didn't turn out quite the way I expected." The whole night had imploded on her. She headed into the living room, which was furnished with several nicely worn matching tan tweed chairs, a contrasting green velvet couch, and a cherrywood coffee table with end tables to match. A huge TV was mounted above the fireplace. Not the place Helen would've placed it, but it was perfect for movie nights, when Will set up a blanket pallet on the floor for the kids so they could watch.

Will followed close behind. "Are you going to see her again?"

"I'm not sure she likes me any longer." In fact, Helen figured Lane hated her right about now. She flopped into the club chair she always chose when they watched movies. It was her favorite.

"Any longer?"

"Yeah. Last night was a disaster." She rubbed her forehead as she contemplated how much to reveal. "I haven't been truthful with her about some things."

"Well, then why don't you just lay it all out and show her who you really are?" Will took his usual spot on the adjacent couch.

"Working on that." She gave him a sideways smile. "I kissed her in the coat closet of the country club the other day." Half-truth. Although she hadn't been the aggressor, she'd enjoyed the kiss fully once their lips touched.

"That's a start." Will was always unbelievably supportive.

"I'm afraid I might have finished it, though." Still annoyed at herself, Helen shook her head.

Will's eyebrows furrowed. "You didn't sleep with her and leave before she got up this morning, did you?"

"No." Helen shook her head. "I didn't get a chance. She found out that I was the catalyst for her ex-fiancée bolting."

"Okay. Now I need to hear a whole lot more of this story." Will leaned forward, laid his forearms across his legs, and clasped his hands together.

Helen went through the details with her brother, her stomach sinking with each word as she saw his expression change from interest to humor, and then to concern.

"Wow." Will relaxed into the couch and balanced an ankle on his knee. "That's quite a series of events."

"Maybe I should've just kept my mouth shut and let them get married." She could have never done that.

"You didn't do it because you wanted to be with Lane, right?" Will had assumed the same thing as Lane.

"No. I don't think so, but I was attracted to her." Helen ran through the events in her head. "Maybe, subconsciously, that's what I wanted all along."

"How long ago was it?"

"A little over six months." She tilted her head from side to side. "Give or take a week."

"Nah." Will crinkled his lips as he shook his head. "If you'd wanted it all along, you would've pursued her by now."

"I tried my best to stay away—ignore her to the point of rudeness." Helen had been so awful to Lane.

"So, what happened? Why'd you give in?" Will smiled as though he could see all the reasons why already.

"I've been working with her on her best friend's wedding." She shook her head as she drew in a deep breath. "Since it was a request from Mom, I couldn't get out of planning this one."

"That's a good sign. Mom buying in to your career." He shrugged.

"It's not about me. She and the bride's mother go way back."

"Gotcha. Is Lane the maid of honor?"

"No. The matron of honor is a disaster, so Lane's been helping me with the arrangements." A total shit show was more like it. "Spending time with her has been really nice, and I let my guard down."

"She enjoyed it as well?" His forehead crinkled.

"I think so." She had to come clean. "I didn't actually initiate the kiss in the coat closet. She did. A week later she kissed me again."

"She'll be back." Will grinned. "This will turn out better than you think." He reached for the remote. "You want to watch the movie from last night? It was pretty good."

"I'll make some popcorn." She got up, went into the kitchen, took a bag from the cupboard, removed the plastic wrapper, smashed it around with her fingers, and tossed it inside the microwave. She pressed the popcorn button and went in search of a couple of Cokes—the only drink that accompanied it well.

She split the popcorn into two bowls, then trapped the sodas between one of her arms and her side and carried everything into the living room. She doubted it, but hopefully the movie would get her mind off Lane.

The popcorn and sodas were gone, and they were about a third of the way into the movie when the kids came running inside, dripping wet. "It's raining."

Will paused the movie and switched to one of the main stations. The radar map on the screen was covered with red and yellow, indicating severe weather, and a timeline to the left of it denoted when the storm would arrive in different areas. She pulled up Lane's contact information and hit the call button. It went straight to voice mail. *Damn it.* She didn't have Iris's number. Helen tried to remember what was on Lane's schedule for today. She'd mentioned she had a wedding, but where was it located? Ah. The Deep Ellum Art Company.

She popped up off the couch, rushed to the TV, and found the time the storm would hit that area. "I need to go."

"You can't go out in this," Will said, staring up at her.

"Lane has a wedding." Helen pointed to the storm path outlined on the screen. "Right there in Deep Ellum."

"Oh, shit." Will stood. "I'll drive you."

"No. I'm fine. You need to stay with the kids." She headed toward the door, then turned back. "Where's Ash?"

"At her mom's. She'll be okay."

"Good." She rushed to the door. She had to find Lane and make sure she was safe.

"Keep me updated," Will shouted.

She didn't respond—couldn't think of anything besides getting to Lane right now.

❖

Helen drove through the area slowly, relieved that the roads weren't blocked off. Thankfully, the storm surge had created downed tree branches but no major structural damage. She came upon the art gallery where Lane had told her the wedding was taking place. The car lurched as she threw it into park. Quickly, she double-parked in front, ran to the entrance, and threw open the door.

When Helen entered and saw Lane standing with the bride touching up her makeup, her heart pounded in her ears, and she became dizzy. Everything tilted a little bit. She'd never been hit by a stronger wave of emotion. Lane was okay. All the crazy scenarios she'd thought up on the way over hadn't happened.

"Thank God you're all right." Helen rushed to Lane and threw her arms around her. "I saw the news and..." Helen squeezed Lane before she released her.

"I understand your concern, but I'm fine. We're all fine. They rounded everyone up and took us downstairs." Lane glanced over her shoulder at the bride. "The bride and groom didn't want to wait for the storm to pass, so they performed the ceremony in the basement."

"Young love can be so very sweet." Helen stared into the pools of green staring back at her, searching for some indication of forgiveness in them. There was none. "I should go."

"Absolutely not." A strange voice pulled Helen from the moment—the bride. "You're not going anywhere. I've never seen such a heartfelt show of love." She took Helen's arm and guided her to an empty seat, then motioned for her to sit. "Please join us in celebrating our day." She turned back to Lane. "You are so fortunate to have someone who cares about you so much." The bride seemed enchanted by Helen's concern for Lane.

"Seems that way, doesn't it?" Lane waited for the bride to move out of earshot. "But you'd never have known that last night." *Ouch.* Apparently, she was still upset with her.

"I'll just go." Helen stood.

"No. Stay." Lane put her hand on Helen's shoulder. Heat seared through her at the contact, but Lane's expression didn't give away her feelings. "We're going to have to talk sooner or later."

People still seemed to be milling about, not sure what to do. The groom went to the stage and grabbed the microphone from the holder. "Listen up, people. The storm's over and we're hitched. The only thunder coming our way now is happening on the dance floor. Let's rock this place." The music started, and everyone seemed to relax.

The bride wiggled her fingers at Lane and Helen. "You two should dance."

Lane shook her head. "I'm not a very good dancer."

Helen knew that wasn't true. Lane just didn't want to dance with her.

"It's not about being perfect. It's about enjoying the dance." The bride put a hand on each of their shoulders and pushed them together. "Make sure your wife takes care of you just as well as you take care of her."

Helen needed to clear up this misunderstanding. "Oh, she's—"

"Not going to have to worry about that," Lane said, glancing at Helen. "I'll make sure she's taken care of." She let Helen lead her to the rhythm in a small circle at the edge of the dance floor.

The knot in Helen's stomach tightened again. "I feel like you mean that literally, and not in a good way."

Lane rolled her lips together. "What you did was wrong. You should've come to me about Belinda."

"I—"

Their motion stopped, and Lane put her fingers over Helen's mouth. "I know it's hard for you, but don't talk. Just listen, okay?"

Helen nodded, Lane returned her hand to Helen's shoulder, and they continued to dance.

"*If*, and that's a big if, whatever this is between us progresses, you have to be straight with me about everything." Lane stared into Helen's eyes. "No secrets—no lies. Understood?"

"Understood." Relief rushed through Helen, and the knot in her stomach loosened. Another chance was all she wanted. She'd thought Lane might be done with her, but she didn't seem to be...yet. She would wait to see if the other shoe dropped after they were away from this setting. For now, she would remain hopeful. She focused on Lane's sparkling emerald eyes, and everyone else disappeared as they danced. They were in a room full of people, but she felt like they were entirely alone.

CHAPTER TWENTY-TWO

L ane pulled up in front of Iris's house and killed the engine. Helen and Lane had parted ways soon after their dance. Helen had left fairly quickly, and Lane hadn't stopped her. Even though she'd felt the depth of Helen's concern deep in her heart today, Lane still wasn't quite sure if she wanted to move forward with whatever was happening between them. It was clear now that Helen was only trying to protect her, but Lane didn't need, or want, protection from anyone, did she?

She pressed her head to the steering wheel. She was so confused. Her only options at this point were to move forward or to cut off all contact with Helen. Neither one seemed appropriate or possible right now. She was still angry about the situation but had persistent feelings for Helen. Burying those feelings would be hard, considering the two of them worked in the same circles and would still see each other frequently.

Lane went into the house and dropped her bag by the end of the couch. Iris was watching TV with her feet propped on the coffee table. "What are you doing here? I thought you were having brunch and hanging out with Harvey's family all day."

"Change of plans. Harvey's dad wanted to go golfing, and the rain stopped, so I didn't object." Iris stretched and reached for the bottle of water on the coffee table. "I had one too many mimosas anyway. So, I came home and took a nap."

"The perils of Sunday brunch." Lane dropped onto the couch next to her. "Helen showed up this morning."

"At the wedding?" Iris straightened in her seat. "Why?"

"She said she was concerned about me in the storm." Lane blew out a breath. "And I kinda believe she was." She remembered the tightness of the Helen's hug, the emotion in her voice when Helen had found her, the warmth that filled Lane while she was in Helen's arms.

"Damn it." Iris slapped her hand to the couch. "I knew I should've canceled brunch with Harvey and gone with you."

"Helen had help from the bride. She thought it was sweet that Helen was worried enough about me to show up." Something stirred inside her.

"You have to admit, it was kind of sweet." Iris scrunched her nose.

"Yeah. It was." Lane was all mixed up now. "You know that feeling you told me about? The one in your stomach—the tingle—the magnificent jolt it sends throughout you?"

Iris nodded but didn't speak.

"Now, when I think of Helen, I have that all the time. I want to be on top of her, under her, between her legs." She rubbed her forehead as she took in Iris's stunned look. "I'm sorry. That was too much information."

Iris blurted out a laugh. "I've been waiting so long for this day, when you realized that sex isn't just a chore that you suffer through for your partner—when you actually want it."

"Jesus. I don't just want it. I crave it—I crave her." Lane shot up and paced the living room. Each time she'd kissed Helen, she'd wanted to press her against the wall, slip her hand into her pants, indulge in the slickness awaiting her. She longed to push Helen out of her comfort zone—push herself into immeasurable bliss. It didn't matter where they were or who they were with. The urge was overwhelming.

Iris grinned and slapped her hands together. "I never expected the person to make that happen would be Helen, but *damn*, this makes me happy."

"I shouldn't feel this way after what she did." But she did. God help her. She did.

"Did you talk to her about that this morning?" Iris's tone was soft and nonjudgmental.

Lane nodded. "I told her we couldn't have any more secrets or lies."

"And?" Iris waited.

"She said she understood, and we wouldn't." Lane hoped Helen was being honest. She seemed to be.

"Well, there you go. All is right in your world again." Iris sighed.

"Not completely. I'm still angry at her." Lane didn't like the fact that Helen had taken her future into her hands without talking to her.

"Oh. Well. That'll fade once that passion takes over." Iris grinned. "I'm so excited for you."

"That makes one of us." Lane flopped back onto the couch. "Maybe I should invite her over to my parents' house for Sunday dinner. Let them grill her."

"That'd be an experience." Iris chuckled. "Can I come?"

"Absolutely not. I don't need to worry about you cheering her on all night." It would already be a madhouse if all her brothers and sisters showed up.

Iris let out a laugh. "You know me too well. What if I promise to keep my mouth shut and just watch?"

"I don't need that either." Lane frowned. "Nothing like making someone feel welcome by having your best friend stare at her all night."

Iris waved her hand in the air. "And I'd never be able to do it."

"It's too late for that anyway."

"You know she'd come." Iris pulled her lips into a lopsided grin. "At this point, she'd be afraid to say no." Iris adjusted to face her. "She'd think it's a test. I know I would."

"She probably would. I don't think I'm ready to allow her that far into my life just yet."

"I can't wait to see this play out." Iris grabbed Lane's forearm. "What am I going to do for entertainment when you find a place of your own?"

"You're going to marry Harvey." Then Lane would be all alone again.

"Oh, right." Iris seemed indecisive. "Maybe you should stay here. Keep the place for yourself. At least I'd have a familiar place to visit."

"What's going on?" Lane hadn't seen Iris so unexcited about her engagement to Harvey.

Iris let her head drop back onto the cushion. "He's just been really busy with work lately, trying to make partner at the law firm. A lot of late nights. And then golf today with his dad. We haven't had much time alone together."

Lane shifted to face Iris. "Why didn't you tell him not to go?"

Iris tilted her head and looked at Lane sideways. "I don't tell Harvey what to do."

"You haven't changed your mind, have you?" Lane hoped that wasn't the case. Iris and Harvey fit perfectly together as a couple.

Iris shook her head. "No. I just don't want our life to be like this permanently." She sat up and took another swig of water.

"I'm sure it won't be." She rubbed Iris's back. "He's just trying to get to the spot in his career where he can take a breath and enjoy life… with you."

"Maybe." Iris had never sounded this down about her relationship with Harvey before.

Lane wondered if something else was going on that she wasn't telling her. She felt a bit selfish. Here she was asking Iris for advice, and it seemed Iris needed some advice of her own.

CHAPTER TWENTY-THREE

A s Helen drove through the gates and up the driveway, she glanced at Lane to see her reaction to the estate. She could usually get an idea of what a woman was thinking when they first approached the property. The mouth drop was usually the first indication of surprise. Lane hadn't blinked an eye at the ostentatious iron gates as they opened. Hadn't glanced at any of the ornate statues as they passed. Hadn't even opened her mouth as they neared the house. All Helen's previous girlfriends had expectations of high society and money. Lane didn't seem to want any of that. Had she just referred to Lane as her girlfriend? She was getting way ahead of herself. She should just be thankful that when she'd called Lane earlier in the week, she'd accepted her invitation to swim today.

Helen parked in the circle drive and killed the engine. "My brother and his kids might come over later. Hopefully they've made other plans for the day. If not, we can have a quick swim and get out of here once they show up." She pushed open the door.

"We don't have to leave. I love kids. I mean, unless you want to." Lane got out of the car and retrieved her bag from the back seat.

That was news Helen didn't have. Did Lane want kids of her own? Did loving them mean she wanted them?

They headed into the house, sandals clicking on the tile as they echoed within the massive foyer. Helen watched Lane walk in front of her, her flower-patterned sundress flowing as she moved her gorgeous legs.

Lane stopped momentarily, taking in the room. "Your parents have a beautiful home."

"I agree." It *was* beautiful but could be uncomfortable at times. "Did you grow up here?"

"I did." Helen scanned the room to spot any signs of her parents being home. They were supposed to be out of town until Monday. "However, I spent a bit of time away at school." She glanced over her shoulder. "There are a couple of rooms just down the hall where we can change." Helen led Lane toward the guest room just on this side of what used to be her room. Her brother's and sister's rooms were on the other side of the house.

"When you're done changing, go back down the hall and through the living room. To your left will be a door that leads to the backyard." Helen backed out of the room.

"Thank you." Lane smiled.

Helen pulled the door closed and then raced into her own room to put on her swimsuit. She didn't want Lane to be uncomfortable and needed to be changed and outside before Lane was. She stripped her clothes off quickly, opened the dresser drawer, and pushed the pile of her sister Gwen's bikinis aside to find her blue board shorts and the red athletic swim bra she kept at the house. She pulled on the shorts and wiggled into the top before she looked at herself in the mirror and sucked in her stomach. She liked the way the top held her breasts securely, but recent years of too much work and not enough exercise had given her a little tummy pooch that she'd neglected. She turned to the drawer and rummaged through it. All her shorts were the same, just different colors, so this was it. Lane would get the true Helen experience. She stepped out into the hallway to find Lane's door still closed, so she continued to the backyard to the towel closet in the cabana and plucked a couple from the top.

Helen had just settled into a lounge chair when Lane came out of the door dressed in a black-and-white cover-up.

"If you want, we can sit in the sun to warm up a bit before we get in." Considering the cover-up, Helen thought Lane might be nervous about being almost naked in front of her.

"I think I'll dive right in, if it's all right with you." Lane pointed to the pool. "That water looks delightful." She pulled off her cover-up and dropped it onto the chair next to Helen.

Just the sight of her sent a glorious surge of heat to Helen's midsection. It was amazing how good a plain purple one-piece suit could look on a woman. It seemed Lane was perfectly comfortable in her own skin. She was getting used to that—looked forward to it, in fact. Lane was a beautiful woman, and Lane in a bathing suit was just icing on the cake.

"Okay then." Helen stood, sucked in her stomach, and cursed herself for not being more diligent at her exercise regimen. She couldn't help noticing Lane's eyes grazing across her. Seemed the attraction might be mutual. She waved Lane ahead of her. "After you."

Lane padded across the concrete and around the pool to the diving board, while Helen waded into the shallow end of the water. Helen watched as Lane walked to the end of the board and bounced like a professional diver before she launched from the board with a perfect dive into the pool. Lane swam underwater and then emerged near her in the semi-shallow area. Everything changed into slow motion like a scene from an eighties movie. The movement of her hair slinging back throwing water into a perfect circle above her head as she rose—and the breasts usually hidden under loose dresses—were the center of the show.

The cool water covered Helen's head as she sank into it. She closed her eyes to clear the vision from her mind, but that only made it worse. She pushed off the bottom and swam to the end of the pool, did a flip turn, swam back to the shallow end, then came up for air.

"Wow. That was fast. You're quite the swimmer." Lane's voice broke through the water in Helen's ears.

"Was on a team when I was younger." She shook her head, and the water flew from her short hair.

Lane's mouth dropped open as she stared. Then she blinked and swam to the diving board. She grabbed the ends with her hands and suspended herself there. "I used to dive."

"Oh, yeah?" Helen swam closer, treaded water in the deep end. "What club?"

"No club. Public pool."

Helen chided herself. What an elitist thing to say. Not everyone was born into privilege. She knew that, yet she asked one simple question that told Lane she regarded herself as upper class. "Sorry. I didn't mean to sound pretentious." She swam closer, clasped the edge of the pool under the diving board.

"Don't even worry about it. My parents eventually got a pool. Not one near this size." Lane adjusted her grip, turning to face Helen before she glanced around the yard. "We both know we come from different backgrounds." She pulled herself up and down, using the board for pull-ups. "You don't have to hide who you are, but sometimes I wonder how we got to this place...you and I."

"What do you mean?" Helen clasped the edges of the diving board, walking her hands, bringing her within inches of hanging from Lane.

"I mean, this." Lane moved closer, their hands touching on the board. Helen recognized the steamy look of want that came across Lane's face before she reached her arm behind Helen's neck and kissed her softly.

Helen tightened her grip on the board when she felt Lane's arms and legs snake around her as she deepened the kiss, their tongues dancing together, softly baiting each other. A jolt of electricity fired all her senses. If it had been real voltage, they would've been instantly electrified.

She heard voices come from the fog in her head and opened her eyes to spot her nieces and nephews running across the deck and come careening into the pool.

Helen groaned. "I'm sorry."

Lane tipped her lips into a smile. "We probably needed that interruption."

"Maybe...but the cabana has a really soft couch." Helen let her voice lilt.

"You'll have to invite me back sometime and show me." Lane gave her a quick kiss. "Now, how about you introduce me to the kids?" She let go of Helen, went under the water, and swam to the shallow end.

"On my list already." Helen dropped into the water, pushed off the side, and followed Lane.

Will came out of the house. "I didn't know you were going to be here." He glanced at Lane. "Hi. I'm Will." He waved.

"I'm Lane." Lane waved back. She stepped out of the pool, and the view became less exciting as she wrapped herself in a towel before she walked to one of the loungers on the side of the pool near the midpoint.

Helen climbed out of the pool, grabbed her sunglasses from the table, and glanced back at Lane. "I'm going to grab a water. You want one?"

"That'd be great." Lane smiled.

Will followed Helen to the mini fridge. "Did we interrupt something?" He must've seen them kissing. "Seems like you worked it out. Are you two a thing now?"

"We were just swimming." Would've been doing a lot more if his timing didn't suck. "I think we're okay, but I'm sure she still has some reservations." She opened the fridge and took out a couple of waters, then held one out to Will. "I thought you were taking the kids to the zoo today."

Will waved her off. "I did. They were antsy in the heat, so I thought I'd bring them over to burn off some energy." Will snuck a glance at Lane. "Sorry. I didn't know you had plans here today. You want us to leave?"

"That would be weird." She looked over at Lane, then lowered her sunglasses from the top of her head to hide her stare. "It's fine. She's okay with kids." It did change her plans, though.

"Cool." Will grinned. "They wanted to get here right away to start early on their sunburns."

Even though the kids were blond, like their mother, Ash, they had the kind of skin that seemed to burn but then tanned quickly. Helen and Will both fared better in the sun than the rest of the family. She supposed they had more melanin in their skin protecting them from the UV rays, like their father.

Will stared at Lane. "So this is the woman who has your interest?"

Helen nodded. "Stop staring."

"It's hard not to. Your girlfriend is cute." Will headed to the deep end of the pool.

"She's not my girlfriend." Helen followed closely behind. "We work together. I ruined her wedding, remember?" Helen couldn't take her eyes off Lane. Will was right. It was hard not to stare.

"Yet, she's here, spending time with you, outside of work, on a Saturday afternoon." Will wasn't stupid. Helen hadn't brought anyone around since her last breakup, and she rarely brought women to the pool, never coworkers. Denying there was something happening between them was pointless. She'd already divulged enough of the situation with Lane to him.

"I'm trying to branch out—make new friends." Will arriving with the kids early wasn't in her plans.

Her sister Gwen came through the door to the patio, and Helen's anxiety kicked up a notch. She could handle Will and his children, but Gwen was a different story. Gwen walked toward them as her own kids got into the shallow end.

Helen took the lounge chair next to Lane as Will launched from the diving board and did a cannonball in his usual fashion, sending water out of the pool, soaking Gwen's shorts. "What the hell, Will?"

Helen grabbed Lane's hand as she bit her lip to prevent from laughing. "They have a love-hate relationship."

"Now that you're already wet, you should come in," Will shouted from the pool as he made his way to the edge and hoisted himself out.

Gwen stood there for a minute and glanced at Helen, then at Lane. "Who are you?"

"This is—"

"I'm Lane." She stood and held out her hand. "I work with Helen."

"Hmm." Gwen didn't take her hand, only raised an eyebrow as she assessed her briefly before she glanced at the pool. "You kids behave while your Uncle Will is watching you." She turned and went back inside.

Lane let her hand drop to her side. "Who was that?"

"My sister, Gwen." Helen hadn't expected Gwen to be friendly, but she could've at least been polite. "I'll be right back." She stood and followed Gwen into the house. This was so not the party she'd intended to have today.

CHAPTER TWENTY-FOUR

Lane watched Gwen walk across the jumbo-sized concrete pavers that created the patio floor and disappear through the sliding-glass door, and then she sank onto the lounger. She'd never experienced such intentional rudeness before. "Is she always like that?" Dressed in khaki capri pants and a V-neck T-shirt, the woman had a demeanor that could send anyone scrambling. Not to mention her stare—twice as terrifying as Helen's. If Gwen hadn't had long, dark hair, Lane would've thought she was looking into Helen's gorgeous blue eyes, but she saw no warmth in Gwen's.

Will nodded. "With pretty much everyone." He sat on the lounger next to her. "Don't take it personally. Gwen can intimidate someone without even a word. When we were kids, that single raised eyebrow could make us both cower."

"I can see that." Lane had plenty of self-confidence, but Gwen was super intimidating. Just like Helen. It was a defense mechanism, Helen had told her—to keep her feelings for Lane in check. Why would Gwen be threatened by Lane?

"She's been doing it to Helen and me since we were kids. I don't pay much attention to her now, though Helen still cares what she thinks." He pointed toward the door. "That right there was meant to irritate Helen."

Lane wasn't familiar with this type of family dynamic, had never experienced it herself. At least not since high school cliques, and those girls weren't her family. She had a sudden urge to protect Helen.

Lane stood, wrapped her towel around her torso, and fastened it above her chest. "I'm going to see if Helen needs reinforcements." Lane glanced at Will. "You coming?"

"I need to watch the kids while they're in the pool." He held his hand above his eyes to shield them from the sun as he looked up at her. "Good luck." He grinned like she was walking into a tiger pit.

Lane stopped at the door, gauged both Helen and Gwen's body language, and had second thoughts for only a minute before she propped her sunglasses on the top of her head and went inside. She was disappointed when she entered the kitchen to see that Helen had put on an oversized T-shirt. She'd been enjoying the view much more than she should've. But if a lean, muscled figure presented itself in her presence, she had a habit of looking. She probably hadn't been discreet enough to hide her glances from Helen, or anyone else for that matter. Maybe that was what this was about. Had Gwen noticed? Was she raking her over the coals for bringing her here?

Helen and Gwen had the same confident posture, almost the same build, although Helen was a bit taller. When Helen became aware of Lane's presence, she immediately stopped talking. She seemed uncomfortable. Maybe she should've stayed outside.

Gwen tilted her head and placed her hand on her hip. "How old are you?"

"Gwen. You of all people know it's inappropriate to ask a woman her age." Helen seemed surprised at the question.

"Don't you think that's something you should know?" Gwen returned her attention to Lane and raised her eyebrows. "Twenty-nine, thirty?"

"I'm flattered." Lane laughed. "I'm thirty-two."

"And Helen is forty-four." She moved the hand from her hip and held it palm up at Helen. "That's a twelve-year age gap."

"So now we know you can do simple math." Helen's ability to use passive-aggressive humor to shoot back was perfect, but her irritation was beginning to show.

Lane held up a hand to Helen. She was more than capable of speaking for herself. "I've never put boundaries around my friendships. They limit personal growth." She pointed to the hallway. "Is the restroom that way?"

"Yes. It's right around the corner." Helen smiled slightly as she moved toward her, led her into the hallway, and pointed to the open door. "That was priceless."

"Thanks." Lane went inside and started to close the door, but on second thought, she left it open a smidge and leaned against the wall to listen.

"There's a bathroom in the cabana. That's what the *kids* use." Gwen's voice floated through the hallway.

"Can you just act like a normal person for once? Why do you insist on embarrassing me? No matter what you think about me, you should treat anyone I bring home with respect."

"Aren't the people you associate with all part of who you are?" Gwen's voice lilted, ridiculously condescending. "Why should I treat them any differently?"

"You're not going to do this to me today." Helen's voice lowered a bit. "I like her, and I'm not going to let you ruin it for me."

Lane's belly tingled. Helen *liked* her. Amidst whatever confrontation she was having with her sister, Helen had told Gwen that she liked her. That meant *something*, right? She was just about to sneak down the hall when she heard the front door open and someone walk into the foyer. She ducked back into the bathroom, peeked through the small crack in the doorway, and saw an older man and woman crossing the living room. Helen's parents? She padded to the end of the hallway and watched them as they entered the kitchen, then slowly followed them. The man was tall, like Helen, with long legs sprouting beneath his khaki Bermuda shorts. A light blue short-sleeved polo shirt stretched across his broad shoulders. The man was fit for his age. His short silver hair was parted to one side and textured just a bit on top to add extra height. The woman was a little shorter but still tall and wore white capri pants, a sleeveless salmon V-neck, and wedge sandals. Her shoulder-length blond hair bounced as she walked with confidence across the room. Definitely Helen's parents.

"I thought you were out of town until tomorrow." Helen went straight to her father and gave him a hug. "Hi, Daddy."

Helen's father kissed her quickly on the cheek and released her. "That was the plan, but your mother feels a cold coming on, so we came home early." He turned slightly to glance at Lane. "I hope we didn't interrupt anything."

"No. Absolutely not." She motioned for Lane to come closer. "This is my friend, Lane."

Her dad held out his hand. "Nice to meet you, Lane."

Lane took his hand and met his strong, firm handshake with her own. "Nice to meet you as well."

He motioned to his wife. "This is Helen's mother, Caroline."

Caroline dipped her chin. "It's nice to meet you."

"Same," Lane responded, chiding herself for not saying something wittier.

"I hope you had a nice swim." Helen's mother glanced at the towel still wrapped around her.

Lane touched the wet strands of hair on her shoulders. "Yes. It was lovely." Did she actually say lovely? "I'm going to go change." She glanced at Helen and hooked a thumb over her shoulder.

"Me too." Helen brushed by her parents and followed Lane down the hallway "I'm sorry. I didn't expect the whole world to show up today." It was clear that Helen hadn't expected any company today.

"It's your family, not the whole world." Lane smiled. "I'm looking forward to getting to know them."

"You might regret saying that soon." Helen chuckled as she opened the door with one hand and let her other land on Lane's back.

The low sound of Helen's laugh along with the touch of her hand sent warmth searing throughout Lane. "They can't be all that bad, can they?" Although, after the kiss in the pool, Lane had hoped for more time alone with Helen.

"You'll see." Helen backed out of the doorway. "I'll meet you out here in a few minutes. I don't want you going into the lions' den alone."

Lane leaned against the edge of the door. "Okay." She watched Helen walk to the next room before she closed the door and began tearing off her clothes.

Surely Helen was joking. What could be so bad that Helen needed to accompany her into the kitchen—to shield her from her family? Her brother, Will, seemed nice enough, although he had given Lane the same impression about Gwen.

She changed into her sundress before she searched through her bag and found a hair clip. Meeting Helen's family today was unexpected, and she clearly wasn't prepared. She raked the brush through her wet hair, pulled it back into a ponytail, and clipped it up before she assessed herself in the mirror. They were going to get the organic Lane. She hadn't worn much makeup besides waterproof mascara, and she hadn't brought anything additional with her. She packed her wet suit in her bag and slung it over her arm before she crossed the bedroom to the door, pulled it open, and found Helen in the hall waiting for her. Helen was wearing the same navy mid-thigh shorts she'd arrived in but had changed from her pink polo to a mint-green sleeveless Columbia button-down shirt that exposed her defined, tanned arms.

"Sorry." Lane swept a stray hair from her face and fastened it to the others pasted to her head. "If I'd known I was going to meet your family, I would've prepared better."

"Don't worry about them. You look perfect." Helen glanced at her bag. "You're not leaving, are you?"

"No. Just going to drop this by the front door so I don't forget it."

"Great." Helen turned to lead her to the kitchen.

"Wait." Lane touched her arm.

Helen spun around, and Lane almost ran into her. Closer proximity than she'd expected.

Lane cleared her throat and backed up a step. "What are the children's names?"

"Billy and Ava are Will's kids, and TR and Lizzie belong to Gwen."

"Lizzie looks like your sister." She hadn't met Will's wife but thought she might be blond, since both Will's kids had light hair. "Do you think Will and Gwen's respective partners will show up as well?"

"Ash, Will's wife, probably will. I don't expect to see Robert, though. He works a lot."

"Oh? What does he do?" Lane wondered what was more important than his family on a Saturday afternoon.

"Real estate broker." Helen looked over her shoulder. "Has to keep Gwen happy, and money seems to do that. Come on." She took Lane's hand and tugged her toward the kitchen.

An amazing warmth radiated from Lane's fingers up through her arm, down across her chest, and settled in her midsection. It was probably a good thing that Helen's family had shown up, or they would be making good use of the couch in the cabana Helen had mentioned.

CHAPTER TWENTY-FIVE

When they got back to the kitchen, they saw only Gwen, who was paying attention to her phone more than anything else. Helen had known what Gwen's reaction would be to Lane, and regretfully, she didn't disappoint. Thankfully, at the moment, she was more focused on her own fucked-up life than Helen's.

"Mom and Dad changing?" Helen asked.

Gwen nodded as she typed in a text. "They're hungry."

The kids burst through the door, with Will right behind them. "Mommy, can we get pizza?" Lizzie asked. She definitely had the same features as Gwen. Ava was almost a carbon copy of Ash. Lane would see that once they met.

TR chimed in. "Pepperoni for me."

"And me," Billy said, seeming to go along with whatever TR wanted. Hero worship was strong between them.

Helen glanced at Lane. "Pizza okay with you?" She'd planned something much different, but that would be impossible now.

"Absolutely." Lane watched the kids interact. "They all seem to get along really well, considering their closeness in age."

"They do—most of the time." Will pulled open the refrigerator. "I see a couple of nice steaks in here." He turned to Helen. "We interrupt something?" He poked her, knowing full well she'd planned on them being alone today.

"Mom must've had those delivered for when they arrived home." She crossed the kitchen, took the package from him, and tossed it onto the shelf. "You know how Dad likes to grill." She'd brought steaks, mushrooms, squash, and potatoes by the night before, hoping that the afternoon of swimming would turn into a romantic evening. She wasn't the best cook, but she knew how to grill.

"Dad doesn't grill. That's my job, and they're not supposed to be home until Monday." Will wasn't letting up. Was he trying to sabotage her date? *Traitor.*

"Yet, they're home. Must have planned ahead." Helen cocked her head toward the other room. "Since there's not enough steak for all of us, let's get pizza." She smiled at Lane as she closed the refrigerator door. "How about some wine?"

"Red for me." Will took out his phone. "You like anything special on your pizza, Lane?"

"I'm not particular." Lane refocused her attention from the kids to Will.

"Anchovy pizza for Lane." He hit the screen and held the phone to his ear.

"Well, don't order it just for me. I'm happy to share with the youngsters."

Helen raked her teeth over her bottom lip to prevent a laugh. It was good to see that Lane had a sense of humor and could take what Will dished out.

"We want anchovies." Ava smiled up at Lane before they spun to look at Will. "Is it like pepperoni, Dad?"

"It's a bit saltier." Will pulled his lips into a cockeyed smile. "I'll see if they have any." He bumped Gwen with his shoulder. "Should I order enough for Rob?"

Gwen shook her head and dropped her phone to the counter. "He'll get something later at home." She proceeded to the cabinet and took out six wineglasses.

Gwen was clearly unhappy that her husband wasn't going to join her, as usual, which wasn't a surprise to anyone else in the room. Will hit another button on his phone and headed around the corner. Helen could hear him placing the order as she opened two bottles of wine and poured each of them a glass.

"Unfortunately, they were out of anchovies, so I ordered a supreme and a couple of pepperonis instead." Will dropped his phone onto the counter and picked up his wine and drank. "This is good." He checked the label on the bottle.

"Is Ash coming over?" Helen needed an ally.

"She'll be here in a bit. Had some errands to run." He topped up his glass.

"It'll be good to have someone in the house on my side," Helen said. Ash and Will were the only ones who supported Helen when she'd decided to go into the event business. The two of them knew how it felt to be happy in their professional and home lives.

Helen sat at the breakfast bar and sipped her wine as she watched Lane interact with her family at the table. She was relaxed and talkative as usual. Gwen's bad behavior hadn't seemed to faze her at all. Plus, she'd been successfully conversing with her parents while Gwen was wrapped up in her phone. Given the way Gwen had been furiously texting for the past five minutes, she seemed to be having a heated text exchange with Robert.

Suddenly she heard her mother ask, "How do you two know each other?"

"We're working together on Darcy Hampton's wedding." Helen quickly fielded the question.

"Yes." Lane smiled. "She's my best friend."

Caroline took a minute before she spoke, which made Helen worry about what was going to come out of her mouth next. "I'm afraid I put Helen in a tight spot there. Three months is very short notice for planning." Caroline sipped her wine.

"It is, but I think we've got it covered." Lane looked at Helen and winked as though they were partners in crime, keeping the deepest, darkest secret between them, and goose bumps rushed over Helen's skin.

Billy sprang from the hallway running. "Grandpa, the toilet is leaking again."

"Tell your dad to shut off the water valve." He frowned. "You can use the other one upstairs. It's a Saturday, and I'm not paying triple the normal cost."

"Do you mind if I take a look?" Lane asked as she headed into the bathroom. "My dad owns a plumbing business. I work in the office now, but I used to help him out on service calls when I was younger."

"You don't need to worry about that," Helen's dad shouted after her as she raced down the hallway.

Gwen's eyebrows flew up. "I thought Helen said you worked with her?" Half-listening as always, Gwen had the details wrong.

"She provides makeup services for brides." Helen followed closely behind Lane. "He's right, you know. We have plenty of bathrooms upstairs in this house. Plus the one in the cabana."

"I know, but this one is the most convenient for the kids while they're in the house." Lane straddled the toilet, and all sorts of unbidden images shot through Helen's head. "Do you have an adjustable wrench and a small container to put under the toilet to catch the water?" She stared up at Helen.

"I'll get it." Billy flew down the hallway.

Helen cleared her throat. "I think I should shut the door instead and adjust you."

"That's not a bad idea." She leaned her head back, hooked Helen's head with her hand, and kissed her before she started feeling around the bottom of the tank again.

"I'll check on where Billy is with getting the wrench." Helen had no idea what kind of tools were in the house, but if there was anything useful it would be in the bottom drawer in the kitchen. It was a catchall.

Helen's mom met her at the entrance to the hallway. "Your friend really doesn't need to worry about the toilet. I'm sure we can get along without it for a couple of days." Her voice was soft but demanding. In other words, *Stop her now. We don't fix our own toilets.*

"That's what I told her." She found a wrench and slammed the drawer shut. "But who am I to turn down free labor?" She took a plastic container from the cabinet before she brushed past her mother as she hurried down the hallway to the bathroom.

Lane met her at the door and took the supplies. "It's the water fill hose under the tank. I called my dad to come change it." She sat and placed the container under the shutoff valve. "Luckily, he's in the area and will be here in about five minutes."

"That's not necessary. No need to disturb your father on a Saturday." Helen's parents wouldn't be thrilled about that either. "My parents will have it fixed on Monday."

"My dad isn't busy. He just finished picking up some things at a butcher shop nearby." She checked the floor to make sure it was dry. "It won't take long. He just has to be back in time to man the barbecue for my mom."

Helen glanced over her shoulder to see if her mother was still hovering.

Lane's eyebrows drew together. "Are you embarrassed that my family is in the plumbing business? Is that why you don't want him to come over?"

"Absolutely not." Helen shook her head. "I respect anyone who has the fortitude to make a good living for themselves." Her family, on the other hand, had a different measure of success.

Lane's lips curved into a beautiful smile. "Me too."

This was the exact reason she'd purposely brought Lane over when she'd thought her family wouldn't be there. She didn't intend to hide her family, but she didn't want Lane to see her as something she wasn't—rich and spoiled.

Chapter Twenty-Six

L ane made sure the water valve was closed tightly before she stood, washed her hands, and dried them.

Helen remained in the doorway and said, "Please don't listen to anything my family says about me. They're not my biggest cheerleaders."

"They should be. You're awesome at what you do." Lane had seen her in action and was beginning to admire her hard work.

"You're good for my ego. I should keep you around." Helen leaned closer and brushed Lane's lips softly with her own.

Lane was amazed at how such a simple, light kiss could ignite a fire so deep in her belly. It wasn't lost on her that, besides the additional kiss after Lane had ambushed her in the coat closet, this was actually the first time Helen had kissed her without Lane initiating it. Helen was slowly lowering her walls.

"And keeping it in check." Lane gave her a sideways grin.

"Yes. I need that." Helen took Lane's hand and led her down the hallway.

Lane's phone chimed. "My dad's here." He'd made it sooner than she'd expected. "I'll get the door." Lane rushed by Helen and let her father in.

Lane's father glanced around the foyer. "Fancy place to spend your day."

Lane cringed at the comment, knowing Helen was right behind her and probably heard it. "This is my friend Helen. It's her parents' house. We just came over to swim."

Helen held out her hand. "Nice to meet you, Mr. Donnelly."

He accepted the greeting, nodding as he shook her hand. "Nice to meet you too." He glanced down the hallway. "Where's the hose that needs replacing?"

"It's right down here." Lane led him to the bathroom, then turned back to Helen. "I've got this if you want to go back to your family."

"I don't mind staying." Helen shrugged.

Lane smiled lightly. "Dad gets a little cranky if too many people are in his way."

"Gotcha. Let me know when he's done, so I can say good-bye, okay?" Helen raised her eyebrows.

"Absolutely." Lane was happy that Helen wanted to engage with her father, but this particular setting wasn't the best to do it in.

"So, your friend has money?" Her father spoke as he removed the water-fill line.

Lane found the new hose in his bag. "No, Dad. Her family has money."

He handed her the bad line and took the new one from her. "Does she do anything for a living?"

"She's not like that, Dad. She runs her own business. She's a wedding planner. I work with her quite often." Lane hoped he didn't put two and two together and realize Helen was the woman she always bitched about.

"Wait." He glanced over her shoulder. "Is she the one you always complain about?"

No such luck. "Yes, but I was wrong about her. Turns out she's really nice."

"I certainly hope so. Because this is a lot." He wiped the line with a rag he'd taken from his bag and then turned on the water valve.

"I know, but her place is nothing like this." That wasn't true. It was still upscale and fabulous, but not nearly as big.

"You've been to her place?" He glanced over his shoulder as he felt under the tank for leaks. "How long have you been seeing her?"

"Not long. It's still new." That was more information than she'd wanted to provide, but her dad would continue to probe if she didn't.

"Okay." He stood and dropped his tools into his bag. "You should bring her over tomorrow. I'll tell your mother to plan on one more at Sunday dinner."

"But, Dad…"

"No buts. You're here with her family." He washed his hands and dried them. "She needs to meet yours as well."

"Okay. I'll bring her. Only if you promise not to grill her about her family and upbringing."

"No need for that. I can already see it." He glanced around as they left the bathroom and entered the foyer.

"And don't do that either." Seemed her dad was just as judgmental as Helen's. She hadn't expected that.

"Do what?" He shrugged.

"Make assumptions about her and her family." Her father looked past her and nodded, indicating someone behind her—Helen. *Shit.* She'd probably heard the whole conversation. She spun around. "All done. I was just getting ready to find you."

"Here I am." She smiled at Lane before turning her attention to her dad. "Thank you so much for making the repair on your day off. Can I pay you something?"

He shook his head. "You get the friends-and-family discount." He opened the door and stepped outside.

"Thanks again, Dad," Lane said, waving as she closed the door. "I'm sorry about that, Helen. He had questions."

"Not to worry. My family isn't any different. It's not unexpected for both our families to be curious about us, and our worlds."

"Join the club, right?" Lane raised an eyebrow and headed toward the kitchen. She was just as curious as the rest of them.

Everyone was still in the kitchen except for the kids. Lane took the seat she'd left at the table, and Helen scooted onto a bar stool.

Lane hoped the pizza would arrive soon and everyone's mouths would be full to avoid more awkward conversation. She'd never been this nervous around someone's family before. Helen's warning about them had put her on edge.

"Leak resolved," Helen said.

Helen's father glanced at Lane. "Send us the bill, and we'll get him paid right away."

"No worries." Lane shrugged. "It was an inexpensive part and a simple fix."

"Well then, please thank him for us." He looked at Caroline. "Maybe you can get his address and send a thank-you card."

"Yes, of course." Helen's mom agreed. "Send that to me, won't you, Helen?"

"I'll be happy to." Helen glanced at Lane and winked. "Lane can bring one of his cards to the next event we work together."

"Or sooner." Lane grinned. She didn't plan to wait very long to see Helen again.

"I'm not sure why you insist on planning parties for people." Helen's mother relaxed in her chair and took a drink of wine.

"Mother." Helen let out a quick breath. "You just asked me to plan one as a favor to you, and it's not the first time you've done that."

"Someone has to do it." Gwen chimed in. She seemed to be critically passive-aggressive.

"She's very good at it." The words flew out of Lane's mouth in response. "Brides love her. They wait months to get on her schedule."

"I agree." Will winked at Helen. "If she'd been doing it when Ash and I got married, I would've let her plan the whole thing." He seemed to be her only ally.

"I'm not sure how Ash would've felt about that." Gwen crossed the kitchen and took a seat at the table beside her mother.

"I have to agree with Will." Lane knew the hard work that Helen put in to planning weddings. "In fact, my fiancée engaged Helen to plan our wedding." Why in the world did she bring that up?

"Oh?" Gwen's voice rose as she turned her attention to Lane. "Are you getting married?"

"No. That didn't work out as I'd planned." Lane glanced at Helen—saw the terror in her eyes. "But Helen handled everything wonderfully…even the cancellations."

"I see." Gwen's smug smile faded "I'm sorry to hear that." She took another sip of wine and focused her attention back on her phone.

"If I'm so incompetent, Mother, why did you ask me to take on the Donnelly wedding?" Helen moved the conversation back to herself, which Lane was more than grateful for.

Her mother shrugged. "I didn't say you're not good at it. I just think you might be better at something else."

"Like what?" Lane let her lips fly again. She really wanted to know what Helen's family thought a better fit for Helen would be.

"She would've done great in real estate if she'd only put in the effort," Gwen said, nonchalantly, not looking up from her phone.

"That would've meant working for a workaholic tyrant," Helen said flatly.

"Robert isn't that bad, is he?" Helen's dad asked.

"I wasn't talking about *him*." Helen shrugged. "I stayed in real estate as long as I did because of Robert."

"You have to work hard to build a good clientele." Gwen looked up and narrowed her eyes. "Haven't you grown tired of being under someone's thumb?"

"Some thumbs are easier to breathe under than others."

Gwen's mouth dropped open. "Are you insinuating I was a bad boss?"

"I'm not *insinuating anything*. I'm *telling you* that you were horrible to work for."

Lane guessed Gwen was the tyrant Helen was referring to. They seemed to have a lot of bad history, which Lane suspected might have started during childhood. Gwen clearly considered herself superior to everyone in the room.

Lane noticed Helen's mood shift back into the stiff personality she'd experienced previously at events. Understandable, since Gwen wasn't letting up. She listened as Helen's family belittled her job without any rebuttal. She couldn't believe how calm Helen was, just sitting there taking it like it was a usual occurrence. This was not the Helen she knew. How could she let it roll off her back like that? Lane could never do that if someone attacked her livelihood so viciously.

Heat climbed up Lane's neck until it reached the back of it and spread into a massive bonfire. A strong urge to protect Helen surged through her, and she bolted up from her chair and crossed the room. She didn't think. She just moved to Helen, took her face into her hands, and stared into her sad, vacant, eyes that seemed to have glazed over to escape her family's criticism. "Are you okay?"

"I'm fine." Helen nodded.

But Lane knew she wasn't fine at all and was overwhelmed by a sudden urge to hold her—kiss her—keep her safe. She let loose and pressed her lips softly to Helen's, hoping the kiss would relieve Helen's sadness. Helen seemed to stiffen at first, but then relaxed into it, letting her hands land on Lane's waist. When Lane broke away, Helen seemed a little stunned, and everyone else sat with their eyes wide and their mouths hanging open.

Lane backed away slowly and turned to face the family. "You all need to stop belittling Helen. This woman makes people the happiest they can be on their wedding days. She does all the difficult tasks involved and handles anything that doesn't go right. I've seen her take a bride from a raging panic to glorious bliss in a matter of minutes." It had been a slow progression over the past few weeks, but Lane had gone from hating this woman to admiring her.

"You don't need to defend me." Helen pushed out of the bar stool and rushed past Lane and into the next room. She seemed angry at Lane, not her family, and she had no idea why. "I told myself long ago I would never depend on anyone, and that includes my family."

Lane followed. "I was just trying to help—tell them how great you are at what you do."

Helen spun around. "I can handle my family. I don't need your help."

Apparently, she needed to fall in line. She flicked her fingers at her forehead in mock solute. "Message received, ma'am."

Helen bit her bottom lip and blew out a breath. "Look. I'm sorry. I appreciate your concern. I really do, but my family can be a handful."

"I saw." Lane rolled her lips in. "Do they do that to you all the time?"

"No." Helen shook her head. "But their expectations of me are different from my own, and they don't include my current career path."

"And…" Lane raised her eyebrows.

"And the pressure to conform can be brutal." Helen paced across the room.

Lane followed and stilled the anger in her voice. "But you haven't…conformed…have you?"

"I have in the past." Helen sighed. "That's why I have a string of degrees and a much-too-long resume."

"Oh." Lane hadn't known about the degrees. "It's not a crime to try different careers until you find the one that suits you best."

"No, but it does give them ammunition for criticism." Helen raked her fingers through her hair. "Especially my sister, who's known what she wanted to do since she was twelve."

Lane didn't know quite what to say at this point. "Fuck them." She kept it simple, hoping Helen didn't get angry with her.

Helen laughed. "You've read my mind." She took Lane's hand. "You want to get out of here? Get some burgers?"

Lane moved toward the door, where she'd left her bag. "A burger sounds great." She would eat chocolate-covered bugs if it got her out of this lions' den.

"Leaving so soon?" Gwen's voice came from behind. She and Will were standing in the kitchen doorway.

"Can I tag along?" he asked.

Lane didn't wait for Helen to answer. "As long as you leave the judgment at the door."

Will held up his hands in surrender. "No judgment here." He turned to Gwen and hooked a thumb over his shoulder. "I like this one."

Gwen chimed in. "Me too. Anyone who can hold her own with this family has my respect." She stared momentarily. "Why don't you two stay? I'll can the passive-aggressive jokes."

"I'm okay with staying." Lane glanced at Helen. "It's up to you."

Helen squeezed Lane's hand. "Let's go eat dinner in peace." She glanced at Gwen. "You can take the leftovers to your invisible husband. Or does he expect you to cook for him when he gets home?" Seemed Helen could get in a few good jabs of her own.

Helen didn't wait for Gwen's reaction. She opened the door and let Lane exit ahead of her. Helen circled the car to the driver's side while Lane got into the passenger side.

"I can't believe your sister treats you that way." Lane glanced sideways at Helen as she slid into the passenger seat.

"She might be my sister, but we're not friends." Helen hit the start button and fired the engine. "Never have been. I don't know why, but she can still make me feel about this tall." She held her fingers about an inch apart.

Lane couldn't believe the strong, confident woman she had butted heads with all this time was so insecure around her family. Was she insecure with her romantic partners—or during sex? That was something she wanted to find out.

Helen put the car into gear. "What are you in the mood for?"

"I'm actually craving pizza now." Lane chuckled. "Can we just go to your place?" She chewed on her bottom lip. "Order it from there?" She'd been planning to take things slow with Helen this evening, but now she was hoping for a different outcome.

CHAPTER TWENTY-SEVEN

Having Lane in her house again was more awkward than Helen had imagined. She was way off her game. In all the scenarios she'd thought about, she hadn't come up with one where she was at a loss for words, where the dialogue between them stilled. She'd always had something witty or savvy to say. But this time she'd been struck with a nervousness and insecurity she'd never experienced before. She was human after all.

Helen cleared her throat. "Can I get you something to drink?" She went into the kitchen and took a couple of glasses from the cabinet.

"Sure." Lane moved farther into the room. "Do you have any sparkling water?" She seemed to be assessing her.

"I do." Ice spilled to the floor as Helen fumbled to put it in the glass. *Get a grip, Helen.* She took in a deep breath as she opened a new bottle of Perrier and poured. She crossed the room to Lane and held out the glass. "Here you are."

Lane took the glass from Helen and sipped. "I don't believe I've ever seen you nervous before."

"Not nervous. Just tired." A total lie. It was apparent that she wasn't nearly as in control of her emotions as she'd thought.

Lane set her glass on the marble coffee table before she moved closer. "Are you sure?"

Helen shook her head. "Honestly, I'm not sure of anything right now, except that I've lost my appetite for anything food-related." She placed her glass next to Lane's.

Lane smiled. "Good, because so have I." She moved closer, slowly unzipped her own dress, and let it drop to the floor.

Helen was stunned by the beautiful woman standing before her in only a bra and panties. "Are you sure about this?" Helen didn't want to rush things with Lane, but she hoped to God she said yes.

"If you'd asked me that question last week, I would've said no." Lane's green eyes sparkled with emotion. "And I'm still not sure where we're going with this, but I *am* sure that I want to be with you tonight."

In all of Helen's wildest dreams, she hadn't imagined a scenario where Lane had done the seducing. She took in the gorgeous sight before her. Lane had hidden her assets well. She was a beautiful treasure that Helen wanted to discover—inch by inch. Lane removed her bra and panties, letting them drop to the floor on top of her dress. It was like the perfect birthday present had just been unwrapped in front of her. Lane stepped closer, out of the clothing piled at her feet. Helen reached for her, impatient for what was to come—all the things she wanted to do to Lane—the pleasure she planned to bring her—fantasies she'd kept locked away for so long.

Lane took her hand, squeezed it. "Not yet." She raised an eyebrow as her eyes darkened and her lips pulled into a sideways smile. "Turn around." She circled her finger slowly in front of Helen.

It was a difficult ask with Lane standing so magnificently naked in front of her, but Helen complied, turning slowly, letting Lane take control. She forced herself to stand waiting as Lane reached around her and unbuttoned her blouse before letting it slide from her shoulders, all the while kissing the back of her neck. Shivers ran down her spine as Lane's delicate touch floated across her arms, hesitating only momentarily before she went to work on the button and zipper of her shorts. Once unfastened, they dropped easily from her hips.

"Oh, my." The words whooshed out of Lane's mouth, her steamy breath pulsing against Helen's back between kisses. "Somehow, I knew you weren't wearing panties."

Helen let out a quiet, guttural sound in her throat as Lane let her fingers glide across Helen's back, unfastened her bra, and slid the straps down her arms. She immediately moved her hands to Helen's bare waist, then around to her stomach while pressing her warm breasts into Helen's back. A red-hot bolt of electricity zapped her entire midsection and shot straight between her legs.

"You're so soft." Lane's wet hot lips trailed from one shoulder to the other as she traced the crease at the top of Helen's thigh with her fingers, then moved to a more sensitive spot.

Helen tried to still herself as she quivered uncontrollably. "You're killing me." She felt Lane's breath against her as a throaty laugh escaped Lane's lips.

"I know, and that's the best part." Lane kissed her shoulder. "I want to savor you, kiss every part of you, touch you until you can't stand it anymore."

She took in a shaky breath. "You've almost succeeded."

"Almost?" Lane laid her head on Helen's shoulder blade and gazed up at her.

How could Lane be so sweet yet so seductive? Helen couldn't help but get caught up in her. Her butt tingled with each slight brush of the small patch of hair covering the magnificent crevice between Lane's legs. She'd only glimpsed it but couldn't wait to explore its depth, feel its cover tickle her nose. Lane reached around and cupped a breast in each hand. That was all Helen could stand. She quickly spun, wrapped her arms around Lane, and pressed her lips hard against hers. Lane's tongue explored her mouth with urgency. With Lane's breasts pressed firmly against her, she wedged her thigh between Lane's legs. The slickness she felt as Lane ground against her had Helen almost ready to come. Thank God she had a huge, oversized couch.

Helen inched backward until she felt the cloth behind her calves, then bent her knee and placed her leg on the couch for balance. She was good at multitasking, but these particular tasks took more concentration. Lane's soft breasts pressed harder against her own as Lane trailed her lips across Helen's jaw, nipping at her neck as she made her way to Helen's collarbone. Helen quivered and almost lost her balance when Lane pushed her fingers between her folds and inside, then circled her clit with her thumb. She let out a whimper, and Lane returned her mouth to hers.

"God, you're so wet." Lane's low, sultry voice in her ear sent another gush between her legs.

"You have no idea." Helen had been waiting for this moment for so long. She tensed as Lane shoved her fingers deeper, then dragged them out slowly, raking across the perfect spot. Tongues and hands battled for control as friction built between them, and they tumbled onto the couch. She wanted Lane under her, but the resistance she felt told her Lane wanted otherwise. She would give in this time because she needed some kind of release, and if Lane was set on being in control, Helen would let her be—for now.

Lane sucked a nipple into her mouth, sending another bolt of red-hot arousal through Helen. An involuntary moan of protest came from Helen when Lane left her nipple and quickly replaced her mouth with the fingers that were making the magic happen down below. She went back to Helen's mouth, nipping at her lip before kissing her deeply. Helen squirmed beneath her as Lane moved her mouth back to her nipple and trailed a feather-light path to her stomach with her fingertips—those magical fingertips. She shuddered as Lane skimmed her fingers across the dark patch covering her center and then moved a leg between her legs, spreading them farther apart.

Lane glanced up, made eye contact, and pressed her tongue to her top lip, and Helen's arousal spiked. God, Lane was sexy. Helen's response was staggering. She was amazed at how wet she was, and Lane seemed to be using her arousal to her advantage. She slipped a finger inside, drew it up through her folds, circled, and took it back down and inside again. As she continued the rhythm, Lane seemed to become more delighted with each whimper that came from Helen's mouth.

Helen was almost there—twice—and Lane had slowed her efforts, taking the anticipation higher. If she didn't let her come soon, Helen was going to take control and do it herself. She reached down and stroked her own clit.

Lane engulfed Helen's fingers with hers. "That's right. Show me."

Helen swirled her fingers over the most sensitive spot before she removed her hand and let Lane take over again. "Harder—and don't stop...please." The orgasm began building again.

"There's the girl I know." Lane's low, sultry voice pushed Helen's arousal up a notch.

Helen couldn't hold in the gasps her heaving chest and rapid breathing caused as Lane continued her rhythm. This sensation was a thousand times better than anything she'd been able to produce alone. Suddenly her vision blurred, and she skyrocketed into a spiraling orgasm she wanted to ride out for hours. She tried to slow it down, savor it, but Lane made that impossible.

"Good?" Lane stared up at her with her eyebrows raised.

"Spectacular." Helen ran her fingers through Lane's hair, then took a strand and wrapped it around her finger, marveling at all the things Lane made her feel—all the things Lane knew to do to make Helen's body come to life into a ridiculously pleasurable orgasm. Sex with Lane went above and beyond, and she had no explanation for it. Maybe it was anticipation, the over-the-top longing every time she saw her at each event, or the impact of her trying to keep her distance and knowing that she was off-limits.

Lane nipped lightly at Helen's nipple with her teeth, producing an involuntary spasm in Helen's belly before she smiled and laid her head on Helen's chest. Helen could remain in this spot forever, but she had some pleasure to give first.

CHAPTER TWENTY-EIGHT

When Helen arrived home after her mid-morning appointment, she was disappointed not to find Lane there. She'd imagined her curled up in one of the club chairs reading a book or, better yet, still in bed. That was an impractical thought, since her meeting had lasted much longer than she'd expected. She entered her walk-in closet, took a pair of navy-blue capri pants from one of the lower-level hangers, along with a white V-neck shirt and oatmeal jacket, and hung them on the back of the door. She changed from the slacks, blouse, and flats she was wearing and assessed her outfit in the mirror.

The jacket was too much. It was Sunday dinner with Lane's family, not dinner at the country club. Lane had invited Helen sometime during the night, and Helen had agreed to come. She took off the jacket and replaced it with a denim overshirt before she sat on the built-in bench and slipped on her white Classic Chucks, sans socks. She assessed herself once more before she glanced at her watch. This would have to do—she was late.

Helen headed back into the bedroom, stopping to stare at the perfectly made bed, where she'd left Lane tangled in the sheets this morning. She hadn't wanted to leave Lane—hadn't wanted to stop making love to her, but she'd had a planning appointment with a couple. When she mentioned canceling, Lane reminded Helen of her own words. *If you cancel, you'd be letting the bride know that you're unreliable and giving her time to see someone else.* Why did she have to be so sensible? All she'd wanted to do today was explore Lane's body again—push her into another screaming orgasm. The way Lane let loose and succumbed to every one of Helen's touches was magnificent. And when Helen finally buried herself between Lane's legs, the climax was spectacular. The experience was just as good as Helen had expected. She'd finally crawled out of bed, leaving Lane sleeping soundly, and slipped into the shower. Lane was still fast asleep when she'd left. Helen had offered to take her home, but Lane said she'd call an Uber, choosing to use those minutes to snuggle rather than be on the road.

Helen's phone rang, ripping her from her thoughts. Thinking it was Lane wondering where she was, she raced into the living room and found it on the counter where she'd left it when she arrived home. She was disappointed to see her sister Gwen's name on the screen.

"Hey, Gwen. Can I call you later? I'm on my way out." She needed to get moving. Lane seemed excited to introduce Helen to her family. Evidently, Sunday dinners were a big event in Lane's family. Even as they'd grown older and farther apart, they still made it a priority to spend time together.

"Listen. I'm sorry about the way I acted in front of your friend last night." Gwen's voice was void of sincerity. Apologetic Gwen didn't show herself very often. Something was up.

"Lane. Her name is Lane." *Unbelievable.*

"Right, but you're not really serious about her, are you?" Gwen's voice rose.

"Why wouldn't I be?" Anger brewed within Helen.

"She's a lot younger than you, for one." Gwen reverted to her usual condescending tone.

"Ten years is nothing these days." Helen blew out a breath. "You should know." Robert was at least ten years older than Gwen.

"That's different. I met him when we were both much younger. Lane's probably thrilled that she's found a woman who can support her. That makeup business can't possibly make enough money to sustain a decent lifestyle."

"I think she makes more than you know. Not that it's any of your business." Helen knew for a fact that brides paid a good amount to look beautiful on their special day. She probably made a good living working for her family business as well.

"I'm sure it does." Gwen's voice lowered, her condescension clear. "She probably has a nice little apartment on the south side of Dallas—has a roommate to split the costs. She drives a modest sedan, possibly a Honda or Toyota. Her idea of a night out is dinner at the local Mexican restaurant and drinks at the local lesbian dance club later." She hesitated for a moment. "Am I close?"

Gwen was probably spot-on, but Helen refused to give her the satisfaction of letting her know she was correct. "Do you honestly believe she's dating me for my money?" Helen was letting Gwen get into her head.

"Of course she is." Gwen chuckled. "I mean, she's sweet and all, but she's nowhere near the type of women you usually date."

"Maybe that's why none of them have worked out before." High-maintenance women had become more work than Helen was willing to give.

"Don't get me wrong." Gwen blew out a short breath. "I'm not saying you shouldn't have some fun with her. Just cut her loose before anything gets serious."

Too late. Things had gotten serious for Helen before Lane even knew it. "Leave it alone, Gwen."

"Have you she slept with her yet?" The sound of ice dropping into a glass came through the phone.

"I can't believe you just asked me that." Helen had never found it easy to talk to her sister about sex, so she refused to confide in her now. Wouldn't tell her how absolutely amazing it was. "Why can't you just be happy for me?"

"I will be when you stop twiddling your life away on senseless careers and start one where you can find the right woman. Someone of your own caliber."

What did that even mean? "I'm hanging up now." Helen hit the end button before Gwen could respond. Her sister was so much more pretentious than she'd realized. But now, Gwen had her rethinking whether she should go. She sat on the couch while text after text came through from Lane.

Are you on your way?

Is everything okay?

I'm starting to get worried.

Then the phone rang. Helen sent it to voice mail and then turned it off. She sat there for over an hour second-guessing herself. Lane didn't seem like someone who was after money in a relationship. Helen couldn't imagine Lane as a master manipulator, although Belinda had given her a huge budget to plan their nuptials. From her discussions with Lane regarding her relationship with Belinda, she'd seemed genuinely hurt when Belinda broke it off. She didn't have extravagant tastes, and from what Lane told her, Belinda had chosen pretty much everything for their wedding. She hadn't said a single thing about Helen on her social media, something that most of her previous girlfriends had done immediately. She hadn't once asked Helen for money, and when Lane had come to her apartment, her attention had immediately gone to Helen's bookshelf. The warmth she felt when she was with Lane spread throughout her, erasing all the doubts Gwen had provoked. She knew deep down that Gwen was wrong, but she had a way of making Helen question every decision she ever made.

"No." Helen bolted from the couch. "Gwen is completely wrong about you." She rushed to the door, hoping she hadn't blown any chance she had with Lane for good this time.

CHAPTER TWENTY-NINE

Lane could tell her mother was getting anxious. The sauce was ready, as were the sausage, meatballs, and pasta. She was a stickler for serving her food hot, the way Lane's father liked it.

"Let's eat," Lane's mother announced as she appeared from the kitchen and set a couple of baskets of bread on the table. She glanced at Lane. "Your friend can join us when she gets here."

Lane stood behind as everyone filed through into the kitchen, lined up at the stove, and started filling their plates.

"I'm sorry, honey." Iris smiled softly. "It doesn't look like she's going to show."

"She wouldn't do this. Not after last night." Lane was sad and a bit confused as to why Helen hadn't gotten there or even answered any of her messages.

"Last night?" Iris moved closer and lowered her voice. "You didn't tell me anything about last night."

Iris had spent the night at Harvey's, so she'd had no way of knowing that Lane hadn't come home last night. "We…"

Iris's eyes widened. "You had sex with Helen?" She blew the words out with a squeal.

"Shush." Lane put her finger to her mouth. "I don't want the whole family to know."

"Oh, honey." Iris shook her head slowly. "I sure hope that wasn't what all this was about. I mean, her not showing up."

"I don't think it is." Lane rubbed her forehead. "I'm worried, Iris. She had a meeting with a client, but that was hours ago. What if she's hurt?" She was worried about herself too. The last time she fell for a woman like this, she'd been left all alone.

"She's probably fine. More than likely, something came up, or she's afraid to meet your family."

"Or she doesn't *want* to meet my family at all." Lane shrugged. "Her family is much different." *And vastly dysfunctional.*

Iris widened her eyes again. "When did you meet them? You've really been holding out on me."

"Yesterday. We went swimming at her parents' house, but I don't think she was expecting everyone to be there." Lane was sure of that. "Then they all showed up." Lane threw her hands in the air. "They're an interesting bunch." She glanced at her phone. Still no response from Helen.

"Enough of that." Iris took Lane's phone from her and tossed it into Lane's bag. "Harvey and I are going out later with some of his friends from work. If Helen doesn't get here soon, you should come with me. Get your mind off her."

"I don't think that's a good idea. I'll probably just go home or stop by Helen's to see if she's all right." She should really go now.

"Absolutely not." Iris was emphatic. "You'll just be letting her see how desperate you are."

Lane *was* desperate. After last night she'd thought they had something special, the beginning of something that would last.

"Some of Harvey's friends are female." Iris sang the words. "One of them is really pretty."

The thought of going out with other women made Lane's stomach clench. "I don't want to meet anyone new." She grabbed her bag and rushed to the door. "I need to find Helen."

Iris followed closely behind. "You need to figure out if it's love or lust. Otherwise, you're not going to be able to move forward or backward."

"I'm not sure if it's love yet, but I'm afraid it's much more than lust."

"Oh, God." Iris sighed. "I didn't know." She grabbed her bag as well. "I'll go with you."

Lane pulled open the door and found Helen standing on the porch, hands by her side like she'd been waiting for someone to answer. Lane's stomach dipped as she let her gaze roam the landscape before her. Such a gorgeous butch.

"I'm sorry I'm late." Helen gave her a tentative smile. "It took me longer to get here than I thought it would." Helen seemed to notice her bag. "Are you leaving?"

"I was coming to find you." Lane backed up and set her bag next to the couch. "What happened? I was worried."

"I'm sure she just got caught up with something work-related." Iris crossed the threshold and ushered Helen inside. "I'm glad you made it."

"Me too." Helen seemed relieved.

"Is everything all right?" Lane sensed Helen's hesitation. "You promised no more secrets."

Helen bit her bottom lip. "I'm embarrassed to admit that I let my sister Gwen get into my head. She hit me with all the reasons why we shouldn't be together, and I started thinking that maybe she was right."

"Oh my God. That's ridiculous." That confession stung a little more than Lane expected. She'd been slighted before, but this time it somehow seemed more important. "The only two people who know whether we should be together are you and me."

"I know. I'm an idiot. The more I thought about it, the more I realized her way of thinking is skewed." Helen smiled softly.

After yesterday, Lane understood Helen's family dynamics and wouldn't fault her for them. "Don't worry. My family will probably think I'm too good for you too." Lane winked. "Or that you're after me for my plumbing skills."

Helen stared into her eyes and seemed to breathe a sigh of relief. "I'm definitely after you for those."

Lane placed a hand on Helen's back and nudged her into the dining room. "Mom, this is Helen." Lane glanced at her. "She got hung up with a bride-to-be."

"You're giving me more grace than I deserve," Helen whispered.

"I know. Blame it on last night." Lane gave her a sly smile and ran her hand across Helen's ass, then cupped a cheek in her hand and squeezed.

Helen jumped and then coughed. "I'm so sorry I'm late for dinner. Something smells delicious."

"There's plenty left on the stove." Lane's mom pointed to the kitchen. "Lane will help you fix your plate."

Lane took Helen's hand and led her into the kitchen. "I hope you like spaghetti and meatballs." She pointed to the pans on the stove. "There's Italian sausage too."

Helen turned to Lane and took both her hands. "I don't know what to say."

"Don't say anything. Let's just eat, and we can discuss all those second thoughts, on both our sides, later." Lane picked up a bowl and placed a helping of noodles in it. "Meatballs and sausage?" She raised her eyebrows.

"One of each, please."

Lane filled a bowl for herself as well before she motioned Helen back toward the dining room. "There's Parmesan on the table." She glanced at the small round table in the kitchen. "Would you rather eat in here?"

"No. I've been looking forward to meeting your family all day." Helen's actions hadn't indicated that attitude.

"Good. I saved you a spot next to me." Lane handed her the bowl and nudged her forward. "You're going to get the full Donnelly family experience tonight. Just like I got the Trent experience yesterday."

"Does that mean I get the same after-dinner experience too?" Helen gave her a sideways smile.

"We'll see. That's still up in the air." Lane pulled out a chair at the dining-room table and motioned for her to sit.

Lane's dad gave Helen a wave as he ate, as did Amy, who'd met her after Lane's meltdown over Belinda. She'd sworn her sister to secrecy regarding that morning. Lane went around the table introducing Helen to her remaining two sisters, two brothers, and their respective partners, each one welcoming her. Helen was never going to remember all their names. That would have to come with time. Time. It seemed she was planning a future with Helen without knowing if Helen wanted one with her.

CHAPTER THIRTY

Helen sat at her desk making notes on a new booking. It had been a long week for her so far, and it was only Wednesday. She'd received several new requests from prospective clients to meet regarding her wedding-planning services. Staying busy helped keep Lane from invading her thoughts. She'd thought she was in love before, but it had never felt like this. The constant longing to be near Lane—to hear her voice—was overwhelming. Helen was thankful that Lane had been so forgiving...again, although she hadn't heard from her all week and wasn't sure she truly had forgiven her for having second thoughts, or if Lane was just giving her time to be certain about what she wanted. Helen hadn't had time to dwell on the lack of contact. In fact, since Sunday she'd barely had any time to talk to Lane, let alone see her, but she really wanted to be with her.

"Danny, Bobby, Maria, Emily, Amy..." She tossed her pen onto the desk. "I'm never going to remember all their names." Except for little Matty, who had crawled up into her lap after dinner. Apparently the two-year-old had never met a stranger he didn't like. Helen wondered what they all thought of her—Lane's ridiculously rude friend who was late for dinner. The only one she'd had much interaction with was Lane's father. And Amy. She smiled. That was over breakfast when she'd taken Lane home drunk, and she'd admitted that she liked her.

The distance over the past few days had been necessary. It had been a wonderful evening, but also saddening. Lane hadn't gone home with Helen after dinner—she hadn't asked her to. Lane seemed to have noticed Helen's mood change. It wasn't intentional. The sadness had hit her out of the blue. Being included in Lane's family dinner should've made her happy, but it had done just the opposite. The relationship Lane had with her mother and father was so wonderful. They were clearly supportive and embraced both her lifestyle and her chosen career path. Helen's family only seemed to tolerate hers. How could two families be so different?

The phone buzzing in her pocket got her attention. She took it out and groaned as she looked at the screen. This was the third time Audrey had called. Helen really didn't want to deal with her antics today, but she was Darcy's sister. She hit the green button and put the phone to her ear. "Hello. I've been trying to reach you." A total lie.

"That's not true. I've called you several times, and you haven't answered."

Helen ignored the bait. She wouldn't argue with Audrey. "What can I do for you?"

"I need to know where we're at on Darcy's wedding plans." It sounded like Audrey was in traffic.

"I'm at my office. Why don't you come by, and we can discuss it."

"I can't. I'm on my way out of town." Unavailable again. "The band agent tells me that you haven't booked the band I chose yet."

And she wasn't going to. "No. Lane and I were thinking Darcy wanted something more traditional for music. Lane recalled her talking about a DJ in the past." She'd already put down the deposit on a fairly popular DJ she'd used before.

"Lane isn't the matron of honor. I am."

"I'm aware, but Darcy asked her to help."

"Sounds to me like she's getting in the way." A horn honked in the background. "Just book the band. I'll be back on Monday, and we can go over the rest of the arrangements."

"Sounds good. Have a safe trip." The line went dead. No way was Helen changing her plans for the music. Booking a heavy metal band for the country club would be a disaster. She clicked a few keys on her computer, bringing up a Google search. There had to be some sort of ordinance about it that would prevent Audrey from pushing them into it.

Helen's phone buzzed again. It was a bride-to-be she'd spoken to earlier in the day. She hit the button and sent it to voice mail. Wasting any more time talking to her would only send her anxiety racing. The woman wanted all the services she provided, plus wanted her to engage all her vendors for half the cost. Then she had the bright idea that it was okay to charge the guests to fund the wedding. Helen shook her head. It wouldn't be the first time she'd had that request, but Helen wouldn't do that. Sharing your special day with the people you love was a privilege, and no one should be expected to pay for it except the bride and groom.

She put all thoughts wedding out of her head and focused on making plans for tonight, then typed in a quick text to Lane. *Have dinner with me tonight?*

Who is this? Lane was too funny.

The woman who gave you the best orgasm you've ever had. Helen hit send and then immediately flushed. The sex between them had been mind-blowing.

Oh...her. I wondered when you'd be in touch. Lane added a fire emoji at the end. *Do you mind picking me up around six at 555 Main Street?*

I'll be there with bells on. Helen had no idea where that was, but she'd find it.

Bubbles appeared, and another text came through from Lane. *I'm glad you texted...I miss your face.*

The immense joy that spread through Helen when she read the text was unexpected, not something she'd felt with any woman she'd been involved with. Helen couldn't wait to get through the next couple of tasks so she could finally see her.

Time passed quickly, and Helen glanced at the address Lane had given her for her family's plumbing business before she packed her bag and headed to the door.

She pulled up in front of the business and sat in the car for a moment. This relationship was really moving forward, and she was happy about it. She wanted to be here at Lane's place of business to pick Lane up and do anything and everything with her. The music stilled when she hit the power button. She took in a deep breath before she got out of the car and walked up the pavement to the business, glancing at the letters written across the sign above the door. *Donnelly Plumbing, Family Owned Since 1985.* It was clear that Lane took pride in being part of her family's successful business, and Helen thought that was wonderful.

Lane's dad met Helen at the door. "Your parents having any more plumbing issues?"

"No. None at all. Thanks for taking care of it for them."

"Tell them they can call me anytime." He raised his hands palms up. "No need to wait on someone else. I can take care of it for them right away."

"That's sweet of you, but I would hate to bother you again." Besides, her parents would expect him to do the job at wholesale rather than pay him for his time—a pattern that helped the rich get richer.

"It's no bother. I'm happy to do it for any friend of my baby girl." He handed Helen his business card. "I wrote my personal number on the back."

"Thank you." Helen slipped the card into her pocket.

Lane came from a back office looking radiant. "Sorry. I just had to finish one last account and then shut down the computer. I hope my dad's not boring you with interesting plumbing facts." She slung a large bag over her shoulder.

"No. Not at all. I find plumbing fascinating."

Lane laughed. "Clearly, you need to get out more." She went to the door. "I'll see you tomorrow, Dad."

Helen hit the button on the key fob, and the car chirped as the doors unlocked. "You didn't tell me you did the books for your dad's business."

Lane pulled the back door open and put her bag inside. "You didn't ask." She looked over the top of the car at Helen and grinned before she got in.

"Fair enough." Helen got into the car and fired the engine. "Where to?" They hadn't decided where to eat.

"Your place. I'm cooking tonight."

"Well, now I'm excited." The thought of taking Lane home with her sent a thrill through Helen.

"You weren't before?" Lane's mouth dropped open. "Careful. You might not get dessert."

Helen chuckled. "How about, I'm more excited." For both dinner and all the things she planned to do to Lane after.

"That's better." Lane smiled at her, and glorious feelings flooded her. It wasn't like Helen to be public about her romantic interests, but with Lane, she wanted everyone to know they were dating—wanted to splash it all over social media.

"I honestly wasn't sure if you'd want to see me again. After

Sunday night—showing up late and all." The second thoughts were completely gone now.

Lane's green eyes sparkled, a bit of moisture clouding them. "I get it. I really do. I wonder how this is all going to play out as well, and sometimes it scares me too. But I want to see it through." Lane reached across the console and took Helen's hand.

Warmth washed through Helen as she realized Lane understood her and was possibly the woman she could be with for the rest of her life. She only hoped Lane felt the same.

CHAPTER THIRTY-ONE

Lane danced around the kitchen as she took several items from the grocery bag and carried them across to the sink. She'd planned to make something more extravagant the next time she wound up at Helen's for dinner, but Helen's invitation had come late, which meant she would prepare one of her favorite standby meals. Thankfully the market near the plumbing shop had all the ingredients she needed to make her Roma tomato and vegetable pasta.

"How can I help?" Helen handed Lane a freshly poured glass of wine.

"You're doing plenty standing right there looking gorgeous." Lane held up the glass before she sipped.

Helen's cheeks reddened, which made her look even more beautiful. "I'd really like to help you."

"Do you have a colander squirreled away somewhere here? I could use that and a cutting board."

"On it." Helen pulled open a cabinet, took out a colander, and set it in the sink, then proceeded to the other side of the kitchen and slid a large wooden cutting board from its place between the wall and a couple of celebrity cookbooks.

"Do you like to cook?" Lane hadn't noticed the books when she was here before.

"I do, but I don't have a chance very often." She set the board onto the counter. "Cooking for one isn't much fun."

Lane dumped the bag of Roma tomatoes into a colander and ran water over them before she removed them and set them on the board.

She peeled a small onion and proceeded to chop it into small equal chunks, then did the same with the tomatoes.

Helen emptied the rest of the ingredients from the bag, which included zucchini and yellow squash, basil, garlic, vegetable broth, Parmesan cheese, and a loaf of sourdough bread. "Can I prep the basil and garlic for you?"

"That would be lovely." Lane grinned as she continued chopping tomatoes. "Can you point me in the direction of a large sauté pan?"

Helen pointed. "To the left of the stove."

Lane pulled open the cabinet and widened her eyes at the huge variety of pans. A would-be-chef's paradise. She took out a medium-sized pan, found the matching lid, and set it on the stove. The Viking gas range ticked as she turned the knob to light the burner. "I would kill for one of these."

"No need for violence." Helen gave her a twisted grin. "You're welcome to use it anytime." The board rattled as Helen smashed several cloves of garlic before she reached across the counter to the salt container, took a pinch, and sprinkled it onto the garlic, then began chopping the cloves finely. She dried the freshly washed basil before she chopped and cut it in with the garlic. "What's next?"

"We'll need boiling water to cook the pasta." Lane pointed to the box on the counter.

"On it." Helen filled a pot with water, placed it on one of the other burners, and added a few pinches of salt.

Lane drizzled olive oil in the bottom of the sauté pan and rotated it to cover the bottom before she added the onions and stirred. "I'm ready for you." She tipped her chin toward the garlic-basil mixture.

Helen scraped the green pulp from the board with the knife and, with her finger, pushed the remnants from the blade into the pan. The pan sizzled, and the wonderful scent of garlic and herbs filled the air. Once the onions became translucent, Lane cupped the chopped tomatoes in her hands and dropped them into the pan.

"You make this often?" Helen watched her intently.

Lane nodded. "It's my go-to comfort food." She poured half a carton of broth into the pan and then covered it.

Helen poured the box of pasta into the water. "I can see why. It smells wonderful." She set the timer on her watch.

"Now we let it simmer while the pasta cooks." Lane glanced around the kitchen, trying to locate the loaf of sourdough bread. "We need to warm the bread also."

"Already in the oven."

"Aren't you the prepared one?" Lane hadn't seen Helen do that. She must've gotten that ready while Lane was dealing with the tomatoes. It seemed they got along in the kitchen together as well as they did in bed. "I like this." Lane waggled her finger between them. "You and I working together in here."

Helen moved closer, leaned in for a kiss. "I like you and me together, period."

Lane lost herself in the kiss. Those were words Lane had never, in her wildest dreams, thought she'd hear from Helen—never expected them to send chills through her the way they did. Lane's world had been sideswiped by an evil queen who, in reality, had turned out to be her princess charming.

The timer buzzed, and their moment was interrupted, thankfully, or they would've abandoned dinner, and the dish would be ruined.

Helen drained the pasta. "Where do you want this?"

"Right in here." Lane lifted the lid off the tomato mixture.

The sauce splashed onto Helen's blouse as she poured it into the pan. "Whoops." Helen set down the pan, wet a towel, and dabbed at several spots to remove the sauce.

"This still needs to sit for a minute to soak up the juices." Lane placed the lid on the pan and turned off the burner before she captured Helen's lips with her own, indulging in the sweet taste of wine on Helen's tongue. All thoughts of dinner flew from her head as the kiss drove her over the edge. "Why don't I help you change?" She began unfastening the buttons.

"Absolutely not." Helen grasped Lane's hands. "I don't want to ruin your meal."

"It's always better the second day." Lane kissed her again.

Helen broke the kiss and touched her lips lightly several times. "I totally believe that, but I want to have plenty of energy for the tasks I plan to perform tonight."

"Oh, really?" Lane raised an eyebrow and then spun back to the stove. "Then let's get this night moving." She plated the pasta. "I might fight you for first up on those." Her stomach growled loudly. Apparently, it wasn't going to let her abandon dinner either.

"What was that?" Helen chuckled.

"I'm starving. I haven't eaten since this morning," she said shyly. "Except for a power bar around two."

"Wait. You were going to forgo food for pleasure?" Helen took the bread out of the oven, put it into a bowl, and carried it to the table. "I can't have you passing out on me."

"I would literally be putty in your hands." Lane winked as she grated fresh Parmesan on each serving.

Helen carried their wineglasses to the table. "I should've known. You haven't touched your wine."

"I want to enjoy it with the meal." She, in fact, didn't want to get tipsy tonight. She had plans after dinner to spend the remainder of the night exploring all the dips and swells of Helen's body.

"I can't wait to try it." Helen picked up the bowls, held one up, and took in a breath. "This smells fantastic." She set the bowls on the table before she pulled out a chair for Lane.

Lane smiled widely when Helen complimented her on the meal. "I don't know why, but it feels good for someone to brag about my cooking."

She sat in the chair Helen offered, and Helen took the adjacent spot.

"It should feel good. You've created a delicious meal." Helen forked a few bowties and slid them into her mouth. "Oh my God. This is delicious. Five stars, easy."

"When I cooked for Belinda, she usually didn't act like she enjoyed it." Lane shook her head. "She was so concerned about calories, she had an aversion to eating."

"Her loss." Helen forked another bowtie, along with a chunk of zucchini, and held it up. "I'm enjoying this meal more than any I've had in any restaurant."

"Even the ravioli at Basilico?"

"Yes. Even though I adore that meal." Helen placed her hand on her heart. "This is so much better."

Lane tilted her head. "You're going to get really lucky tonight."

"Ooh. Great meals come with perks. I like it." Helen ripped off a piece of bread and trailed it through the sauce in her bowl. "I bet this meal doesn't taste half as good as you."

Lane picked up her wine, sipped, and relaxed into her chair. She stared at Helen above the rim of the glass. "Eat fast, and you can find out."

Chapter Thirty-Two

When Lane awoke, she was sideways in the bed, with Helen's arm and leg draped across her. "Good God," she mumbled. Helen had fucked her—satisfied her completely and then fucked her again, stretching her wonderfully sore muscles. No regrets about this exercise. She didn't play like this often, but she really enjoyed it with Helen. Sex with Belinda had never been like this—never been close to this kind of passion.

The thought of Helen under her tongue again made Lane's stomach flutter. She remembered Helen's heels digging into her legs as she settled between her thighs, nails digging into her shoulders as Helen's hips lifted into her, begging for more—for her to delve deeper, the flutter moving south, turning into a burning pulse as pressure built. When Lane ran the flat of her tongue across Helen's clit, the glorious cry that had escaped her lips pushed Lane closer to climax. Lane had been ready to come again immediately. When Helen had taken her again, her muscles had pulsed and tightened around Helen's fingers. A spike of pleasure had rushed through her as Helen had sucked a nipple hard into her mouth, raked it with her teeth as she pumped into her.

She stretched and found the wonderful soreness of her muscles again. Helen was definitely not insecure during sex. All the ways she'd touched her last night had proved that fact. Helen's eyes were closed, and she appeared completely relaxed now, her expression nothing like the pleasure Lane had seen on her face during the night. Lane watched her sleep, listening to the soft breaths coming from her chest as it rose and fell. Lane wasn't done with her yet. She traced a finger around Helen's nipple and saw it come alive.

Helen opened her eyes and smiled. "Good morning."

"Good morning." Lane raised her eyebrows as she pinched Helen's nipple. "Ready to go again?"

"The answer to that question will always be yes." Helen rolled onto her. "You first."

Lane had never experienced such easy and pleasurable lovemaking with any woman. "Do you spend this much time pleasing the other women you sleep with?"

Helen propped herself up on her elbows, her expression sobered as she stared into Lane's eyes, her own impossibly blue. "I'm not sleeping with any other women."

Lane believed her and regretted asking the question. Honestly didn't know why she had. "I like it when you look at me like I'm the sexiest woman on the planet." Lane trapped the tip of her tongue between her teeth.

"Good, because you are." Helen's eyes darkened. "I've thought that for a long time."

"You know just the right things to say." That was a tidbit Lane had pondered since Helen had told her that was why she'd been so cold to her in the past—she was trying to hold back while Lane was engaged to someone else. In recent weeks, Helen had exposed herself to Lane on the deepest level. Lane had seen the real Helen, not the one she presented to everyone else, and she liked her. Not even Helen's family saw her in such a vulnerable state.

CHAPTER THIRTY-THREE

Helen sat behind her desk, closed her eyes, and recalled the scent of Lane's hair—imagined her face buried in it around Lane's neck as she brought her to orgasm. The woody floral scent of amber was lovely, one she would always associate with Lane from now on. She was beginning to really like their nights together—waking up with Lane in her arms. It had been over a week since she'd spent the night solo in her bed. She'd been so used to sleeping alone she hadn't realized how lonely she was, and now she was growing accustomed to having Lane around—making love to her nightly. That wasn't a bad thing, was it?

The door to her office burst open, and Darcy stood in front of her desk with her hands on her hips.

Helen popped out of her chair. "Are you okay?"

"No. I'm not. I'm angry." Darcy let her arms drop to her sides. "Audrey tells me that you've been excluding her from the some of the wedding arrangements I asked her to handle."

Oh, shit. Helen had known that decision would eventually bite her in the ass. She remained calm. "Why don't you have a seat, and we can discuss Audrey's participation." She walked to the chairs in the corner of the room.

"I don't want to sit. I want an answer." Darcy didn't budge.

"Okay." Helen went back to her desk and picked up the binder she'd made for Darcy's wedding. "First off, Audrey isn't available to go with us. When we've made plans to meet, she's either not shown up or, in the event that she does, is too busy to participate and leaves soon after she arrives." *Barking orders on the way out.*

Darcy narrowed her eyes. "This is all Lane's doing because I didn't choose her as my maid of honor." She paced across the room.

"I wouldn't say that at all." How did Darcy jump to that conclusion so quickly?

Darcy spun back around to face her. "That's what Audrey said, and it's certainly what it looks like."

"She seriously wanted to serve carnival food at your wedding. The heavy metal band choice was the last straw. Lane and I were both shocked—that's when we decided to circumvent her." Helen's voice rose. "Is that the kind of wedding you want? I doubt it's the kind of wedding your parents are expecting to be held at their country club." Helen's mother would come unglued if she let that happen.

"I can't believe Lane would do that to my sister—to me. I should've known this would happen. She's been really different since her wedding turned out to be a failure."

Was that what Darcy called it? Helen had much stronger words for it than that—catastrophe, for one, which was not Lane's fault. "I don't think that has anything to do with it." Helen needed to defuse this situation quickly. "It's clear that you and Audrey don't have the same tastes, and since she doesn't have time, we thought we would just move forward and do it ourselves."

"It has everything to do with it. Lane is trying to live her wedding dreams through mine, and I won't let that happen." Darcy spun and rushed out of the office, heels clicking on the hardwood floor.

"Wait." Helen rushed after her. "That's not it at all." Audrey had really fed Darcy a load of bull and apparently given her some reason to believe it.

"She's going to have to explain herself to me," Darcy said over her shoulder.

"Please don't do anything rash. She *is* your best friend."

"I'm not so sure of that right now." Darcy was gone, and Helen couldn't stop her.

"Shit." Helen raced back into her office, found her phone, and hit the button for Lane. It rang a few times and then went to voice mail. "Lane. It's Helen. Call me back. I need to talk to you now." She typed in a quick text message. *Call me. Audrey is causing trouble.* She had to warn Lane before Darcy got to her. Helen's phone rang in her hand.

Thinking it was Lane, she hit the button quickly and pressed it to her ear. It wasn't Lane.

❖

Lane was helping with inventory in the back warehouse when she heard Darcy's voice in the front area of the plumbing shop. What was she doing here, and why was she being so loud? That was a silly question. Darcy was never quiet. Excited to see her, Lane highlighted her place in the spreadsheet, put down her tablet, and headed through the doorway.

Once in the front area, she could see Darcy, who was pacing back and forth in front of Emily, Lane's sister. Emily looked Lane's way, widened her eyes, and clenched her teeth. Darcy was clearly upset about something.

Lane rushed toward them. "I didn't expect to see you here today. What's wrong?"

"I'm angry, so angry I can hardly speak." Darcy fisted her hands in the air in front of her. "I trusted you to do the right thing, and you just couldn't do it."

"What couldn't I do?" Lane was truly confused.

"All I asked you to do was help Audrey with the arrangements for my wedding, and instead you totally excluded her."

"What? That's not true. I've asked her to help—to participate in everything I've done, but she's never available." Lane's stomach knotted.

Darcy shook her head. "God. How could I have been so stupid?" She continued to pace. "Helen said you'd been purposely planning without her this whole time."

The back of Lane's neck tingled. How could Helen have blamed this all on her? "We aren't purposely excluding her." Darcy seemed to be spinning out of control and reaching crazy conclusions, and Lane couldn't stop her. "Neither of us thought Audrey was serious about any of it. She rarely showed up for the appointments. So, Helen and I agreed to continue doing some of the legwork without her...for her."

"You should've run that decision by me first. Now my sister is hurt, and my mom is livid." Darcy bolted forward and held a finger in front of Lane's face. "As of now, *you* are out of the planning."

Lane felt dizzy as she blinked back tears. "And the wedding? Am I out of that as well?"

"That's still up in the air. I'm not sure I can get a replacement this late in the game." Darcy spun and strutted toward the door. "I expected more from you."

A replacement? Was she that interchangeable? "Darcy, what can I do to fix this?" Lane pleaded, tears streaming down her cheeks.

"Stay out of Audrey's way." Darcy stopped and turned before exiting. "I'm not sure we can still be friends after this." She pushed open the door and left the building.

Lane ran out the door after her. "Darcy, please." She grasped Darcy's arm.

"Stop." Darcy yanked her arm free. "Or I'll have to remove you from everything, right now."

"You would seriously do that?" Lane's stomach lurched to her throat.

"After what you did—ruined my relationship with my sister and my mother. Yes. I would seriously do that."

"I didn't intend to—"

"It doesn't matter what you intended. That's what happened. So just steer clear of me for the time being." Darcy jumped into her car and raced out of the parking lot.

What had just happened? Lane stood on the sidewalk feeling light-headed as she wiped the tears from her face. She'd just been reduced from best friend and almost maid of honor to nothing. It seemed best friends meant something different to Darcy than it did to Lane. Maybe she was right. By excluding Audrey, Lane had clearly not been the best friend in this case either.

CHAPTER THIRTY-FOUR

Helen broke the speed limit ten times over as she sped to the hospital. Her mother had barely been able to speak when Helen had answered the phone. All she'd said was, "Get to the hospital. Now." Helen hit the button for Lane, and the phone rang through the car speakers. She let it ring several times before she ended the call and hit the button for Will. After two rings he answered and said, "I'm on my way."

"What's going on?"

"I'm not exactly sure. It was difficult getting anything out of Mom because she was so upset. I think Dad—" Will's voice faded in and out as he spoke. Fucking wireless signal was breaking up.

"You think Dad what?" Helen shouted at the phone.

"I think he had a heart attack."

"Oh my God. No." *Please no.* Anxiety hit Helen hard, her own heart racing, as she fought to keep her wits about her. "Did anyone call Gwen?"

"She's on her way too. I'll see you there. I need to call Ash." The line went dead.

Helen immediately hit the button to call Lane, and it went straight to voice mail. She wanted—needed to talk to her. She couldn't leave a message, not about this. She wouldn't use her dad's emergency to force Lane to speak to her.

"Hey, Siri. Text Lydia," Helen shouted into the windshield. She had to let her boss know she'd left the office in her assistant's hands. Lydia wouldn't like it, but Teigen was capable.

Siri responded with, "What would you like to say?"

"I have a family emergency. I left Teigen in charge. I'll update you later."

Siri read the message back to her, and Helen directed her to send it.

When Helen arrived at the emergency room, she rushed straight to the woman behind the sliding-glass window. "I'm looking for my father, William Trent. He was brought in just a little while ago."

The woman clicked a few buttons on her computer. "He's been taken upstairs to surgery. Take the main elevator to the third floor. The waiting room will be to your right, around the corner and down the hall."

"Thanks." She threw the word over her shoulder as she rushed to the bank of elevators. There she punched the button several times and watched the red numbers change as they each went in different directions. The elevator to her left pinged, and she moved quickly to it, waiting impatiently as people exited.

When she arrived in the waiting room, her mom was sitting all alone in the corner staring up at the TV, which was playing an HGTV home-improvement show. Her usually perfect makeup was smeared around red, tear-soaked eyes.

Caroline shot to her feet as Helen rushed to her and held her in her arms. "What happened?"

Caroline blotted the tears rimming her eyelids. "He was working out as usual and said he felt winded. After he took a shower and then came down for breakfast, he was nauseous." She shook her head. "He's been eating healthy, and his cholesterol is way down." She clasped Helen's shoulder. "You've seen him. He's lost twenty pounds. I thought it couldn't be a heart attack."

Will appeared and gave Caroline a hug before guiding her to one of the chairs to sit. Helen took the chair next to her.

"Then the chest pain began." Tears began to well in Caroline's eyes again. "By the time the ambulance arrived, he was pale, breathless, and in severe pain." She glanced at Helen. "He wanted me to drive him."

"You did the right thing, Mom. They have all the meds to treat him in the ambulance." He might not have survived the drive to the hospital otherwise.

"The doctor gave him nitroglycerine pills to open his arteries and whisked him into surgery. They're putting in a stent to unclog one of them."

"Has he been feeling bad?" Will asked.

"He's been tired, but he's been working more to catch up from our vacation." She shrugged. "We attributed it to that."

"Sometimes the symptoms are hard to see." Helen took her mother's hand and squeezed.

"He had some heartburn after dinner last night. We had Mexican, so we didn't think anything of it." Caroline plucked a tissue from the box on the side table and blew her nose.

Gwen rushed into the room. "Is he okay?"

"He's in surgery. He had a heart attack." Helen noted Gwen's disheveled state, wearing black sports leggings, an oversized cropped purple hoodie, and sneakers. She must've been at the gym.

Gwen came at her hot. "This is partly because of you, you know."

"Me?" The back of Helen's neck heated as she stared up at Gwen.

"Yes. You. All he wanted is for you to be successful—to find a career that meshes with the rest of the family, and you just can't do that."

Was that truly the case? Was she a huge disappointment to her father? Has he been lying to her every time he said he was proud of her for following her own path?

"Gwen. Stop." Caroline's voice was firm. "Your sister did nothing to make this happen." She squeezed Helen's hand. "Your father had a partially blocked artery, and they're fixing it."

The doctor came through the double doors and walked straight to Caroline. "We were able to insert the stent without any issues. He's awake and doing well."

Caroline put her hand to her chest. "That's such a relief. Can I see him?"

"Of course." The doctor glanced at each of them and held up two fingers. "Just two of you for now." He turned to lead them.

"I'm going in first." Gwen grabbed her mother's arm and moved her toward the door.

That wasn't surprising. Each of them had a special relationship with their father, and Gwen had worshipped him for as long as Helen could remember. Pleasing her father had been Gwen's number-one goal as a child, and that hadn't changed much as she'd grown into an adult.

Ten minutes later, Gwen came back through the doors. "One of you can go in now. He said he'd been feeling tired and run-down for a while but chalked it up to work." She grabbed Helen's forearm as she passed. "I'm sorry." Tears streamed down her face.

"It's okay." Considering the circumstances, Helen would give her a pass today, but never again would she let Gwen's opinion define her.

"You go." Will cocked his head toward the entrance.

She pushed through the double doors into the post-op area and spotted her mother standing near the third bed. Caroline waved her forward as she came closer.

"Hi." Relief rushed Helen when she saw her father, eyes open, smiling at her mother. "How are you feeling?"

He placed his hand over his heart. "Like they lifted a million pounds from my chest."

"They probably did." Helen gripped her father's hand, letting the warmth of it heat the ice that had formed in hers in the waiting room. "They took good care of you?"

He nodded. "They gave me what they called a twilight anesthesia. I was awake for the whole thing but didn't feel anything."

Helen drew her eyebrows together. "Really? That sounds scary."

"It wasn't at all. There was a big screen where I could see everything they were doing. I found it fascinating." At least her dad was feeling good about the procedure.

Helen glanced at her mom and then back at her dad. "I've been thinking about my future and was wondering if you'd like me to join you in the firm." That was impulsive, but she would do it if she truly was part of the reason for her father's stress.

He scrunched his eyebrows together. "Your sister's been getting to you again."

She nodded. "But still, I can come back if you need help, and if that's what you want."

"Is that what you want?" He raised his eyebrows. "Will it make you happy?"

"No. Not really." Helen shook her head. She hated it—the legal profession was boring and unfulfilling—she'd never learn to love it.

"I've never been happier doing anything else than what I'm doing right now."

"That's all that matters to me…no matter what your sister says." He smiled and squeezed her hand.

"Thanks, Daddy." She leaned in and gave her father a hug, letting his love and warmth fill her.

"Besides, you'd never get to see that girl you fancy. Lane? Is that right?"

"I'm not sure I'm going to see much of her anyway."

"That's too bad. She seemed to care for you." He kept eye contact. "Why else would she go up against your sister the way she did."

Her mother laughed. "Not just Gwen. She put us both in our place, didn't she?"

"She did at that." Helen smiled softly, saddened by the reality of the situation.

"You should call her," her father said. "Turn on the Trent charm."

Her mother chimed in. "We'll have her to a proper dinner after your father recovers."

"Sure." That probability was slim, but she would try to talk to Lane and explain what had happened with Darcy. "I should go and let Will come in for a bit." She kissed her dad on the cheek. "I'm really glad you're okay, Daddy." She turned and headed across the room, hit the metal plate on the wall to open the double doors, and walked through them to where Will and Gwen were waiting on the other side. "You can go in. He's doing good." She touched Will on the shoulder as she passed but didn't stop. She headed straight to the elevator and out of the hospital. There was no way she could spend another minute with Gwen, apology or not.

When Helen got into her car, she couldn't stop the tears. She gripped the steering wheel and sobbed ugly, heaving sobs for several minutes. She'd almost lost her father and couldn't have done a thing to prevent it. She focused on her breathing to calm herself. In and out, in and out. It took a few long minutes, but she felt her anxiety subside and loosened her grip on the steering wheel. Yet she still couldn't clear her unease totally. She felt nauseous. Helen's dad was her hero, the only one who ever supported her in her job choices, her career path. She couldn't lose him.

It wasn't lost on her that Lane had been the first one she'd called after she'd received the call from her mother. Why had she done that? Because she needed a safe spot, and Lane had become that for her. She let loose of the steering wheel, wiped away her tears, and composed herself before she took her phone from her bag. She had a missed phone call, a voice mail from Lane, and several text messages on the screen.

Answer your phone.

Are you too much of a coward to even speak with me?

I think we need to take a break.

Helen hit the button, and Lane's angry voice blared through the speakers. Not the sweet tone she was accustomed to. "I can't believe you told Darcy I excluded Audrey. You've made her hate me." Lane sniffed, and Helen imagined the tears on her face. "Was that your goal? To separate me from my best friend? You promised me I could trust you. You're no better than Belinda. I can't be with someone who lies to me." Helen felt Lane's words deep in the pit of her stomach. The mixed emotions in Lane's voice hurt more than she could've imagined.

She typed in a simple message. *I'm sorry.*

She would make this right with Darcy, but that would probably be the end of her and Lane. Helen closed her eyes and blew out a breath as she dropped her phone into her bag. She couldn't deal with this mess right now. Her whole world had almost fallen apart. Lane was so angry that she wasn't sure anything she would say would make her listen. Her own heart wasn't strong enough for this kind of stress. She wiped the tears from her eyes, got out of her car, and walked back into the hospital.

CHAPTER THIRTY-FIVE

L ane couldn't eat, couldn't sleep. Her stomach churned. She'd been crying nonstop since last night. Now she felt more than empty inside and didn't know how to fix it. She'd been stunned by Darcy's accusations and furious that Helen had led her to believe that Lane was the one at fault. The fact that Helen wouldn't answer her calls told her everything, but Lane had only herself to blame for trusting her. She should've fought her feelings—known better than to fall for someone who saw the world in such a black-and-white manner. That wasn't completely true. Recently, Lane had seen a very different side of Helen, the soft, vulnerable part she hid from the rest of the world, so much more of Helen than she'd intended—much more than she'd expected. It was that Helen she'd fallen in love with.

"You're up early." Iris came from her bedroom.

"Couldn't sleep." She swiped at her eyes as the tears began to well again. She'd thought she was all out of them.

Iris rushed to the couch and sat next to her. "What's wrong?"

"Darcy threw me out of her wedding." She blubbered the words through a sob. In that moment, she'd felt ambushed and helpless, unable to stop it from happening.

"What?" Iris's eyebrows rocketed up. "Why would she do that?"

"She found out that we were excluding Audrey from the wedding planning, and Helen blamed me for all of it." Lane couldn't get Darcy's stare out of her mind. Her eyes had burned through her like lasers.

"What the hell?" Iris scrunched her eyebrows together. "Why would Helen do that?"

"I have no idea, but she did." A tornado of thoughts swirled around in her brain. Lane couldn't place all the blame on Helen. Lane had been an equal partner in the deception.

"Have you talked to her?" Iris tucked her leg under herself as she sat sideways on the couch.

"Tried to call her. Texted multiple times." Lane shrugged. "All I got back was a text that said I'm sorry."

"Whoa. That doesn't seem like Helen." Iris lightly rubbed her back.

"I've never been so hurt and humiliated in my life." And to some degree, it was her own fault.

"Well, we both know that's not true." Iris smiled softly. She was right.

"It's a close second." Lane had let Helen into her heart, and now she felt broken and betrayed. She was a huge, messy jumble of emotions. Lane wiped her face with the palms of her hands and shook her head. "I've been living in this fairy tale like nothing else matters, ignoring the fact that we come from very different worlds."

"Stop that." Iris rolled her eyes. "It doesn't make any difference what worlds you come from if you love each other."

"Yeah. I know. But that doesn't help me much right now." Tears spilled from her eyes again. Lane didn't understand how a woman she'd just fallen for could impact her this way so quickly.

Iris squeezed Lane's forearm. "You have to talk to her."

"Too late." Lane held up her phone to show her the final text she'd sent to Helen last night. *You showed me who you were when we first met. I don't know why I thought you would change.*

"Oh, honey." Iris gathered Lane into her arms. "There has to be an explanation—some misunderstanding. There just has to be."

"I'm not sure there is. Otherwise, she would've called me back yesterday." The disappointment she'd seen in Darcy's eyes had rocked her to her core. Her heart had hammered in her ears as the back of her neck had burned, and the room had suddenly grown smaller.

Iris slipped her foot from under her and stood. "How about I call her to find out what's going on?"

"No." Lane grabbed Iris's hand. "Let it alone. I need resolve this situation with Darcy first."

Iris sank back onto the couch. "You don't have to choose, you know."

"Sure feels like it." In the state Lane was in now, she didn't really know which woman was more important to her.

She'd truly wanted to pursue a relationship with Helen, but she'd just watched a lifelong friendship with Darcy disintegrate because of her involvement with Helen. None of it made sense, and she wasn't sure she could repair either relationship.

CHAPTER THIRTY-SIX

After an overnight stay in the hospital, Helen's father was back at home recovering. The house had quickly become crowded with family members, which meant emotions were running high, and Helen didn't have much to do besides argue with Gwen. So, back to work Helen went.

She had arranged to meet Darcy at the country club to go over some of the last details for her wedding and had asked her to bring Audrey along so they could finalize everything. She wanted Darcy to be aware of the choices Audrey was making for her. She hadn't heard from Lane since she'd effectively broken it off with her but hoped Darcy had made amends with Lane, and she would be there as well. It would be awkward, but Helen would get through it.

Darcy was already in the banquet room when Helen arrived. Audrey was absent again, and Lane was nowhere to be seen either. Helen strolled across the room toward her and set her bag on one of the tables.

Darcy gave her a solemn smile. "I'm sorry to hear about your father. I'm glad he's doing okay."

Helen scrunched her eyebrows together. She hadn't told Darcy what had happened.

"My dad told me. Your mom let the board know."

"Oh." That made sense. "Thank you." Helen glanced around the room. "Where's Lane?"

"After the way she's treated my sister, I don't want her help any longer...If you can call it that."

"Are you kidding me?" Helen didn't usually speak to clients harshly, but after the week she'd had, she needed to at this point. "You still believe Audrey?"

"She's my sister. I have to."

"You absolutely *do not* have to believe anything Audrey tells you, and you shouldn't. Apparently, she's lied to you about this whole process."

Darcy's eyes widened and her nostrils flared. "What makes you think I won't fire you right now?"

"Go ahead." Helen straightened. "In fact, maybe it would be better to let Audrey take care of everything from here on out." Helen glanced around the room. "Where is she, by the way?"

"She couldn't make it."

"Surprise, surprise." Helen rolled her eyes and blew out a quick breath. "During your rehearsal dinner, your wedding, and your carnival-themed heavy metal reception, I want you to think about your choice when your best friend isn't there supporting you and helping with all the details." She grabbed her bag. "I'm done fighting this battle for you."

"Wait." Darcy seemed to panic. "Audrey really tried to ruin my wedding?"

"And my reputation along with it."

Darcy stood stone-faced, apparently taking Helen seriously this time. "I can't believe Audrey would do that."

"Listen. I'm not sure what's going on between you and your sister, but the things Audrey was suggesting would've been very inappropriate for this venue and the type of guests you and your fiancé invited to the wedding. Lane is the *only reason* your wedding is going to be a gorgeous success."

Darcy chewed on her bottom lip. "I've made a big mistake with Lane, haven't I?"

"Yes. I believe you have." That was an understatement.

Darcy blew out a breath. "Can you help me fix it?"

"You're on your own for that one. Unfortunately, Lane isn't speaking to me."

"Yeah. I guess she was pretty upset about what I said to her. I'm sorry I messed that up." Darcy rolled her lips in. "I think she really likes you."

"I'm not so sure about that now." Helen felt nauseous as she recalled the voice mail Lane had left—the tremble in her voice as she told Helen that she'd broken her trust once again. The full-out sob that came through the speaker as Lane told her she couldn't be in a relationship with someone who lied to her.

"I take full responsibility for excluding Audrey," Helen said. "Talk to Lane. Let her know she's still your best friend." Helen's heart hurt more than it ever had before, but her father had just survived a heart attack, and her trouble with Lane didn't seem so important now.

❖

Lane crossed the restaurant to the table where Darcy was sitting. She'd been surprised to receive the text from Darcy mid-morning asking her to meet for lunch. She hoped she wasn't still angry with her but was pretty sure she wouldn't be included in the wedding.

"Thank you for coming." Darcy smiled softly. "I wasn't sure you would."

"Of course I would. No matter how you feel about me." The knot in Lane's stomach tightened as she took the seat across from her. "You're still my best friend, Darcy."

"I'm sorry. I've been horrible to you." Tears welled in Darcy's eyes. "I lost sight of who has my best interests at heart—who's been there for me from the beginning."

A huge weight lifted from Lane's chest, and she had to stop herself from getting up and comforting Darcy. "No. I'm sorry. Instead of ignoring Audrey, I should've let you in on what she was planning." She *had* done that wrong.

"I know now that you were just trying to spare me the anxiety of dealing with what Audrey was trying to do. Essentially ruin my wedding."

Lane nodded. "I believe she was trying to do just that."

"She was probably getting back at me for not being very involved in her big day." Lane shook her head as she looked at the ground. "I guess I'm a little self-centered."

"You? Noooo." Lane grinned.

"It's not intentional. I don't think before I act." Darcy swiped at her tears with her fingers.

"I'm okay with taking second fiddle to you." Lane raised her eyebrows. "But I wasn't okay with you choosing Audrey over me."

"Yeah. That was a mistake." Darcy fidgeted with the silverware. "Would you consider helping me again?"

Lane truly wanted to help but was unsure of whether she should. "I don't know if that's a good idea." She leaned back in her chair. "Audrey and I don't see eye-to-eye on anything."

"Not as a part of the bridal party, as my maid of honor."

"What about Audrey?" Would Darcy be able to handle that conflict?

"Audrey and I had a conversation about it all, and she's agreed to step back and be a bridesmaid."

That would've been an interesting conversation to hear.

The knot in Lane's stomach loosened. It seemed Darcy did value her friendship after all.

"I'd love to help."

"And be…"

"Your maid of honor. Yes. I'd love that too." She wanted nothing more.

"I'm so glad to hear it." Darcy reached across the table and squeezed Lane's hand. "Thank you for forgiving me for being such a dolt."

"Wow. This a first." Lane glanced around the half-full restaurant as she pointed her fingers at Darcy. "Darcy Hampton over here calling herself a dolt."

"I threatened to fire Helen, and then she quit."

"Seriously?" Lane hadn't expected to hear that. "What are you going to do?"

"We worked it out." Darcy relaxed into her chair. "She told me how instrumental you've been in all the arrangements." Darcy stared into Lane's eyes. "Helen really cares about you."

"I'm not so sure about that." The betrayal Lane felt was still strong.

"She said she'd stay on only if I reconsidered your involvement." She swept the droplets of sweat from her water glass. "She gave you credit for the food, music, and cake choices."

"We made those together. I hope you like all of them." Helen had laid out all the choices, and Lane had just helped her decide.

"They're perfect. You two should go into business together." Darcy smiled. "Unless you're against mixing business with pleasure."

"You threw us together intentionally, didn't you?" Lane was familiar with Darcy's attempts at matchmaking.

"I did." Darcy chuckled. "But I didn't know how much trouble you two would cause together."

"So, you're admitting that all of this is your own fault?"

"I guess it is." Darcy laughed, opened her menu, and glanced at it briefly before looking up at Lane. "Don't let me fuck it up for you."

"I'll see what I can do, but she hasn't been in touch since this situation exploded." Lane's shoulders felt lighter. It seemed Darcy's angry reaction had spun her out of control without letting anyone give her the facts. In response, Lane had immediately gone into defense mode and pushed Helen as far away as she could. What a mess.

"Oh. I forgot to tell you." Darcy dropped her menu to the table. "Her dad had a heart attack."

"What?" Fear tingled through Lane. "Is he okay?" That was why Helen had gone MIA on her—hadn't been in touch at all. It had nothing to do with the wedding.

"He's fine. They put in a stent, and he's recovering at home."

Oh my God. Lane had no idea why she'd turned on Helen so quickly. Heart preservation was her first thought. What was she going to do now? She'd been totally wrong about Helen...again.

CHAPTER THIRTY-SEVEN

When Lane arrived at the bridal suite, everyone was set up at their makeup stations facing the wide, connecting mirrors on the wall, and Iris was working on one of the bridesmaids. Since this wedding had a larger wedding party than usual, they'd brought in another makeup artist to assist.

"This new girl is excellent. She's already taken care of half the group." Iris touched Lane's chin, moved her face from side to side. "You look beautiful today."

"Thank you. Sorry I'm late." Lane glanced at the rest of the bridesmaids. "Looks like you have it all under control." Her anxiety was through the roof.

Iris patted Lane's shoulder. "Take a breath and relax."

Lane sat in one of the makeup chairs and scanned the room through the reflection in the mirror. Helen had to be here somewhere. They'd compared all their bookings, and they both had this event on their calendars.

Lane had been avoiding the inevitable. It had been several days since Darcy had forgiven her and filled her in on Mr. Trent's heart attack. Other than a short text exchange regarding Helen's father's condition, she hadn't been in touch. When Lane had found out about Helen's father, she'd wanted to run to her, comfort her, but she'd still been angry at Helen for misleading Darcy even after Helen had taken the blame.

The whole situation had thrown her into protection mode—she didn't want to get hurt again. She knew how selfish that was, yet she couldn't bring herself to see Helen. She still had mixed feelings about it all—how she'd immediately concluded that Helen had thrown her under the bus to save her own career. The way she'd reacted had been horrible. What did that say about her? Seemed like Lane was the coward now.

"She's here. Just went to check on the guys." Iris took Lane's hand and squeezed. "I gather you haven't talked to her yet?"

Lane shook her head. "No." She'd jumped to a completely wrong conclusion—just as Darcy had done with Lane. She had to apologize, especially if she was going to work with Helen in the future. She would swallow whatever pride she had today and make that happen.

"No time like the present." Iris stared into the mirror and moved sideways to give Lane a view of the door.

Lane's stomach leapt into her throat when she glimpsed Helen as she entered the room. Her usual wardrobe seemed to have changed. Helen wasn't in her typical stiff pencil skirt and jacket. Instead, she wore a lovely sleeveless silk-charmeuse cocktail dress. Her defined, tanned arms popped against the sea-green color, and her sparkly belt wrapped her waist nicely. Helen looked absolutely gorgeous.

A tingle overtook her anxiety as Helen came toward her. Lane had dreamed of this scenario so many times since her conversation with Darcy last week. One minute she wanted to throttle Helen, and the next she wanted to run to her—sweep her up into her arms and tell her everything would be all right. By the end of the night, she hoped to have her emotions in check enough to move forward.

"It's good to see you." Helen smiled. "I'm glad my conversation with Darcy sank in."

"She told me you cleared everything up." Lane chewed at her bottom lip. "Took responsibility for it all."

"I was in charge, and you were only along for the ride." Helen drew in a deep breath. "I didn't want to break up a lifelong friendship."

"Even if it meant losing her business?" Lane needed to know just how important she was to Helen.

"Yes. Well." Helen looked away briefly. "Higher stakes were involved." She swallowed hard before she crossed the room to the champagne bucket. Helen popped the champagne bottle and brought several glasses to the makeup counter. She poured the bride a glass and then proceeded to pour both Lane and Iris a glass before she continued to the bridesmaids.

Lane's stomach tightened. Now she knew. "Guess we've moved up in the hierarchy."

Iris glanced at Lane in the mirror. "You need to talk to her."

Lane shrugged. "This isn't the time or place. Maybe later."

"Don't be so hard on her." Iris frowned. "We both know you'll feel better after you forgive her."

Forgiving Helen wasn't the issue. Lane had already done that. Forgiving herself and opening the door to her heart again was the challenge.

❖

The ceremony had been beautiful, Lane thought, but she hadn't been able to keep her eyes on anything but Helen. They were well into the reception when a random guest spun out onto the dance floor and stumbled into the bride. Helen immediately went into action, whisking the guest into her arms and dancing him off the floor to a table where she sat him in a chair and left him with a couple of his friends while she went to the coffee bar.

Helen was her hero in every way. Why was she hesitating to forgive herself for so quickly jumping to the conclusion that Helen had sold her out? Lane took in a deep breath and headed to the perimeter of the room. She was determined to resolve these feelings here and now.

Lane's eyes were completely locked on Helen as she moved and didn't see the woman who crossed her path. "Oh my God, I'm so sorry." Liquid spilled across her chest as she grasped at the woman's arms to prevent them both from falling. Lane blinked several times when she realized who it was. "Belinda...*What* are you doing here? Are you a friend of the couple?"

"Yes...I mean, no." Belinda shook her head. "I came as a plus one, and when I saw you, I just had to talk to you. I've been attending every wedding I can just to see you." Belinda swirled the red cocktail straw in her drink and glanced up at Lane as she took a sip. The glassy look in her eyes told Lane this wasn't her first. "I've been miserable since you left."

"You're drunk." She'd thought Belinda knew they were done—completely over.

"They say alcohol brings out your true feelings." Belinda touched

Lane's shoulder before she let her hand trail slowly down her arm. "Can we please try again?"

"I can't be involved with someone who wants me only when she's drunk." Lane glanced around the room for someone who might be looking for Belinda. "Where's your date?"

Belinda flipped her hand up. "I have no idea."

"You haven't changed at all." Lane looked for Helen. She wasn't where she'd seen her before. "Fuck."

"Yes. Please." Belinda grinned.

Lane rolled her eyes. "Oh, God." She needed to pass Belinda off to someone so she could find Helen. Then there she was, right in her view, the person she needed now and forever.

Helen seemed hesitant as she moved forward. "Can I help with something?"

"Just leave us alone." Belinda lunged forward. "Haven't you done enough?"

Lane put up her hand. "Stop, Belinda. You need to move on." She glanced at Helen. "I have." The knot in her stomach loosened. It was amazing how the truth could do that.

"You have?" Helen's eyebrows rose above searching blue eyes.

"Of course I have." Lane's anxiety was completely gone. "Isn't that obvious to you?"

"Not really. I thought maybe after what happened that you'd changed your mind about us."

"I just needed time to think…sort out my feelings." Lane rubbed the back of her neck to calm the tingle erupting across it. "That doesn't mean we don't still have some issues to deal with."

A woman appeared. "I told you not to bother her." She whisked Belinda away.

"Seems someone else is doing my job tonight." Helen laughed.

"I'm so sorry to hear about your dad." Lane touched Helen's cheek. "I should've called as soon as Darcy told me."

Helen put her hand on Lane's, removed it from her cheek, and held it tightly. "He's doing well. Can't keep that old ticker down." She smiled softly before her expression changed. "We don't have to get married. We don't even have to live together if you don't want to, but I don't want to lose you."

"I don't want to lose you either. I'm sorry if it took me too long to realize that I feel the same." She pressed her lips to Helen's. It had only been a week or so, but she'd missed their softness. "Even though we have some issues, I think we have something worth working on. I didn't have that with Belinda." She glanced over to see the woman Belinda came with struggling to control her. Thankfully that wasn't Lane's job anymore.

"That woman isn't going to have any of that with anyone." Helen laughed as she took in the same scene.

A swell of contentment rushed over Lane. "I need you to take me home, Helen—now." Lane grasped her other hand. "I want to make love to *you*—the woman I love."

"But I need to—"

"Don't do it." Lane stared into her eyes. This was one time Lane refused to allow Helen to micromanage anything. "Let someone else handle the rest of the night."

"Okay." Helen led Lane across the room to where Teigen, her assistant, stood observing the guests. "I need you to wrap this one up."

Teigen smiled widely. "Really?"

"Really." Helen glanced at Lane. "I have plans."

"I won't let you down." Teigen straightened her posture, ready for the challenge.

Lane tugged Helen toward the exit, stopping momentarily only to give her a long, passionate kiss. "If there's an emergency, she can call the fire department. Anyone but you."

Suddenly everything was right in Lane's world. She was going forward with Helen, the woman she loved with all her heart, and she didn't intend to let any time go to waste.

Epilogue

Helen watched Lane dance so freely, having the time of her life at her best friend's wedding. She followed her gorgeous legs as they moved, then let her eyes travel up, tripping momentarily across her breasts before landing on Lane's luscious, full lips. They spread into a wide smile, and when Helen ventured to gaze farther, she was caught in beautiful emerald-green eyes. The all-too-familiar feeling danced in her belly.

This woman was her forever girl, and she needed to tell her. She pushed through the crowd on the dance floor and took Lane in her arms. She was absolutely stunning—more gorgeous tonight than Helen had ever seen her, if that was even possible. Thin strips of eyeliner traced her eyelids, and Lane's green irises danced with the sparkle Helen had become accustomed to over the past few months and loved. Lane tugged her closer, and Helen melted into her.

When the tempo moved into a faster rhythm, Helen immediately threw Lane out into a twirl and pulled her back against her. "We might have to leave early."

"I'm game for that." Lane trailed her finger down Helen's arm. "I can't wait to get you out of this dress."

Helen pressed her lips gently to Lane's. "Can't we just sneak out now? No one will notice, will they?"

"Patience, love." Lane's eyes grew darker. "One more hour, and you'll be at home under my tongue."

A red-hot jolt of arousal shot through Helen. Lane was the only one who could produce that sensation in her. "You're such a beautiful tease."

"I think we both qualify in that area," Lane murmured before covering her mouth with her own. The kiss was soft, demanding, and sweet all in the same moment—the most amazing kiss ever.

Helen wanted nothing more than to spend the rest of the evening alone with Lane, wrapped up in her until dawn. She planned to do that every night for the remainder of her life. It was amazing that only a few months ago, Helen had thought a life with Lane would never be possible, yet today, she had everything she'd ever wanted with the woman she'd only dreamed of having it with.

About the Author

Dena Blake grew up in a small town just north of San Francisco where she learned to play softball, ride motorcycles, and grow vegetables. She eventually moved with her family to the Southwest, where she began creating vivid characters in her mind and bringing them to life on paper.

Dena currently lives in the Southwest with her partner and is constantly amazed at what she learns from her two children. She is a would-be chef, tech nerd, and occasional auto mechanic who has a weakness for dark chocolate and a good cup of coffee.

Books Available From Bold Strokes Books

Digging for Heaven by Jenna Jarvis. Litz lives for dragons. Kella lives to kill them. The last thing they expect is to find each other attractive. (978-1-63679-453-2)

Forever's Promise by Missouri Vaun. Wesley Holden migrated west disguised as a man for the hope of a better life and with no designs to take a wife, but Charlotte Rose has other ideas. (978-1-63679-221-7)

Here For You by D. Jackson Leigh. A horse trainer must make a difficult business decision that could save her father's ranch from foreclosure but destroy her chance to win the heart of a feisty barrel racer vying for a spot in the National Rodeo Finals. (978-1-63679-299-6)

I Do, I Don't by Joy Argento. Creator of the romance algorithm, Nicole Hart doesn't expect to be starring in her own reality TV dating show, and falling for the show's executive producer Annie Jackson could ruin everything. (978-1-63679-420-4)

It's All in the Details by Dena Blake. Makeup artist Lane Donnelly and wedding planner Helen Trent can't stand each other, but they must set aside their differences to ensure Darcy gets the wedding of her dreams, and make a few of their own dreams come true. (978-1-63679-430-3)

Marigold by Melissa Brayden. Marigold Lavender vows to take down Alexis Wakefield, the harsh food critic who blasts her younger sister's restaurant. If only she wasn't as sexy as she is mean. (978-1-63679-436-5)

A Second Chance at Life by Genevieve McCluer. Vampires Dinah and Rachel reconnect, but a string of vampire killings begin and evidence seems to be pointing at Dinah. They must prove her innocence while finding out if the two of them are still compatible after all these years. (978-1-63679-459-4)

The Town That Built Us by Jesse J. Thoma. When her father dies, Grace Cook returns to her hometown and tries to avoid Bonnie Whitlock, the woman who pulverized her heart, only to discover her father's estate has been left to them jointly. (978-1-63679-439-6)

A Degree to Die For by Karis Walsh. A murder at the University of Washington's Classics Department brings Professor Antigone Weston and Sergeant Adriana Kent together—first as opposing forces and then as allies as they fight together to protect their campus from a killer. (978-1-63679-365-8)

Finders Keepers by Radclyffe. Roman Ashcroft's past, it seems, is not so easily forgotten when fate brings her and Tally Dewilde together—along with an attraction neither welcomes. (978-1-63679-428-0)

Homeland by Kristin Keppler and Allisa Bahney. Dani and Kate have finally found themselves on the same side of the war, but a new threat from the inside jeopardizes the future of the wasteland. (978-1-63679-405-1)

Just One Dance by Jenny Frame. Will Taylor Sparks and her new business to make dating special—the Regency Romance Club—bring sparkle back to Jaq Bailey's lonely world? (978-1-63679-457-0)

On My Way There by Jaycie Morrison. As Max traverses the open road, her journey of impossible love, loss, and courage mirrors her voyage of self-discovery leading to the ultimate question: If she can't have the woman of her dreams, will the woman of real life be enough? (978-1-63679-392-4)

A Talent Within by Suzanne Lenoir. Evelyne, born into nobility, and Annika, a peasant girl with a deadly secret, struggle to change their destinies in Valmora, a medieval world controlled by religion, magic, and men. (978-1-63679-423-5)

Transitioning Home by Heather K O'Malley. An injured soldier realizes they need to transition to really heal. (978-1-63679-424-2)

Truly Enough by J.J. Hale. Chasing the spark of creativity may ignite a burning romance or send a friendship up in flames. (978-1-63679-442-6)

Vintage and Vogue by Kelly and Tana Fireside. When tech whiz Sena Abrigo marches into small-town Owen Station, she turns librarian Hazel Butler's life upside down in the most wonderful of ways, setting off an explosive series of events, threatening their chance at love…and their very lives. (978-1-63679-448-8